Unwound

"Colby? Colby?"

Debbie's panicked voice preceded her down the staircase and sent Tori's pulse racing once again. "Debbie, what's wrong?"

"Colby . . . he's not in his bed . . . he's not upstairs anywhere." Debbie rushed through the parlor and into the kitchen, lights flipping on in every room she entered. "With that sleeping pill I gave him he shouldn't be wandering around. He shouldn't even be a—"

A low guttural moan escaped Debbie's lips as she stopped halfway through the kitchen, her feet moving backward as she bumped into Tori. "Oh no . . . oh no . . ." Her voice trailed off, only to return in a shriek as she pointed at the floor in front of them. "Oh no!"

Stepping around her friend, Tori stared at the knife jutting from the linoleum kitchen floor with a hastily scrawled letter beneath its handle.

Careful not to touch anything, Tori leaned in as close to the note as possible, her stomach churning violently as her gaze fell on the faint red spatters that dotted the otherwise ordinary white stationery paper. Faint red spatters that looked a lot like—

"Oh my God. Debbie, call the police . . . now."

D0047551

Berkley Prime Crime titles by Elizabeth Lynn Casey

SEW DEADLY
DEATH THREADS

Elizabeth Lynn Casey

BERKLEY PRIME CRIME, NEW YORK

THE BERKLEY PUBLISHING GROUP
Published by the Penguin Group
Penguin Group (USA) Inc.
375 Hudson Street, New York, New York 10014, USA
Penguin Group (Canada), 90 Eglinton Avenue East, Suite 700, Toronto, Ontario M4P 2Y3, Canada
(a division of Pearson Penguin Canada Inc.)
Penguin Books Ltd., 80 Strand, London WC2R 0RL, England
Penguin Group Ireland, 25 St. Stephen's Green, Dublin 2, Ireland (a division of Penguin Books Ltd.)
Penguin Group (Australia), 250 Camberwell Road, Camberwell, Victoria 3124, Australia
(a division of Pearson Australia Group Pty. Ltd.)
Penguin Books India Pvt. Ltd., 11 Community Centre, Panchsheel Park, New Delhi—110 017, India
Penguin Group (NZ), 67 Apollo Drive, Rosedale, North Shore 0632, New Zealand
(a division of Pearson New Zealand Ltd.)
Penguin Books (South Africa) (Pty.) Ltd., 24 Sturdee Avenue, Rosebank, Johannesburg 2196,
South Africa

Penguin Books Ltd., Registered Offices: 80 Strand, London WC2R 0RL, England

This is a work of fiction. Names, characters, places, and incidents either are the product of the author's imagination or are used fictitiously, and any resemblance to actual persons, living or dead, business establishments, events, or locales is entirely coincidental. The publisher does not have any control over and does not assume any responsibility for author or third-party websites or their content.

DEATH THREADS

A Berkley Prime Crime Book / published by arrangement with the author

PRINTING HISTORY
Berkley Prime Crime mass-market edition / March 2010

Copyright © 2010 by Penguin Group (USA) Inc.
Cover illustration by Mary Ann Lasher.
Cover design by Judith Lagerman.
Interior text design by Laura K. Corless.

All rights reserved.
No part of this book may be reproduced, scanned, or distributed in any printed or electronic form without permission. Please do not participate in or encourage piracy of copyrighted materials in violation of the author's rights. Purchase only authorized editions.
For information, address: The Berkley Publishing Group,
a division of Penguin Group (USA) Inc.,
375 Hudson Street, New York, New York 10014.

ISBN: 978-0-425-23341-2

BERKLEY® PRIME CRIME
Berkley Prime Crime Books are published by The Berkley Publishing Group,
a division of Penguin Group (USA) Inc.,
375 Hudson Street, New York, New York 10014.
BERKLEY® PRIME CRIME and the PRIME CRIME logo are trademarks of Penguin Group (USA) Inc.

PRINTED IN THE UNITED STATES OF AMERICA

10 9 8 7 6 5 4 3 2 1

If you purchased this book without a cover, you should be aware that this book is stolen property. It was reported as "unsold and destroyed" to the publisher, and neither the author nor the publisher has received any payment for this "stripped book."

To Dr. Barry A. Singer, MD, Heather Popham,
and the rest of the folks at the
MS Center for Innovations in Care . . .
Thank you.

Chapter 1

Tori Sinclair had always prided herself on being a relatively calm person—the kind of woman who kept a cool head and a professional demeanor at all times. The kind of woman who steered clear of mindless watercooler drivel in favor of more intelligent and meaningful conversation.

And, technically, she still was that woman.

But only because the Sweet Briar Public Library didn't have a watercooler.

What it did have at that moment, however, was Colby Calhoun—the dark-haired, smoldering gray-eyed hunk of manhood that left women drooling in his wake for miles.

It didn't matter one iota that his brow was furrowed in distress or that his hands were flipping through a pile of books at mach speed, completely oblivious to the eyes of nearly half of the Sweet Briar Ladies Society Sewing Circle who'd stopped by for a quick chat yet stayed to gawk. It didn't matter that the nearly crater-sized dimples that made them all swoon hadn't appeared even once since he arrived. And it didn't matter that he'd bypassed his infamous chest-enhancing button-down shirts in favor of a ragged old run-of-the-mill T-shirt.

The only thing that mattered was the great view he afforded over the ever-growing stack of books that graced the information desk. Books Tori knew she should shelve, but couldn't bring herself to move. Not before he left anyway.

"Would you just look at those hands? And those eyes? How on earth Debbie can drag herself out of bed every mornin' when that's lyin' next to her is beyond me." Margaret Louise Davis leaned her plump sixty-something frame against the maple counter and sighed. Heavily. "Because if it were me, I wouldn't move. Ever."

"If it were you, my dear twin, he wouldn't look like that."

"Leona Elkin!" Tori reprimanded sharply, her voice echoing across the large room and drawing more than a few disdainful looks in their direction. Feeling the instant heat to her cheeks, she raised an apologetic hand in the direction of her patrons then pinned her friend with a disapproving look to rival all others. "What an awful thing to say to your sister. Margaret Louise is a—" She stopped, cast a slow glance down her friend's polyester-clad body as she searched for the perfect description. Something that would do justice to the warm and witty woman who'd grown to be one of her dearest friends despite their age discrepancy of nearly thirty years.

"A what, Victoria?" Leona prompted as her carefully tweezed eyebrow arched upward in amusement.

"A-a study in perfection," Tori offered. She tilted her head to the left, a strand of light brown hair grazing her cheek as she considered the woman who had stood by her side through thick and thin, helping her to not only consider Sweet Briar as home but to embrace it as well. "She's the most amazing cook I've ever met . . . she-she's laugh-out-loud funny without even realizing it . . . she has the most infectious smile I've ever seen . . . and she's the epitome of what a grandmother should be." Raising her own eyebrow in triumphant fashion, she folded her arms across her lilac-colored blouse and leveled a look of challenge at her self-proclaimed mentor. "So there."

"Very good, Victoria. I can see my coaching has been relatively successful thus far. You've managed to put just the right positive spin on my sister's qualities like the good southern girl in training that you are. But let us not forget that southern girls are only sweet and kind when a man is not involved. Which, of course, there is." Leona gently swept her pink-tipped fingers through her salon-softened gray hair and peered at the object of their bickering over her stylish glasses. "And no matter how many of my noteworthy qualities may be running parallel through Margaret Louise's body, one thing remains unchanged. That"—she gestured her bejeweled hand toward the well-built man hunched over an open book in the corner of the library before bringing it to rest on her fraternal twin's shoulder—"would never look twice at this."

"And he'd look twice at you, Leona?" Rose Winters, the oldest of the group, pulled her cotton sweater tightly against her frail body and snorted.

Tori couldn't help but giggle as Leona's mouth gaped open and the color drained from her cheeks. "I-I wasn't saying he'd look at me."

"That's good. Because if you were, I'd have to rethink your recent lack of judgment," Rose hissed as she raised a bony finger in Leona's direction. "First, your despicable fling with that detective from Tom's Creek . . . and now this?"

"Despic-flin-I-didn't," Leona sputtered.

Margaret Louise's eyes danced as her face stretched into a mischievous smile. "Oh yes you did, Twin. You were all fired up 'bout Daniel McGuire from the moment you laid eyes on him. I believe you said somethin' about a uniform and snug packaging at the time."

"And don't forget his gun. She really liked that part, remember?" Tori interjected around nibbled lips that threatened to release an entirely too-loud laugh.

"It was despicable," Rose interrupted firmly, "because you let your replaced hormones run amuck in favor of your friendship with Victoria." The retired schoolteacher jutted her chin into the air as she stared pointedly at Leona. "And while you may hide your age better than the rest of us old-timers with your fancy clothes and Poga-fied rump—"

"Yoga-fied, Rose," Tori whispered.

The elderly woman waved her off, opting instead to continue her tirade. "No matter what you do, Leona, no man that looks like Colby Calhoun is going to see you as anything other than what you are—an old snooty woman. Who can't sew her way out of a paper bag."

"We're working on that though, aren't we Leona?" Tori cast one final look across the room at Colby Calhoun before draping an arm around the thinner and more poised version of Margaret Louise. "In fact, we have our first lesson tonight, don't we?"

The burst of pale crimson that had risen to Rose Winters's cheeks for all of about thirty seconds retreated behind the normal pale pallor of her wrinkled face. "You're teaching Leona how to sew?"

"And she wants to learn?" Margaret Louise chimed in with blatant disbelief.

"She's willing to learn." Tori gently tapped the side of Leona's head with her own and squeezed the older woman's shoulder. "Isn't that right, Leona?"

"If you intend to hold me to a concession made under duress, Victoria, I guess I'm willing."

"She won't show up," Margaret Louise said with a knowing shake of her head. "Learnin' to sew means listenin', and my sister is as contrary as they come."

"I take offense to that." Leona placed her hands on her hips and leaned forward, her eyes locked on her sister's.

"Why? It's true."

"It is not," Leona argued. "I've learned things. Lots of things."

"Name two . . . no, three." Margaret Louise ticked off three fingers on her right hand with the index finger of her left. "Name three things you've learned in the last five years."

"I've learned my twin sister has gotten even more aggravating with age," Leona hissed through clenched teeth. "I've learned how to run a business . . ."

"That's true. Elkin Antiques and Collectibles is well respected," Rose grudgingly acknowledged from the sidelines.

"And I've learned that just because someone carries the detective title doesn't mean he's particularly adept at detecting the truth . . . or what, exactly, makes a woman such as myself purr." Leona folded her arms across her chest with defiance. "That's three."

"So you named three, congratulations. I'll bet anything you won't add sewin' to that list."

"Anything?" Leona prompted.

"Anything."

"How about dinner every night for a month? Delivered to my door?"

Tori laughed. "Getting tired of eating out every night, Leona?"

The woman flicked her hand off to the side. "Sweet Briar is hardly a mecca of fine dining, dear. There's not a restaurant within fifty miles of here that knows what good wine means." To her sister she said, "Do we have a deal?"

"And if you don't learn?" Margaret Louise asked, her eyes twinkling merrily.

"An antique from the shop."

"I was thinkin' more along the lines of you watchin' all

seven of Jake's young-uns one evening so I can take him and Melissa out for supper."

All eyes stared at Leona as her pallor drained to the color of freshly fallen snow. "All seven?"

"*All* seven."

"Even the baby?"

"Molly Sue is number seven. So, yes, she's included." Margaret Louise's pudgy hand patted Tori on the back. "I think I just freed up your evenin', Victoria."

"No you haven't, because I accept that bet." Leona's chin rose into the air as she inhaled through her cosmetically altered nose. "And, as for what we were talking about before my character was called into question, I'm not old, I'm aging. There is a difference.

"In fact, as you astutely pointed out, Rose, I'm aging much better than either of you two"—she slowly and deliberately let her gaze roam between the elderly spitfire and her own sibling—"and I'll take *snooty* over *backwoods* any day. At least I've been to the places Colby writes about. Unlike the two of you, who seem to think Sweet Briar, South Carolina, is the be-all-that-ends-all."

"That's because it is. You just try and show me another town—anywhere—that has the kind of rags to riches history Sweet Briar has. A history that saw this town destroyed by fire at the hands of those blasted Yankees and watched it rebound stronger than ever thanks to hard work, sheer determination, and the undying dedication of its founding fathers." Rose stared back at Leona, her thick glasses magnifying her eyes to nearly twice their original size.

"'Undying dedication'? Isn't that a bit much?"

"It's *fact*, Leona. And you can't do it, can you?"

Leona crossed her arms in delicate fashion as her chin tilted upward once again, this time in quiet defiance. "Do what?"

"Find a more impressive history than Sweet Briar's anywhere in these parts." Rose stamped her penny loafer–clad foot ever so slightly as she waited for a response.

"I'm sure, with a little research, I could—"

"Find nothing," Rose finished with authority. "So you can take your fancy cruises and your airplane rides all over the world, Leona. I'll take a town like this—one that was reborn on hard work and pride—any day of the week. Especially if it comes with someone like that." The woman's bony finger rose into the air, effectively aiming their collective focus back where it had started—on the dark-haired hunk sitting in the middle of the library.

"Amen." Leona sighed. "Do you think he's working on his next novel?"

Tori shrugged as she forced her attention back to the books in front of her, her hands expertly sorting each title into the appropriate pile. "He could be, I guess. But I suspect it's more likely his newspaper column on account of the time he spent in local history."

"I'll get those, Miss Sinclair." A petite woman with dark skin and even darker eyes breezed her way between the sewing circle members and the counter, setting down one stack of books and retrieving another. "I'm sorry I'm late. Duwayne's car broke down off Route 25 and I had to go and fetch him. I can come in on Saturday if that'll help, Miss Sinclair."

"It's not a problem, Nina. Things have been relatively"—she ran her gaze across the smattering of patrons around the room before returning it to her assistant's worried face—"quiet here so far."

"If you can call us quiet," Margaret Louise piped in from her spot against the expansive countertop that surrounded three and a half sides of the information area. Within the boundaries denoted by the counter stood the branch's main reference computer, a few filing cabinets, and a stool.

"True. I forgot about these three." Tori motioned with

her head toward her sewing circle buddies. "They stopped by to—wait. Why did you three stop by?"

"You haven't figured that out yet?" Nina asked as her endearing yet tentative smile began to surface. "How long have they been here?"

"About as long as he has." She lowered her head slightly, raising her eyes in the direction of the man they'd been gawking at for the past thirty minutes.

"He . . ." Nina looked over her shoulder, her timid smile giving way to a blush that began halfway down her neck before she finally turned back. "Ahhh."

Tori laughed, the sound quiet yet still enough to turn a few heads in their direction. Including Colby Calhoun's.

Great.

Shaking her thoughts back to a semirespectable place, Tori squeezed Nina's hand gently and motioned toward the stack of books the woman had set down on the counter. "What are these?"

"There was a message on the machine in your office when I came in. Those are just a few titles Ella May Vetter asked us to set aside. She said she'd be in later today to fetch 'em."

"Oh. Okay." Tori pulled a small slip of paper from a rectangular pad and scrawled the woman's name across the surface. "Not a problem."

"So what exactly does someone like Ella May Vetter read?" Rose asked, her raspy voice suddenly light and giddy.

"Oooo, let's see." Margaret Louise's chunky hand reached across the counter, scooted the stack of books to within an easy reach. "Hmmm. Well . . . there's *Ten Easy Steps to Turn Your House into a Home*, *Sew Deadly*, *Misery*, *Peter Rabbit*, and—get this—*Keep Your Man Lusting*."

"*Keep Your Man Lusting*?" Leona asked through lips that twitched. "You can't be serious."

Margaret Louise pulled the bottom book from the pile and held it in the air. "I can and I am. See for yourself."

She set the book back down on the counter and slid it across to her sister. "Maybe there really is a man."

"There is. And has been for quite some time. He just resides in her head," Rose offered as she, too, peered at the book Margaret Louise had placed in front of Leona. "That one is—and will always be—a strange duck. Or should I say bunny."

Giggles erupted among the group.

"Who?" Tori asked feeling more than a little left out. Sure, she'd only been in Sweet Briar less than six months, but the circle members had done a fairly good job of getting her up to speed on the who's who of the tight-knit town. Ella May Vetter, though, was a name she hadn't heard before.

She watched as Leona slowly scanned the library, her heavily lashed brown eyes darting from one face to the next before coming to rest squarely on Tori. "Now dear, we realize you're used to lunatics every five feet where you're from and, in all fairness, I've certainly seen my fair share while traveling . . . but here, in Sweet Briar, we have just one. And her name is Ella May Vetter."

Choosing to ignore the comment about her years in Chicago, Tori leaned closer. "Lunatic?"

Three heads nodded in unison with Nina grudgingly adding her own silent affirmative.

"Oh, c'mon, how bad can she be?" Tori asked.

"Well, she lives in that big old Victorian off Lantern Drive. You know . . . the white one with the—"

"Polka-dot mailbox?" Tori supplied as a picture began to form in her mind.

Margaret Louise nodded, taking over where Rose left off as she simultaneously sifted through the rest of Ella May Vetter's books. When she found the title she was searching for, she turned it so Tori could see, tapping her finger on Beatrix Potter's name. "Lest Ella May be known as the clichéd cat lady, she raises *bunnies*. A whole mess of bunnies. She sits on her porch for hours hand-feeding each rabbit their very own organically grown carrot."

"Which, of course, she buys. Oh, and we can't forget the frilly gloves."

She looked at Leona. "Frilly gloves?"

Everyone nodded in sync as Leona offered the explanation that made Rose's eyes roll upward. "Of course. We can't have the carrots carrying any harmful oils from our fingers to the bunnies, now can we?" Leona lowered her voice to a near whisper. "But that's not all. The last time I was in Leeson's Market she was there, gushing about you-know-who as usual."

"You-know-who?" Giving up on any hope of shelving, Tori simply settled on the stool. "Who's that?"

"That, Victoria, is the million dollar question." Rose bent forward at the waist ever so slightly as a deep cough rattled her frail body. "For going on ten years now we've all heard about this amazing man she's been dating. He's smart. Good-looking. Funny. Charming. Well traveled. Even famous. He is—to hear her talk—the epitome of every woman's dream."

She looked from Rose, to Margaret Louise, to Leona, to Nina, and back again. "I don't get it. So what's the problem? I mean the mailbox is funny and the bunny thing is definitely a little weird. But what's wrong with this—this Ella May Vetter woman having a great guy? Milo has certainly made my life a lot more special."

Just the mere mention of Milo Wentworth's name made her smile—a genuine happy smile that started deep inside her soul and had a way of carrying her through an entire day no matter how crazy or mundane it may be. Officially dating for three months now, she found herself eagerly looking forward to each new day just to see what sweet surprise the local elementary school teacher had up his sleeve.

There'd been flowers on her front porch, surprise picnics in the town square, countless nights spent discussing books, candlelit dinners on her patio, and bakery treats at the end of a long day at work.

In short, Milo Wentworth was like opening a great big present with multiple compartments and memorable surprises every step of the way.

"The difference, dear, is that Milo is real." Leona tsked.

"And this man isn't?"

"Darned if we know. And it's been ten years. *Ten years*, Victoria." Rose pushed a trembling hand through her wiry crop of white hair and shrugged. "But whatever gets you through the day, I s'pose."

"If he's famous as you say—"

"I don't say . . . she says," Rose corrected.

"If he's famous as *she* says," Tori amended, "maybe she's simply respecting his privacy."

Rose shook her head, a motion copied by both Leona and Margaret Louise. "No, she's just cuckoo."

"Maybe she's just a private person." Tori had known several of those in her life. And they certainly weren't lunatics. "Sometimes people are just different. They act differently, think differently, and behave differently. But it doesn't mean they're crazy. Or 'cuckoo' as you just said."

Four sets of eyes cast downward like disobedient puppies who'd met the end of a rolled-up newspaper. Rolling her own eyes upward she stifled a laugh. "Look, I'm not getting on you guys. I'm just saying maybe there's another explanation."

"Excuse me, ladies. Victoria, may I have a moment of your time?"

Five sets of eyes flew upward as five throats swallowed simultaneously.

"Uh, hi, Colby. How are you?" She flashed a welcoming smile at the man standing less than two feet away, prayed he didn't notice the way she wiped her hands on her charcoal gray skirt. It wasn't that she was interested in the object of the group's collective fantasizing—she wasn't.

She had Milo. And Colby had Debbie—a circle member closer to her own age whom she both admired and respected. But seeing him up-close was like having a plate of chocolate candies thrust in front of your face with iron-clad instructions not to touch.

Hence the sweaty palms.

"That barbecue you and Debbie threw last weekend was terrific. The chicken was absolutely mouthwatering and the . . . well, you're quite a cook."

"Grill master, maybe. Cook, no. But I'm glad you enjoyed yourself." Sliding a strong hand through his wavy dark hair, Colby drummed his fingers nervously on the counter. "Do you have anything on moonshine? Specifically its flammability?"

"I imagine we would. Let me check." Pulling the stool closer to the computer, Tori tapped in a few words and waited as the sound of heavy breathing filled the air behind her. "Yes, here we go. There's a book written by a Jake Bavaria in the Cooking section that will give you more information. But, based on the title, I'd say it's quite flammable."

"You should check with Gabe Jameson, Colby. He's the resident moonshine expert," Margaret Louise chimed in while Tori jotted the author and title on a slip of paper. "And he gives samples, too."

"Margaret Louise!" Leona hissed in embarrassment.

"Oh please. Like you didn't know that, Twin."

Colby held up his hand as his frown deepened. "I just came from Gabe's. It's why I've been poring over those." He gestured toward the books scattered across the table he'd just vacated, the corners of his mouth dipping even lower as he surveyed the aftermath of his research. "Look, I'm sorry I left things like that. I'll just take care of that real quick."

Tori stopped him with her hand. "It's not a problem. Really."

"If you're sure . . ." His voice trailed off as he closed his eyes momentarily only to reopen them with rapid speed. "Man, I don't know what to do. If I keep quiet I'm perpetuating a lie. But if I don't—"

Cutting himself off midsentence, Colby Calhoun simply hiked the strap of his computer case higher onto his shoulder and made a beeline for the front door, five sets of eyes following his hasty retreat, the lust of earlier replaced by worry and concern for their friend's husband.

"Colby, wait." Margaret Louise took a few steps toward the door then stopped. "If you don't . . . what?"

Slowly he turned around, eyes wide, his voice suddenly calm.

"If I don't, I'm dead."

Chapter 2

If she hadn't been waiting and listening, she probably wouldn't have given the faint thud outside her window a passing thought. She'd have merely chalked it up to the evening paper skittering across the front stoop or an unexpected meeting between one of the resident chipmunks and the new porch furniture she'd added just that afternoon.

But she'd been waiting and listening. For two days.

Turning her sewing machine off, Tori slid out of the white lattice-back chair in the tiny alcove off her living room and tiptoed over to the front door. The last of the sun's rays played across the wooden floor as dust particles danced in the light, reminding her of the housework she'd neglected while waiting for the woman on the other side of the door. A woman who prided herself on her southern manners yet failed to show up for a prearranged meeting or to offer any sort of explanation for her absence.

Though, really, Tori knew the explanation without hearing the words.

Leona Elkin loathed the idea of learning to sew.

Rose knew it. Margaret Louise knew it. Debbie knew it. The whole sewing circle knew it. Yet she, Tori Sinclair, had thought she could defy the odds and change the woman's mind.

Grasping the knob as quietly as she could, Tori turned her wrist to the right and pulled the door open. "Ah ha!"

Leona Elkin straightened up, her hand quickly retrieving a white square box from the small circular wicker table that stood off to the side of the door. "Oh, Victoria, dear, you scared me half to death."

"You're late."

"I uh—" Leona sputtered as a pinkish hue graced her moisturized cheeks.

"By two days."

"Oh. That."

"Yes, that. Must I remind you of your bet with Margaret Louise?" Tori placed her hands on her hips and tapped her foot against the wood floor. "Jake and Melissa have seven children, Leona. *Seven*."

The woman daintily cleared her throat then shoved the box in Tori's direction. "I brought chocolate."

Tori stared at the box, her mouth beginning to water. "Did you say chocolate?"

"I did . . ."

Damn.

I will be strong. . . . I will be strong. . . .

"If you don't learn to sew, Leona, I'm going to have to tell your sister. You do realize that, don't you?"

"Truffles to be exact, dear."

She gulped.

"The freshest batch in Debbie's bakery," Leona continued with an angelic tilt of her perfectly groomed head. "Though, I must say, I didn't catch Debbie in her usual sunny mood. Perhaps something is amiss in the water at the Calhoun home."

Fresh truffles.

Double damn.

"Okay, okay. You're forgiven. Unless"—she glanced toward the little table where Leona had been standing when she flung open the door, reality dawning in an instant—"you were going to leave these out here and take off without knocking."

Leona glanced down at the ground, shifted from foot to foot.

"You were, weren't you?" Tori looked from her friend to the box and back again, disgust in fierce battle with desire.

"Truffles, dear."

Damn.

"Okay, okay. Come in." Stepping to the side, Tori motioned her reluctant student inside, shaking her head in mock repugnance as the woman passed. "Do you at least have an excuse? You know, like you got busy at the shop . . . or you were battling the flu . . . or you had to leave town suddenly to care for a sick friend?"

"No." Leona swept into the cottage in her quietly sophisticated way, one pristinely manicured hand clasping a floral clutch, the other resting gracefully just below her neck. "The shop is fine. I don't get sick. And I have low tolerance for sickly types—that's what nursing homes are for, dear."

Slowly, Tori shut the door and trailed the woman into her home, her lips torn between smiling and grimacing. Leona Elkin was a force to be reckoned with—plain and simple. A true study in extremes if there ever was one.

How she did it, Tori wasn't sure, but somehow, someway, Leona managed to wear an array of different hats, each one fitting her as perfectly as the one before . . . She was ornery, yet sweet. Proper, yet indulgent. Standoffish, yet loving. Intelligent, yet pigheaded. Well traveled, yet southern to the core.

And loyal to a fault . . . Unless a handsome man in uniform happened to cross her path.

But even then, her loyalty would return. Eventually.

"So why didn't you show up Wednesday night like we'd planned?" She set the box on the maple coffee table in the center of the living room and slowly untied the pink string that held it closed. "We were supposed to have your first sewing lesson, remember? We even talked about it at the library that morning."

"You talked, dear. And my sister and Rose did their cute little display of shock at the news." Leona perched on the edge of the blue and green striped armchair Tori had purchased shortly after moving to Sweet Briar.

"But, Leona, we agreed. You said you'd come. You said you'd give sewing a real try." She stopped fiddling with the box of truffles long enough to size up her guest.

"That was said in a moment of weakness—when I felt remorse for abandoning our friendship. But that was months ago, dear . . . the remorse has worn off."

"But you still said you'd come," Tori reminded her friend. "You accepted Margaret Louise's bet."

"That was before Daniel called, dear. A romantic candlelit dinner takes precedence over an evening of poking myself as I try to make some worthless scrap of frumpy clothes I wouldn't be caught dead wearing in the first place."

She couldn't help but laugh as she flipped open the box and reached for a truffle. "Ah yes . . . I get it now. That explains why you didn't call. Southern manners go out the door when a man is part of the equation, right?"

"I don't see a man right now, dear," Leona said through pursed lips.

"What?" Tori looked from the box on the table to the half-eaten truffle in her hand, her face warming ever so slightly. "Oh. I'm sorry." With one quick shove she pushed the rest of the truffle into her mouth and grabbed hold of the box, offering its contents to her guest. "Would you like a truffle?"

Leona shook her head. "A woman must be mindful of her figure, dear."

"Oh." She stared forlornly at the box in her hands. "Then why bring them in the first place?"

"Bribery."

She cocked an eyebrow at her friend. "Bribery? Don't you mean a peace offering?"

Leona's hand swept its way down the armrest of Tori's sofa, stopping every few inches to pluck a piece of invisible lint from its patterned upholstery. "Why on earth would I need a peace offering, dear?"

Tori walked around the coffee table, tucked her leg underneath her, and dropped onto the love seat. "For not showing up when you were supposed to."

Pulling her attention from the armrest, Leona peered at Tori over the top of her glasses. "I already explained that. I had dinner with Daniel."

"O—kay. Then I give up. Why are you trying to bribe me? With truffles, no less? And how is leaving them outside bribery?" She grabbed the fringed throw pillow from the corner of the sofa and hugged it to her chest. "C'mon, Leona, what gives?"

"What *gives*?" Leona huffed. "Many things give, Victoria. Gumball machines give. Postal carriers give. Wealthy widowers give."

Tori snorted a laugh. "Wealthy widowers?"

Leona waved the question aside as she jogged her head to the left and pointed at Tori's sewing machine. "What are you working on?"

"Working on?" She sat up, looked over her shoulder quickly, and then sunk back into the sofa, her arms still wrapped around the pillow. "Oh. That. Eventually it'll be a halter dress like I saw in a celebrity magazine a few weeks back. The price tag for the store-bought version was outlandish. So, I walked over to Grace's Cut & Sew and found a similar pattern I can make on my own for less than a quarter of the price."

"Have you cut it to your size already?" Leona asked.

Surprised by her friend's sudden interest in sewing, Tori released the pillow and nodded. "Would you like to see it?"

"That's okay. You tend to favor peekaboo dresses more than I do anyway."

"Peekaboo dresses? I'm sorry, I'm not following." Tori pushed off the sofa with her leg and wandered over to the alcove in the corner of the room, her thoughts trying desperately to keep up with a conversation she'd somehow lost along the way. "What's a peekaboo dress?"

"Dresses that show too much bosom, dear."

Too much bosom?

"Why, the very first time I met you, you were wearing a sundress that attempted to show cleavage."

"Leona! I don't own an inappropriate item of clothing."

Leona clasped her hands together and laid them in her lap. "How perfectly awful for Milo."

Shaking her head against the ludicrous turn of their discussion, Tori simply laughed. "I was referring to dresses . . . you know, attire viewed by the general public. All of which is appropriate for someone my age. And, in case you haven't noticed"—she motioned at the neckline of her pale blue Henley style shirt—"I wasn't exactly blessed with much bosom to begin with."

"Of course I've noticed. Everyone's noticed, dear." Leona tilted her head to the side pensively. "But just because your halter dress wouldn't work for me doesn't mean it can't work for you."

"Wait. You lost me again." She plopped back down on the sofa, this time grabbing the box of truffles and pulling it to her chest, her stomach pleading for a second piece and her sanity granting the request. "Obviously I'm going to make a dress that works for me."

"I was thinking that perhaps *I* could make it for you."

She stopped—midbite—and coughed, tiny remnants of chocolate shooting through her mouth. "Y-you?"

"Yes, me." Leona sat up taller in her chair.

"S-seriously?" Wiping her mouth with the back of her hand, Tori couldn't help but stare at the woman sitting to her left. Had she heard her right? Was Leona Elkin ready to take the proverbial bull by the horns and learn how to sew?

"Well, you'd make it of course, dear. We'd just tell everyone else that I made it."

"Wait! I can't do that!" Tori pushed the box off her lap and onto the sofa. "That would mean lying to Margaret Louise and Rose and Debbie and Georgina . . . and Melissa . . . and everyone else."

"I don't see the problem," Leona said with a quiet sniff. "Believing I made it would make them feel good."

"And it would make me feel rotten." Tori slipped her hands down the outer side of her jean-clad thighs and sat on them, a maneuver she prayed would keep them away from yet another piece of Leona's blatant bribe. "Besides, how would we explain the magazines you'd continue to read during circle meetings when you're supposedly whipping up a dress for me?"

"I'm a temperamental artist? Someone who prefers to create masterpieces of cloth in the privacy of my own home?" Leona reached across the armrest of her chair and grasped the box of truffles in her hand, lifting it to Tori's eye level. "No one would have to be the wiser, Victoria."

"They would all be the wiser, Leona. There's not one member of our circle that would believe you made that dress. Not one." Tori diverted her gaze from the box the woman wielded in her face, determined to resist temptation at all cost. "If it were a lace-edged handkerchief, maybe. If it were a cloth gift bag, maybe. If it were an apron—for someone who actually cooks, of course—maybe. But a halter-style dress . . . as your first project? Never."

Deflated, Leona set the box down and leaned her head against the back of the chair, her thick eyelashes mingling with each other as she closed her eyes. "Maybe if I made a few mistakes . . . crocheted a button in the wrong spot?"

Tori laughed as she reached for Leona's hand and patted it gently. "You don't crochet buttons, Leona. You sew them on. Or, rather, you could once you learn how. And once you do, you'll be thanking me for teaching you."

The woman's eyes snapped open. "Don't push it, Victoria."

She laughed again. "Okay. You don't have to enjoy it. You just have to try it."

"I don't see why on earth I should." Leona lifted her head from the back of the chair and repositioned her glasses on the bridge of her nose. "If I want to give someone an apron, I'll buy one. And if I want a"—the woman scrunched up her nose in distaste—"reusable gift bag, I'll go—I'll go wherever one goes to buy such a thing."

Rising to her feet once again, Tori crossed to the sewing alcove and retrieved the wooden sewing box Leona, herself, had given her just a few months earlier. She set it on the coffee table and opened the top lid. "Sometimes it's the effort of creating something with your own two hands that makes the gift more memorable."

"Memorable, schmemorable. I didn't make that sewing box and it made you cry." Leona scooted forward on her chair just enough so as to peer inside the box at the plethora of colorful threads, laces, and buttons it held.

"True. But we're talking about two completely different kinds of gifts. And besides, once you learn how to sew, you'll have a freshly prepared meal delivered to your door every night for a month. A whole month, Leona." Tori reached inside the box, extracted a handful of colorful buttons, then laid them atop the table for Leona to inspect. "Pick one."

"Why?"

"Because you, my friend, are about to sew."

"Here? Now?" Leona asked as she shrank back in her chair, a look of dread tugging her lips downward.

"Right here. Right now."

"This is why I wanted to simply leave the chocolates and then follow them up with a pleasant phone call, dear. So this wouldn't happen."

"What?" she asked.

"Th-this sewing nonsense."

"You mean the sewing nonsense you agreed to?"

"You northerners sure are pushy." Leona stamped her foot against the wood floor and reached for a truffle, her hand disappearing into the box. "And here I thought you were a kind and thoughtful young woman."

"Well, we could forget it if you really want to. I'm sure Margaret Louise's seven grandchildren would enjoy your undivided attention for a whole evening."

"Where do we start?" Leona mumbled grudgingly.

"Pick one." She grinned as she scooted the buttons closer to her friend. "We're going to start at the very beginning—with buttons."

"Buttons, dear?" Leona peered at her over the top of her glasses. "Isn't that what a tailor is for?"

Ignoring her friend's comment, she handed her a needle, a spool of thread, and a pair of scissors. "Okay, let's take it from the—"

A staccato knock at the front door cut her off midsentence.

"Oh thank heavens." Leona clapped her hands together then smoothed back her hair with unadulterated glee. "A box of truffles to whoever that is."

"You are not off the hook, Leona. Not by a long shot." She stood, walked around the coffee table, and headed toward the front door. Grasping the knob, she looked back over her shoulder at the woman in her living room—a woman who looked as if she'd been handed a winning lottery ticket. "This is a temporary reprieve. Nothing more."

"I've been thinking, dear. Perhaps I do have a sickly friend who needs me after all."

"I'm not buying that one, Leona. I've heard your take on the sickly, and Florence Nightingale you're not." With a turn of her wrist she pulled the front door open, her cheeks rising skyward as Leona's accidental knight in shining armor came into view—all six foot one of him. "Milo, hi! What a wonderful surprise."

"Hi, yourself." Flashing the shy smile she loved more with each passing day, Milo held up a stack of DVDs with one hand and a splay of theater-sized candy boxes with the other. "I was hoping maybe we could watch a movie or something."

"That sounds wonderful but . . ." She nibbled her lower lip inward as she tilted her head to study him, her gaze playing across the burnished brown hair he kept short on the sides yet a little longer on top. "Leona finally showed up and we're just now getting started on her sewing lesson."

"A lesson we can put on hold, dear." Leona breezed past Tori and gestured the young widower inside. "You've both put in long hours at work this week and now it's time to relax—together."

"Leona, it's just a button for crying out loud." Tori folded her arms across her chest. "It'll only take us thirty minutes."

"I could just sit outside here and wait. It's a beautiful night—"

"You'll do no such thing, Milo Wentworth. You'll come in now." Leona reached her arms onto the porch and yanked Milo inside, smiling sweetly at Tori as he acquiesced and stepped into the house. "We'll do buttons tomorrow."

"I work tomorrow," Tori protested.

"Then we'll do buttons on Sunday."

Tori's left eyebrow rose upward. "Sunday is Re-Founder's Day, Leona. It's all anyone's talked about at our circle meetings for weeks now, remember?"

"It's all Rose has been talking about," Leona corrected with a well-timed eye roll.

"It's all Rose and Georgina and Dixie have talked about, too. And don't forget your sister. Margaret Louise has been working on her recipe for the cook-off for weeks now."

Waving off Tori's words, Leona simply shook her head. "The others might be looking forward to the festival, dear, but it's Rose who's gaga about it. To hear that woman talk, Sweet Briar is the Cinderella of southern towns."

"It kind of is," Milo interjected quietly. "This place was incinerated by the Yankees during the Civil War. And now look at it—it's thriving and has been for many, many years. It's almost hard to believe, really."

Shrugging, Leona crossed the living room and retrieved her clutch from the floor beside the armchair. "I guess Sunday is out for buttons, too, then. Such a shame."

Glancing apologetically at Milo with his stack of movies and boxes of candy, Tori joined Leona in the middle of the room. "We still have now."

"No, dear. This wonderfully special gentleman has traveled miles to see you!"

"Blocks," Tori corrected in amusement.

"Don't belittle his efforts, dear. That undermines his manhood," Leona whispered from the corner of her mouth. To both, she said, "He's traveled all the way across town to spend some time with you, dear. I wouldn't dream of interfering with that." Leona grasped the clutch with her long, delicate fingers. "The buttons can wait."

"Why do I feel as if I'm being used as a scapegoat?" Milo asked, the sparkle of amusement in his eyes belying the seriousness of his face.

"Because you are," Tori said as her disapproving gaze

met Leona's triumphant one. "But at least you're getting a box of truffles out of it."

"Truffles? I don't need truffles."

"Oh yes you do." Tori shot a gentle elbow into Milo's side before turning to her friend who was fairly tiptoeing toward the door in an effort to escape. "And as for you, Mizz Elkin . . . we will pick up where we left off. Soon."

"Of course, dear. I can hardly wait." Leona grabbed hold of the doorknob and pulled, the sounds of crickets and katydids filling the tiny cottage. "I'll see you both at the festival, yes?"

Tori looked at Milo for confirmation just as his arm slid around her shoulders and pulled her close, an unexpected public display of affection that sparked a surge of warmth through her body. Grinning, she looked back at Leona and nodded. "We'll be there."

"Perhaps I'll pack some earplugs."

Tori looked a question at the woman—the same question Milo spoke. "For the fireworks?"

"I was thinking more along the lines of Rose's incessant town cheerleading. It gets worse on Re-Founder's Day." Leona stepped onto the porch and looked around, the slight nod of approval at Tori's new wicker furniture barely discernable in the gathering dusk that seemed to envelop their surroundings in mere minutes. "Though I suppose they'll be useful for fireworks as well."

"I love fireworks," Tori offered as she peered up at Milo, the corners of her mouth tugging upward in anticipation of both the movie night ahead and the Re-Founder's Day Festival on Sunday. "Especially the ones that look like fairy dust when they're raining down."

"I was kinda surprised to hear they were doing them at all. Everyone's super paranoid about fire around here . . . even after all this time. But I ran into Colby Calhoun as he was leaving the newspaper office this afternoon and he said the fireworks on Sunday were going to be huge."

"Oooo, yay," Tori said with a squeal. "The bigger the better."

"Was he okay?" Leona asked quickly.

"Who?"

"Colby." Leona shifted her clutch to the other hand and peered over her glasses at Milo. "He seemed rather concerned when we saw him in the library on Wednesday morning. And then today, at the bakery, Debbie wasn't her usual bubbly self either."

Milo shrugged. "Can't comment on Debbie but Colby seemed fine to me. At the time, anyway. Though, now that you mention it, he did seem a little . . . I don't know . . . edgy, I guess. And he didn't ask about school getting ready to start up soon like he normally would . . ." Milo's voice trailed off briefly. "I don't know, maybe he's working through the plot for his latest novel. I've always heard writers can get a little distracted when they're at that stage."

"Colby wasn't just distracted on Wednesday. He was worried . . . scared, even." Leona raised her hand in farewell only to return it to her side just as quickly. "Something is off with Colby Calhoun—you mark my words. That man is rattled to the core about something. And for a man that good-natured and that calm to get rattled . . . well, I think it's safe to say that whatever is brewing is big. Very, very big."

Chapter 3

There was no doubt about it, there were simply days she missed living in Chicago. Missed the sound of the El in the distance and the general hustle and bustle of the city streets. Missed lounging outside Millennium Park on the first warm day of spring or daydreaming her way down Michigan Avenue on a snowy day. Missed the first bite of an Italian beef sandwich and the smell of the city's infamous stuffed pizza around virtually every street corner.

But there was also no denying the fact that Sweet Briar felt more and more like home every day. Her job at the library was fulfilling, her ever-deepening bonds with the sewing circle members brought a welcome sense of inclusion that extended well beyond the confines of their weekly Monday night meetings, and her relationship with Milo Wentworth was progressing better than she could have imagined. Yet, deep down inside, she knew it was more than a dream job, new friends, and a great guy that had allowed the small southern town to grab hold of her heart. It was the pervasive feel of pride and closeness that its residents not only felt but also shared. Readily.

"It's funny how things can change so fast, isn't it?" Tori slipped her hand inside Milo's as they rounded Leeson's Market and headed toward the town square, the sound of voices and laughter growing louder with each passing step. "At Heritage Days in the spring I couldn't have felt more out of place here. But now . . ."

"You belong." Milo stopped walking long enough to raise her hand to his lips for a quick kiss, the daffodil yellow sleeve of her ribbed V-neck shirt slipping down her wrist with the motion. "I hate to sound like a broken record but I knew this town would come around . . . start to judge you on who you are rather than where you're from. You handled the fallout from Tiffany Ann's murder with grace and honesty. And you kept your head held high every step of the way. What's not to love about that?"

She shrugged. "At the time, it was heartbreaking to have everyone pointing at me for a crime I didn't commit simply because I was an outsider—an unknown. But now that that's behind me, I see the loyalty for one another as something rare. Even special."

"It can be. When it's in your favor. But when it's not, it can get mighty ugly." He tugged her across the street, his nose lifting into the air. "Do you smell that?"

She couldn't help but laugh. She smelled lots of things, heard lots of things, saw lots of things. In fact, it was safe to say all five senses were in overload as they stepped through the trellised archway to the town square—the site of every festival Sweet Briar held throughout the year.

"What smell would that be?" Looking up at Milo she grinned, her pulse quickening as his amber-flecked brown eyes locked with hers and tiny dimples appeared in his cheeks. "Wait, don't answer that. Let me guess . . ."

Slowly she pulled her gaze from his, let it travel its way

across the top of people's heads in search of any and all food tents they could see from their vantage point. There was a Polish sausage tent that boasted the inclusion of pepper and onions on an easel-propped chalkboard. There were three different tents selling pork barbecue—one with corn on the cob as a side, one with hush puppies, the other offering straight barbecue with no add-ons at all.

"Look . . . right there." Milo's index finger shot into the air as he pointed at a blue and white striped tent a good hundred yards from where they stood. "It's all I've dreamt about for days—well, except for when"—he looked down at the ground and then back at her, his cheeks sporting a slightly reddish hue—"I'm thinking about you, of course."

"Nice save, Milo. For a minute I was worried you were going to say I fell below a slab of dough on your list of daydreaming subjects."

His mouth gaped open. "Slab of dough?"

"Yeah. That's what those people have on their plates, isn't it?" she asked, pointing at a group of teenagers who'd come from the direction of the blue and white tent. "I've seen them before at fairs like this, but I've never thought they looked terribly appetizing."

Milo raised his palms to his ears and covered them as his lips pursed into a whistle.

"What? Did I say something wrong?"

Slowly, he lowered his hands, his left claiming her right. "First, it's not a slab of dough, Tori. It's a funnel cake. Second, you must not have gotten a very good glimpse at their plates, because if you had your mouth would be watering."

"Watering, huh?" she teased.

"Wa-ter-ing."

"Okay. Lead the way."

Squeezing her hand to his side, he led her through the seemingly endless crowd of residents from Sweet Briar and its neighboring communities—a sea of smiling faces that surely mirrored her own. "I could never get Celia to try the stuff. Mainly because it wasn't green and didn't grow in the ground. But you—you like your junk food so there's hope."

For a brief moment she thought about denying her propensity for unhealthy eating, but she let it pass. What was the point? Some things were just futile. . . .

But still, hearing Milo mention his late wife always stirred an overwhelming need to lighten the moment. Not because he wasn't ready to move on after ten years—he was. But because she ached for the pain he endured all those years ago as he watched his wife succumb to cancer.

Sneaking a look at his face as they neared his destination of choice, she was pleased to see the face-lighting smile that had endeared him to her from the moment they first met. Whatever pain he still carried over his loss had been tamed by hope. And for that she was glad. Very, very glad.

"Oh, hey, would you remind me to grab a paper before we leave?" Milo tilted his head toward a small grouping of people huddled around the Sunday edition of the Sweet Briar *News Times*. "I like to read Colby's columns and I forgot to pick one up on my way to get you this afternoon."

She stopped, gestured toward the white tent just off to their right—a tent that appeared to rival that of any other at the festival in terms of a line. Only instead of food or trinkets, it existed solely to sell papers and subscriptions. "I could get one for you right now."

He tightened his grip on her hand and shook his head. "Oh no . . . you're not getting out of trying a funnel cake."

"I'm not trying to get out of it," she protested. "I just figured you could get in line for that while I get in line for a paper. When we're done, we'll just meet somewhere in the middle."

"You won't take off for the hills?"

"Not before I get your paper."

"Hey!"

"I'm just kidding." Tori jabbed a finger into his side and laughed. "Besides, finding a hill around here would be pretty tough to do. Perhaps the ocean would be better. It's only an hour or so away. . . ."

"Cute. Very cute." He leaned over, planted a gentle kiss on the top of her head. "I'll meet you back here in a few."

"I'll be here." She waved as he started across the matted grass in search of the artery-clogging treat that appeared to be a staple at Sweet Briar's festivals. Why people wanted to eat a plate of fried dough was beyond her, but she'd give it a try if it meant something to Milo.

Pulling her gaze from the back of his head as he disappeared into the crowd, Tori turned and headed toward the ever-growing line at the newspaper tent. Many of the faces she recognized as library patrons, others were simply people she glimpsed at the market or church or a variety of other spots around the small white picket fence town.

She smiled at the forty-something woman in front of her as she took her place at the end of the line. "I can't believe this line. Is the news tent always this busy at a festival?"

The woman shook her head, the emphatic motion dislodging a few strands of red hair from the casually pinned bun at the nape of her neck. "But it's hard not to notice them there folks." She pointed to various clusters of people peering over the shoulders of others to read the paper. "Everyone sure seems to be hankerin' for one, don't they? I reckon there's somethin' good goin' on."

Tori glanced at a group of men standing to the right of the tent as they waited for their buddy at the front of the line to get his copy. He'd barely exchanged money for a paper before they were ripping it from his hand and flipping through the contents with a mixture of determination and dread on their faces.

"Do you have any idea what's going on?" she asked the woman.

Again, the redhead shook her head, her green eyes widening as she did. "Not a clue. But I'm guessing—hey! Watch where you're going, mister."

Carter Johnson, the owner of Johnson's Diner, shoved his way between the two of them, his lips making an angry slash mark across his face as he balled up his newspaper and threw it into a nearby trash receptacle.

"Do you think it's really true, Papa? Do you really think everybody's been lying?"

"I most certainly do not. That kind of talk is rubbish, nothin' but pride-stompin' rubbish." The man, seemingly oblivious to the fact he'd nearly knocked the redhead to the ground, grabbed hold of his grandson's upper arm and fairly dragged him across the grass. "I have half a mind to come back here with a match and set those papers on fire. And while I'm at it, maybe my rifle wouldn't be such a bad idea either."

If the boy responded, Tori didn't hear, as the pair moved so quickly through the crowd they disappeared before her eyes.

"Wow. Ain't he ill as a hornet," the woman said with disgust before waving the man's actions off. "Eh, don't pay him no mind, he's just bein' rude is all."

Without waiting for an answer, the woman stepped forward just as an additional worker sat down at the table and beckoned them to form the start of a new line. Mechanically, Tori followed along, her thoughts a few steps behind. Carter Johnson wasn't a rude man. A little loud at times, yes. A little bit of a know-it-all at times, yes. But rude, no.

And certainly not violent . . .

"One copy or two?"

"Huh, what?"

With a bored roll of his eyes, the teenager behind the counter repeated his question, this time pointing to the stack of newspapers sitting on the table beside him. "One copy or two?"

"Oh, yeah, sorry." Forcing her attention back to the task at hand, Tori reached into her purse and pulled out two singles. "One copy is fine, thanks."

The worker dropped two quarters, a dime, and a nickel onto a paper and slid it across the table at her. "Page three."

"Excuse me?"

Again he rolled his eyes, this time adding a smirk for the benefit of the young girl sitting beside him manning the other line. "Page three. The story is on page three."

"What story?"

"Page three," he repeated before turning his attention to the person behind Tori. "One copy or two, sir?"

Stepping to the side, Tori glanced in the direction of the group of men she'd seen earlier, their mouths now distorted in rage as they, too, balled up their paper and disappeared into the crowd, leaving nothing but a trail of mumbled threats in their wake.

"What on earth . . ."

"Is everything okay, Victoria?"

Startled, Tori looked up, her mind racing to put a name to the rounded face in front of her.

Ella . . . Ella something . . .

"Everything is fine." Her mind continued to cycle through names as she tried to buy herself some time. "I guess I was just lost in my own little world."

The woman reached out, touched her forearm with long slender fingers. "I do that sometimes, too. Mostly when I'm reading though."

Reading?

"I wanted to thank you for setting aside those books for me the other day. I'm not normally quite so lazy."

Setting aside books . . .

"I'd fallen behind on feeding my bunnies and wasn't sure I'd have time to locate all of the books on my own before you closed for the evening."

Bunnies . . .

As her identity came into focus, Tori placed her free hand over the woman's and gave it a gentle pat. "It was absolutely no problem, Miss Vetter. That's what we're there for. I'm only sorry I didn't have more time to chat when you stopped by to pick them up. I was giving a tour of the new children's room to a reporter from a national library publication."

Ella May Vetter clapped her hands together. "A national publication? How wonderful."

"It really is," Tori agreed, studying the woman as she did. There was no doubt about it, Ella May Vetter was a tad peculiar. One only needed to see the petticoat-style dress and Little Bo Peep–curled hair to know that. But just because she did things a little differently didn't mean she was a lost cause as Rose, Margaret Louise, and Leona made it sound. If anything, Tori found her to be sweet and unassuming. "Did you enjoy your selections?"

"Very much. Thank you."

"There you are!" Milo flashed a warm smile at Ella May as he stopped beside Tori with a paper plate in his hand and a hint of powdered sugar on his upper lip. "Hi, Ella May. Are you enjoying the festival?"

The woman nodded as a smile broke out across her face as well. "It's lovely."

"Couldn't wait, could you?" Tori looked from Milo's lip, to the plate, and back again.

"I waited . . . see?" Milo held up the plate, a perfectly formed latticework of powder-topped golden fried dough shimmering in the sunshine.

"Then what's this?" She reached out, swiped a finger across his upper lip, and then held it where he could see.

"I—er."

"Busted!" She tucked the newspaper under her arm and rocked back on the heels of her tennis shoes.

Ella May laughed as Milo's cheeks reddened. "You two are so cute, you remind me of the way Billy and I are together."

"Who's Billy?" The moment the words were out of her mouth she knew the answer. Billy was the guy—the smart, charming, intelligent, well-traveled Mystery Man no one in Sweet Briar had ever seen.

"He's simply the most amazing man ever." The woman sighed.

"Does he buy and hide second helpings of things, too?" Tori asked as she eyed Milo accusingly.

"I did not buy a second helping. I swear. I just"—he looked down at the plate and back up again—"happened to be in the right place at the right time."

"Translation, please?" Tori prompted as she winked a smile at Ella May before looking back at Milo and waiting.

"Dirk Rogers's nephew didn't care for his funnel cake. And Dirk was in a foul mood."

"Dirk Rogers? Why does that name sound familiar?"

"Dirk owns the garage out on Plantation Lane."

Tori nodded. "Okay, so what does his nephew's dislike for funnel cake and his foul mood have to do with you?"

"Someone had to eat it," Milo pleaded. "Wasting food is a sin."

"Ohhh. I see now." Tori crinkled her forehead as she looked at Ella May. "He simply couldn't stand by helplessly as an innocent plate of funnel cake faced an uncertain fate."

"Milo Wentworth is a true philanthropist in every sense of the word." Ella May's near-perfect crack at a straight face, coupled with the words she'd chosen to speak, set Tori into a fit of giggles—giggles that only intensified as Milo rolled his eyes.

"Mock me all you want, ladies. You'll change your tune once you try a bite." Carefully, Milo tore a piece of dough from the creation in front of him and extended it toward Ella May. "Would you like some?"

"No, thank you."

Milo shrugged and held it toward Tori. "You promised."

"I did." She took the sprinkled dough from his outstretched hand and took a bite. "Mmmm. Wow."

"See? I told you." He fixed his gaze on her face for a moment before letting it travel slowly down her soft yellow T-shirt and formfitting stonewashed jeans. "And with your body, you can eat this stuff all day and not worry."

She felt her face redden with a mixture of flattery and embarrassment. Flattery because he liked what he saw and embarrassment because Ella May was still standing there, soaking it all up. "Yeah, but do you hear that sound?"

Milo shook his head, his brows furrowing. "No. What sound?"

"This"—Tori parted her lips ever so slightly and then inhaled deeply—"that's the sound of my arteries clogging as we speak."

Milo waved the comment aside with his free hand. "We're at a festival. We don't hear those sounds at a festival. The only thing we hear is laughter. And an occasional screaming kid."

"I've heard a few expletives myself." Tori pulled the paper from under her arm and held it out to Milo. "In fact, I've heard threats."

"Threats?" Milo swapped the funnel cake for the paper. "What kind of threats?"

"Well, Carter Johnson said he wanted to burn the news tent down."

Milo's head snapped back. "That doesn't sound like Carter at all."

"I know. I thought the same thing."

"Now that you mention it though, Dirk Rogers said something about shoving a computer in places a computer shouldn't be shoved."

Tori gestured toward the paper. "I'm thinking that whatever has everyone so fired up is on page three. At least that's what the kid in the tent said."

"Page three," Milo repeated as he unfolded the paper and flipped back the front page. "Page three—ah, here we go. The only thing here is Colby's—oh no . . ."

"What?"

"Oh no," he mumbled again, as Ella May moved in from one side and Tori from the other. "Oh, Colby, what did you do?"

"What are you talking—" She stopped, midsentence, as the object of Milo's displeasure sprang into view in the form of a bold black headline that stretched from one side of the page to the other.

SWEET BRIAR'S HISTORIC REBIRTH A FRAUD.

A slightly smaller headline sat just below the first.

Moonshine—Not Yankees—to Blame for Town's Incineration

Lenin once said, "A lie told often enough becomes the truth."

While it's anyone's guess what specific event sparked his comment, he could—in theory—have been talking about Sweet Briar.

For well over a century—in homes across our town—the story of Sweet Briar's rise-from-the-ashes rebirth has been passed around the table along with the okra. It's been written on blackboards in the elementary school and preached as gospel on more than its share of Sunday mornings. It's been passed down as truth through the Johnsons, the Rogerses, the Clemmonses, and every other founding family, including my in-laws.

But I'm here to tell you it's all been a fairy tale. Or, to be more blunt, an out-and-out lie.

Well, 90 percent of it anyway.

There *was* a fire. And it *did* reduce Sweet Briar to ash. That part is true. It's just the celebrated how—the part that's been flaunted for generations and generations—that is nothing short of a boldfaced lie.

Yankees didn't burn Sweet Briar to the ground. Gabe Jameson's great-great-grandfather did.

That's right, my fellow Sweet Briar residents, our town didn't rise from the ashes of an enemy attack. We rose from the flames of a moonshine snafu.

Tori sucked in her breath as she scanned the rest of Colby's column, the enormity of his charge bringing a new clarity to Carter Johnson's words. "The matches were for the tent . . . the rifle must have been for . . ." The words trailed from her mouth as reality dawned.

"What rifle? What are you talking about?" Milo asked.

She met Milo's worried eyes with her own. "Matches weren't the only thing Carter Johnson wanted to bring back after he read this. He said"—she swallowed over the sudden lump in her throat, her words growing raspy—"he said a rifle might not be a bad idea either."

"A rifle?" Ella May ran the tips of her fingers slowly down the article in front of them, her gaze never leaving the paper. "Why on earth would he need a rifle?"

Pushing the paper in Ella May's direction, Milo raked a hand through his hair in frustration. "Why? Because Colby Calhoun just destroyed a legacy with the sweep of his pen . . . and placed himself firmly on the top of everyone's Most Hated list in the process."

Chapter 4

From the moment she stepped inside Melissa Davis's home the aura was anything but normal. In fact, if she didn't know any better, Tori would have thought she was at a funeral rather than the weekly sewing circle meeting that had managed to turn Mondays into one of her favorite days of the week.

Gone was the sound of the animated chatter and good-natured gossip that was as much a part of each meeting as the sewing itself. Gone was the verbal banter over who brought what for the dessert table. And gone were the smiles on the faces of women who treasured the opportunity to spend a few hours with close friends while engaging in a hobby they all loved and respected.

Instead, the chatter and gossip had been replaced by the intermittent sound of throat clearing laced with a suffocating silence. Instead of a dissertation about a particular recipe's lineage, covered plates were merely plunked down on the table and ignored, their claim to fame left unspoken. And instead of smiles there were only sullen faces—sullen and angry.

Except Debbie Calhoun's. Hers simply looked sad. Heartbroken, even.

Tori stood just outside the doorway of the family room and studied her friend. The woman's normally upturned lips drooped low and her eyes cast downward as if she were waiting for the floor to open up and swallow her whole. And if the expressions on the faces of the other women in the room were any indication, they were not only waiting but hoping she'd meet with the same fate as well.

Milo was right. The steadfast loyalty she'd grown to admire among the residents of Sweet Briar could, indeed, be a double-edged sword—a sword that was now pointed in Debbie Calhoun's direction.

"Oh, Tori, hi. I didn't hear you come in." Melissa strode down the hallway from the back of the house, an assortment of toys nestled against her side by one forearm, an infant propped atop the other. "I just finished nursing Molly Sue and Jake took the rest of them—plus Debbie's two—to the park to play for a little while. If we're lucky he'll get them nice and tuckered before bringing them back home."

Tori shook her head and smiled, her hands instinctively releasing her sewing box and tote bag in favor of her hostess's most recent addition to the family. "I don't know how you do it, Melissa."

"The secret is to not think. If I did, I'd have to be committed." Melissa released an audible sigh of relief as she handed the wide-eyed baby to Tori. "I apologize for this place"—she gestured around the room with her newly freed hand—"looking the way it does. But housecleaning is an art form I've yet to relearn since baby number seven arrived."

"That's okay. You're focusing on the important part first. Anyone who's spent more than two seconds with your kids knows they're rare—respectful, creative, encouraged, and loved." Tori looked down at the baby in her arms and smiled as they locked gazes. "Molly Sue will be no exception, I'm sure."

"Thanks, Tori, I think I needed that more than I realized." Bringing her mouth within inches of Tori's ear, Melissa lowered her voice to a whisper. "Would you see what you can do about lightening the mood in there? It's been like this since Debbie showed up with Jackson and Suzanna. But before she came . . . wooo, I needed earplugs for the kids' ears so they wouldn't pick up the nasty things being said in this very room."

"That bad, huh?"

"Worse." Melissa looked around briefly then whispered in Tori's ear once again. "I think it's safe to say Debbie Calhoun is public enemy number two."

"Two?"

"The top spot belongs to Colby."

Tori nodded, her heart aching for the woman who sat quietly in her chair, the pattern for a child's summer dress lying completely ignored in her lap. It was hard to see anyone shunned by people who were supposed to be their friends, but it was even harder to see it happening to a woman like Debbie Calhoun—a woman who'd treated her with nothing but kindness and compassion since the day they'd met.

"Here, let me take Molly Sue so you can work your magic." Melissa's free hand swooped in, scooping the tiny infant from Tori's arms and drawing her against her body with ease. "There's an empty seat over by Rose."

"Okay, thanks." With one final smile at the still wide-eyed baby, Tori reclaimed her sewing box and tote bag and stepped inside the family room, the normal round-robin welcome replaced by a few slight head nods and even less eye contact.

To her left sat Leona, busily flipping through the pages of the latest travel magazine she'd received. Beyond her was Rose, the elderly woman's frail frame slumped over one of four portable sewing machines that traveled from meeting to meeting. Georgina Hayes sat on the opposite side of the room, one of her trademark straw hats gracefully poised atop her dark brown hair as she quietly worked to secure the first of many buttons on the navy blazer she'd been fussing over for weeks. Beside her was Beatrice Tharrington, the youngest of the group, who diligently worked on a patchwork quilt for one of her charges, her mouth serious, her eyes never leaving her latest project.

And then there was Debbie, tucked in a corner by herself, her shoulders slumped downward as she stared—unseeingly—at the birthday dress she planned to make for her ten-year-old daughter, Suzanna.

Squaring her shoulders against the glares she suspected she'd receive, Tori bypassed the empty spot beside Rose and claimed the less comfortable folding chair to the left of Debbie. "So where is Margaret Louise tonight? Playing hooky?" Without waiting for an answer, she set the sewing box at her feet and placed the tote bag on the empty snack table between her and Debbie, offering a wink of encouragement to the woman as she blathered on. "Or do you think she got lost?"

She knew it was a ridiculous question—the kind of inquiry akin to asking whether a librarian was familiar with the Dewey decimal system. But desperate times called for desperate measures, and the present situation lurking over the heads of the Sweet Briar Ladies Society Sewing Circle more than qualified as desperate.

"The day Margaret Louise can't find her way to this house, dear, is the day she takes her last breath." Leona looked up from her magazine long enough to acknowledge Tori's choice of seats with a slight nod of her head. "And even then I suspect she'll get herself here before she officially keels over."

"But not before she braids Lulu's hair, reminds Jake

Junior to look after his siblings, reties Sally's shoes, plucks Travis from a dirt pile somewhere, coaxes Julia from her mother's makeup case, teaches Kate how to ride her bike, and makes goofy faces at Molly Sue," Rose muttered as she shot visual daggers in Tori's direction.

"And prepares a five course meal for Melissa and Jake to enjoy at three in the morning after the last of the brood is finally asleep," Georgina added before pursing her lips and returning to her buttons.

The conversation, which would have normally been peppered with laughter, fell flat as everyone said what they wanted to say and then turned back to their immediate task at hand—ignoring Debbie while pretending to sew.

"Okay, so maybe she's not lost. Any other guesses?"

Debbie met her attempt to keep the chatter alive with a shrug and a voice that failed to disguise her sadness. "She'll be along soon. She's at the bakery using the kitchen."

"She's trying to put us all to shame with her dessert, isn't she?" Tori reached into her canvas tote and pulled out the sample cloth gift bag she'd put together after the festival. The project—which had started as a whim—had ignited an idea she was anxious to share with the group.

"She's experimenting with her recipe from the fair, dear, trying to see if she can turn her blue ribbon into ten thousand dollars and the chance to grace an upcoming cover of *Taste of the South* magazine." Leona peered at Tori over the top of her glasses, her hand poised mid-page turn. "It's been a dream of my sister's since . . . well, since I can't even recall."

Setting the gift bag on her thigh, Tori seized on the opportunity to stoke a conversation. "Ten thousand dollars? I had no idea winning the side dish competition at the Re-Founder's Day Festival carried the possibility of a prize like that. Perhaps I should spend more time cooking and baking."

"The festival doesn't have anything to do with this latest contest—not really, anyway." Debbie worked her bottom lip with her teeth, the uncertainty in her voice hard to ignore. "But she was tapped by the magazine because of the contest."

"I'm confused . . ." And it was true, she was. But under normal circumstances Tori would simply wait things out, let the answers reveal themselves in subsequent conversation. This, however, was not normal circumstances and subsequent conversation was not a given.

Unless she cast the hook and reeled it in nice and slow . . .

A hook Georgina Hayes impaled herself on in quick fashion.

"William Clayton Wilder, president and CEO of Lions Publishing—the company that makes *Taste of the South* magazine—just happened to be passin' through Sweet Briar on Sunday as he traveled from a meetin' in Richmond to his summer home in Boca." Georgina positioned the next button on her blazer and held it in place with her index finger.

"Actually, that's not quite true, he was here—"

As if Debbie hadn't said a word, Georgina continued talking, "Somehow he found out about the festival. He stopped by, stumbled across the contest, offered to be a stand-in judge for Martha Brinkman, who has the flu—bless her heart—and was absolutely taken by Margaret Louise's Sweet Potato Pie."

Tori clapped her hands together. "Are you serious? Oh how wonderful. I bet Margaret Louise is just beside herself with excitement."

"She's a wreck," Rose interjected from her spot behind the portable sewing machine. "It's Leona who is beside herself."

"Leona?" Tori repeated as her gaze fell on her friend.

"William Clayton Wilder is single, Victoria. Single and wealthy." Rose peered at Tori over the top of her bifocals, her thin lips pursed in a knowing manner. "Though why she'd be interested is beyond me. That man has a reputation for being ruthless with everything from his handling of employees to his unethical publicity tactics."

"She's interested because of what you said in the beginning. He's single and wealthy," Georgina drawled.

She couldn't help but laugh as the mayor's words brought an unmistakable flush to Leona's cheeks. This was one of her favorite parts of any sewing circle—the playful banter and occasional barbs.

"Did you get his number, Leona?" she asked.

The woman simply shook her head, her attention still trained on the magazine in her hand.

"You didn't?" Tori gasped in theatrical fashion. "Why, Leona, I'm shocked."

Slowly, Leona lowered the magazine to her lap. "Have we missed the lesson about southern women respecting their elders, Victoria?"

With a flurry of activity, Rose pushed the wheeled cart that housed the portable sewing machine away from her body and wrapped herself in the baby blue afghan that had been draped over the back of the rattan sofa. "You better bundle up, everyone . . . hell is about to freeze over."

"Good heavens Rose, what ever are you babbling about?" Georgina asked midstitch.

Pushing her stocking feet into the warm slippers she always brought to every meeting, Rose simply shrugged. "I figure if Leona is admitting she's old then hell must be freezing over . . . and surely, if it is, we'll feel some of that chill up here."

Tori laughed as Leona crossed her arms and turned a disapproving glare on the group's oldest member. "I never said I was old, Rose Winters. I simply said I was Victoria's elder."

"Elder, schmelder. You're old and you know it." Rose reached for the cart, pulled it close to the sofa, and hunched over it once again, the bobbin gliding across the flowered fabric in rapid motion. "But you're in luck. Seems this Wilder fella is in the golden years of his career anyway."

"Is he really going to write a cover story on Margaret Louise and her recipe?" Beatrice asked. "That's just so exciting."

"I agree," Tori added, her hope for the meeting rebounding with each new word spoken. "But why is she a wreck?"

"Because she has to find a way to make the recipe uniquely southern in order to be eligible for recognition in the magazine." Debbie's voice, quiet and shaky, brought a hush to the room. "And since I've had virtually no customers in the bakery today, I figured the large kitchen and expansive counter areas might be useful to her as she works through each step of her recipe."

Beatrice beat Tori to her question. "Why haven't you had any customers?"

Slowly, Debbie shifted in her folding chair, her hands clasping and unclasping each other as she seemed to struggle with the best way to answer. Finally she spoke, her words every bit as heartbreaking as the hitch in her voice. "I guess for the same reason Suzanna and Jackson were taunted on the playground this afternoon . . . and for the same reason my husband received a death threat in the mailbox today."

This time Tori's gasp was anything but theatrical as a chill shot up her spine and through her chest. "Colby got a death threat?"

Debbie nodded as she dropped her hands to her sides and began picking at tiny pieces of lint on her pale peach slacks. "It was the most awful thing I've ever read. At first it was kind of written in a rambling . . . strangely whimsical way, bemoaning Colby for making Sweet Briar the laughingstock of the south. But then it simply turned frightening . . ." Her voice trailed off as she stared at the floor beneath her feet.

"What did it say?" Tori leaned forward and stilled Debbie's hand with her own. "C'mon, Debbie, tell us."

Debbie slowly looked up, her gaze traveling from face to face around the room before settling on Tori's. "It said his life as he knew it was about to come to an end."

"An end?" Beatrice repeated, her eyes round with confusion.

"*His* end," Debbie whispered.

Pushing the gift bag sample from her lap, Tori left her chair long enough to offer Debbie a hug. "You've got to know it was just an idle threat made by someone who's lashing out in frustration . . . someone who's not educated enough to vent it in a more suitable way."

Debbie swiped the back of her hand across her face in an attempt to catch a few unchecked tears. "That's what Colby said. But how do you explain the lack of customers at the bakery today and the abhorrent way my children were treated on the playground with parents standing nearby? You can't tell me everyone is uneducated."

"People are angry, Debbie. And rightly so. I'm angry, too." Georgina Hayes stopped sewing and leaned back in her chair in much the same way she did at the town's monthly mayoral meetings. "For longer than any of us have been alive Sweet Briar has been known for its resiliency in the face of adversity. It's a history that has served us well. Yet, because your husband has writer's block where his novels are concerned, he's decided to hone his fiction skills elsewhere and disguise it as truth."

"He didn't disguise anything," Debbie spat through clenched teeth. "He researched everything he wrote. He asked questions. He read books. He spoke online with fire experts. And it killed him to write that piece. But turning his back on the truth simply to save some fairy-tale fantasy would have made him part of the lie."

With a strong shove, Rose pushed her cart out into the middle of the room and stamped her slipper-clad foot on the ground. "So in order to clear his conscience, Colby tarnished a part of history that has made this town proud? Oh no. Georgina is right. Your husband asked the wrong people. This town was burned to the ground by Yankees. No one—not even the midlist Colby William Calhoun—can change history to earn him the notoriety his books have failed to achieve thus far."

"Rose!" Tori heard the anger in her voice yet did nothing to quell it. As much as she adored the prickly older woman, there was no denying the simple fact that she was not only out of line but being unnecessarily cruel.

"Victoria, it's okay. I shouldn't have come, I see that now. But Colby insisted. He said my friends would stand by me until the storm passed." Debbie quietly folded the pattern she'd brought and placed it into the large straw bag propped against the legs of her chair. "I guess he was wrong."

"Debbie, wait. It's only been a little over twenty-four hours. Everyone is still in shock. No one means any harm." Tori looked around the room for backup, her gaze desperately seeking some sort of reassurance from Leona or Beatrice or even the strangely quiet Dixie Dunn. But no one responded, no one met her gaze. Turning back to her friend, she squeezed Debbie's hand and offered another hug, her lips brushing the woman's ears as she spoke quietly into her ear. "I'm sorry, I really am. If it matters, I respect Colby for standing by his convictions. And I truly believe everyone will come around . . . in time."

"They know where to find me when they do." Debbie hiked the strap of the straw bag onto her shoulder and headed toward the doorway that led to the hall. As she reached her destination, she turned and offered a shaky smile in Tori's direction. "Thank you, Victoria."

And then she was gone, audible sighs of relief filling the room in her wake.

Turning toward her sewing buddies, Tori worked to keep

the anger from her voice. "I won't stand here and pass judgment on any of you for what just happened. I'm not from Sweet Briar . . . I didn't grow up here . . . I don't have grandparents and great grandparents who grew up here . . . but what I do have is a friend—a friend to all of us—who just left because she was made to feel unwelcome." Slowly, she let her gaze take in each woman in the room—Georgina, Rose, Beatrice, Dixie, and Leona. "And while I haven't done any research of my own to see where the truth lies, I do know that everyone here will come to regret how that woman was just treated. And when you do, I hope you do everything in your power to make it right."

Stuffing her sample into her tote bag, Tori retrieved her sewing box from the side table and set off in search of Debbie. As she reached the doorway to the hall, she turned around, her voice quiet but steady. "I'll see all of you next week. I just want to make sure Debbie gets home okay tonight. I didn't see her car when I pulled up so I'm guessing she and the kids walked."

"Victoria?"

Slowly she swung her gaze toward the woman who had hurt Debbie the most. "Yes, Rose?"

"That threat wasn't the work of an uneducated person. It was the words of someone who's positively furious. And when folks are that angry, they don't think as clearly as they should." Rose pulled the afghan snug against her body as she pulled the cart close once again. "See that she and the children get home safely—and wait until they're inside before you leave."

Chapter 5

As much as she enjoyed Debbie's children, she was glad they were staying at Melissa's for another hour or so, their attention captivated by a game of chase with Jake and the kids. They needed that time with friends as badly as their mother needed to vent in peace.

Tori drove slowly down the streets of Sweet Briar, her tiny four-door compact easily skirting the occasional street-parked car. "So things were pretty bad at the bakery today, huh?" She maneuvered around a group of kids playing a postdinner game of kickball in the middle of the street and then turned to look at the woman in the passenger seat.

Debbie Calhoun was a pretty woman. Her pale blue eyes sparkled nearly twenty-four/seven, providing a perfect accompaniment to the ever-present smile that graced her face. Even now, with the weight of the world on her shoulders, she still managed to emit an aura of contentment to all but the truly observant. Barely in her midthirties, she not only managed to flawlessly juggle motherhood to Suzanna and four-year-old Jackson with her roles as business owner and doting wife, but also found a way to make it look easy. In short, she was the kind of perfection that normally brought out the claws in other women. But even that, she managed to overcome by simply being herself—sweet and genuine.

Which is why it broke Tori's heart to know that deep down inside Debbie Calhoun was hurting.

"I didn't have a single dine-in customer all day," Debbie said with a shrug as she traced the edge of her seat with her finger. "In some ways it was good—it gave me a chance to get caught up on the books. But it also meant a lot of food got wasted."

"But you had some people purchase items to go?" Tori turned onto Main Street and headed west, the businesses surrounding the town square closed for the night.

Again Debbie shrugged. "That part is actually kind of funny . . . the customers I know best—the ones I call regulars—avoided the bakery like the plague today. Yet the one person who has never liked me, showed up."

Pulling her gaze from the darkened windows of the library as they passed, Tori focused instead on her friend. "There's actually someone in this town who doesn't like you?"

"Don't sound so surprised, Victoria. I'm sure there are many more where Ella May Vetter comes from. She's just one who's never bothered to disguise it."

"Ella May? Really? I'm surprised."

"Me too. We never had a run-in, never had any conflicts . . . yet, still, if we're in the same place at the same time she'll act as if I don't exist. The rest of the circle finds it funny."

"Why do you think she doesn't like you?"

Debbie leaned her head against the seatback and sighed. "The only thing I've been able to figure is she must have overheard the circle making comments about her somewhere along the way. Because, aside from sewing and talking, sharing Ella May Vetter oddities is a favorite pastime for many of our friends."

Tori nodded her head as she turned onto Picket Way enroute to Debbie's home on Tulip Lane. "I've kinda picked that up. Although, to be honest, the first I heard of her was just last week at the library. They were going on and on about her—"

"Man," Debbie supplied. "I know. It's the one subject all Ella May stories eventually lead to. Which is why Rose and Leona and Dixie and the rest of them would have been absolutely beside themselves this evening if they'd been a little friendlier to me."

"How so?"

"Ella May's man is about to become Ella May's husband."

"Are you serious?" Tori turned onto Tulip Lane, slowing the car enough to allow her gaze to focus on Debbie. "Details!"

"She came in to look at my catalog of wedding cakes. She doesn't want anything too elaborate or too big and she wants me to use an organic frosting, of course. And, unlike my sewing circle sisters just now, Ella May was actually polite and friendly."

She couldn't help but notice the way Debbie's voice cracked as Tori pulled to a stop in front of 15 Tulip Lane. Shifting the car into park, Tori turned and removed the key from the ignition before reaching out and gently patting the woman's arm. "I'm sorry, Debbie. I truly am. But I think it's the kind of thing that will die down. Sooner rather than later."

Debbie turned her head and looked toward the pale yellow two-story home she shared with her husband and children—a home Tori herself would love to replicate one day. "Jackson cried so hard when he came home from the playground that I thought my heart was going to break in two. And just about the time we got him settled down, he started with one of his nosebleeds."

"Nosebleeds?"

"Yeah." Debbie waved her hand in the air as she continued to study her home from the passenger side window. "It's no big deal. Colby gets them, too. But it was one thing after the other and it started him sobbing again. And Suzanna . . . she was crushed, too. Her very best friend uninvited her to a sleepover this weekend."

"Oh, Debbie, I'm—"

"On top of all that," Debbie continued, the words pouring from her mouth, "Colby was devastated. He kept saying he hadn't thought the story out enough . . . that he never stopped to think how his need for honesty and truth might affect the kids and me."

"I can only imagine how he's feeling right now. But you have to respect him for taking a stand on something he felt was right."

"I guess." With a quick swipe of her hand, Debbie brushed away one lone tear as it made its way down her cheek. "I just hate to see the people I love hurting. And now, with that letter . . ."

"Idle threats, Debbie, idle threats. Remember that."

Slowly, the woman turned from the window, her lip quivering in the streetlamp light streaming in through the windshield. "I'm trying. I really am."

"I know." Removing her hand from Debbie's arm, Tori reached into the backseat and hoisted her tote bag into her lap. "Want to see something?"

"Sure."

"Ella May called in a stack of books she wanted us to set aside last week. And it got me thinking . . . about the people in the nursing home on the northern edge of town. I know they have an on-site library, but it's mostly books that people have donated over the years—books that were first released decades ago."

"Go on."

Feeling a slight upward swing in Debbie's demeanor, Tori continued on, anxious to do anything she could think of to restore a smile to her friend's face. "The truly house-bound residents simply don't have easy access to books with more recent release dates." Sliding her hand into the tote, she pulled out the sample gift bag she'd intended to share with the circle before things got out of hand. "But, maybe, with the help of a few volunteers on a once-a-week basis, we could fill request orders for the residents."

Debbie snatched the cloth bag from Tori's hands and turned it over in her own. "And you want to deliver each resident's requested books in a homemade sack?"

She nodded.

"Victoria, that's a wonderful idea. Absolutely wonderful." Opening the bag, Debbie slid her hand inside. "We'll need to make them a little bigger—to accommodate several hardcovers if necessary."

"I agree."

"And this would be a wonderful project for the circle to do as a group—like the costumes we made for the dress-up trunk in the children's room at the library."

Again, Tori nodded, a sense of relief washing over her as a genuine smile returned to Debbie's lips.

"Oooh, I think I even have some fabric that would be perfect for some of the sacks . . . cheerful colors that'll make the whole experience even brighter for them." Debbie dropped the bag onto her lap and clapped her hands. "And, even if the circle never accepts me back, this is something I can do on my own here at the house. It might even be something Suzanna can help with as well."

"They'll come around, Debbie. I'm sure of it." Tori nudged her chin in the direction of the house. "It's kind of dark in there, is Colby home?"

Debbie quietly folded the sample bag and handed it back to Tori. "He wasn't feeling very well when I left. He tried to pass it off on a persistent sinus infection, but I know better. He's upset about the fallout of his article and it has him as low as I've ever seen him. So I encouraged him to take two sleeping pills. By the time I left for the meeting with the kids, he was passed out on the bed. I imagine that's where he'll remain until sometime tomorrow morning."

"Then I'll wait here until you get inside." Tori stuffed the gift bag back in her tote and offered the woman a quick hug. "Try to stay positive, okay?"

"I'm trying, I really am." Debbie wrapped her long slender fingers around the recessed handle and pulled, the door swinging open to the curb. As quickly as she swiveled her legs to the street, she stopped and turned back to Tori. "Why don't you come in for just a minute? I'd like to show you the fabric I have in mind for some of the sacks . . . see if it's okay."

"Are you sure? I don't want to wake Colby."

Debbie laughed. "Not even a freight train will wake him right now." Stepping from the car, she leaned down and motioned Tori to follow. "C'mon. It'll only take a moment."

"Okay." Tori set the tote on the now-vacant passenger seat before stepping from the car, her keys safely housed in her backpack purse. With a few quick strides she joined her friend on the sidewalk.

Falling into step with one another, they headed toward the house, the gathering dusk making it difficult to navigate the stretch of porch steps that didn't benefit from the glow of a nearby streetlight. "I'm sorry, Victoria. I could swear I flipped on the porch light as I was . . ."

Tori cast a sidelong glance at her friend as the woman's words suddenly trailed off. "Debbie, is everything okay?"

"The door."

"What?"

Debbie pointed at the partially opened door in front of

them, her voice a nervous whisper. "I pulled the door shut behind me . . . I know I did."

"Are you sure?" Tori asked as she forced her words to sound calm and reassuring. "Is it possible you were distracted by one of the kids? You have a lot on your mind, you know."

"Not enough to be that careless."

She knew Debbie was right. In addition to being a successful entrepreneur, Debbie Calhoun was also meticulous. About everything. Leaving a door half open at a time her family was under fire didn't fit the bill. Not even close.

"I'll call Chief Dallas." Slipping her backpack purse from her shoulder, Tori unzipped it and reached inside, her hand closing over her cell phone. "I'm sure he can be here in a matter of minutes."

"Wait." Debbie stepped forward and turned her ear toward the opening. "I don't hear anything. Do you?"

Tori listened for a moment as well. "No, but maybe we should still call. Just to be sure."

"I don't know, Victoria, maybe I was distracted. Jackson was still so sad . . . and Suzanna's hurt had turned into anger by that point. And I was trying to juggle my sewing stuff and the cookie squares with Jackson's little hand . . . Maybe I really did just leave it open."

It sounded plausible when presented like that, but still, this was Debbie Calhoun they were talking about.

"Really, I think it's okay." Debbie pushed the door the rest of the way open and beckoned Tori to follow, her hand finding a wall-mounted light switch in record fashion. In an instant, the front hallway of the Calhoun home was bathed in light, the only sound coming from the grandfather clock that stood sentry beside the wood planked staircase. "See, it's fine."

Tori watched as Debbie's shoulders drooped in relief, the same sensation running through her own body. "Phew. You had my heart starting to race there for a moment."

"Mine, too." The woman gestured toward the parlor on their left. "Make yourself at home, Victoria. I'm going to grab that fabric to show you and check in on Colby real quick."

"Take your time." Tori's hand found the light switch for the parlor and stepped inside, her pulse beginning to slow to a near-normal rate as she stopped beside the mantel adorned with pictures of Debbie's family. Jackson and Suzanna starred in just about every framed photo, each snapshot documenting various stages of their young lives. In some, they were photographed in posed fashion, in others they were caught in more random, candid moments. But in each and every one they sported genuine happy smiles, a perfect match for the one photo they didn't grace—the one from their parents' wedding day. In that picture, it was Colby and Debbie who were all smiles as the promise of a life together stretched before them.

Tori swallowed over the sudden lump in her throat as she leaned closer to the wedding day photograph. In it, Debbie's dirty blonde hair was swept into a French braid that emphasized her high cheekbones. And Colby was as handsome as ever, though it was easy to see that the subsequent nine years or so with Debbie had served him well.

That was what she wanted one day. A good man to share her life with from that day forward . . .

"Colby? Colby?"

Debbie's panicked voice preceded her down the staircase and sent Tori's pulse racing once again. "Debbie, what's wrong?"

"Colby . . . he's not in his bed . . . he's not upstairs anywhere." Debbie rushed through the parlor and into the kitchen, lights flipping on in every room she entered. "With those sleeping pills I gave him he shouldn't be wandering around. He shouldn't even be a—"

A low guttural moan escaped Debbie's lips as she stopped halfway through the kitchen, her feet moving backward as she bumped into Tori. "Oh no . . . oh no . . ." Her voice trailed off only to return in a shriek as she pointed at the floor in front of them. "Oh no!"

Stepping around her friend, Tori stared at the knife jutting from the linoleum kitchen floor with a hastily scrawled note beneath its handle. "What is that?"

"I th-think it's the letter . . ."

She strained to hear her friend's muted words as she dropped to the ground to examine the knife. "Letter?"

"The death threat."

Careful not to touch anything, Tori leaned in as close to the note as possible, her stomach churning violently as her gaze fell on the faint red spatters that dotted the otherwise ordinary white stationery paper. Faint red spatters that mingled with the red waxy scribbles and looked a lot like—

"Oh my God. Debbie, call the police . . . now."

Chapter 6

If there was ever a time she wished she could hit the Pause button on her life, this was it. Sure she'd have opted to use Rewind—or, more accurately, Erase—during her temporary stint as a murder suspect a few months earlier, but Pause would suffice at the moment.

With Pause, she could mute the incessant whispered chatter of the teenage girls in the young adult section. With Pause, she'd be spared the needling guilt over all the little tasks that needed to be completed before lunch—shelving, returning calls, and planning a theme for the next installment of Toddler Time. And with Pause, she might have half a chance of collecting her thoughts after the roller-coaster ride she'd been on since the frightening discovery at Debbie's house the night before.

"Miss Sinclair?"

From the moment she'd noticed the bloodstains in Debbie's kitchen, all hell had broken loose. A hell that had included a hysterical friend, a probing police chief, a hurried phone call to Melissa's home to head off Suzanna and Jackson's impending return, and the undeniable presence of even more blood than first thought.

"Miss Sinclair?"

As grateful as she'd been that Debbie had heeded the chief's instructions to stay downstairs as he searched the house, seeing the overturned chair and scattered books in their bedroom firsthand hadn't been a whole lot easier for Tori. The condition of the room had answered questions she hadn't really wanted to entertain even as she'd stared at the knife-pierced note.

Regardless of what had happened in the Calhoun home while Debbie and the children were at Melissa's, one thing was certain. Colby had put up a struggle.

"Victoria!"

The sound of her name and the stamp of a foot made her head snap up from behind the computer monitor.

"I'm sorry, Miss Sinclair, I tried to get your attention."

"What? Oh. I'm sorry, Nina, I guess I was woolgathering . . ."

"Miss Elkin wants a moment with you." Her assistant's hand rose into the air and pointed toward the hallway that led to their office and the children's room.

Sure enough, Tori's self-appointed southern etiquette-coach-turned-reluctant-sewing-pupil stood guard, her slight figure set off by the pale pink skirt and jacket she wore with an air of regality.

"Can you handle things up here for a few moments?" She looked from Leona to Nina and back again, her gaze drawn to the conflicting emotions playing on the elderly woman's face.

"Of course. Take your time. If I need anything, I'll buzz you."

"Great, thanks. I won't be long." Tori stepped out from behind the information desk and made her way over to the woman whose pursed lips suggested irritation while concern ruled her eyes. "Leona, is everything okay?"

"You tell me, dear." Linking arms, Leona Elkin fairly tugged Tori down the hall and into the tiny office she shared with Nina. "It's true, isn't it?"

She stared at her friend as the woman continued on, her mouth moving at warp speed. "Rose called me first thing this morning. At first I thought maybe it was all wishful thinking on her part after the article, but seeing you just now . . . I knew it had to be true." Leona pushed the door closed and led Tori to the pair of cushioned chairs in the corner of the room. "But, dear, no matter how difficult a morning you might have, you must always—always—apply makeup to de-emphasize your flaws. Which today"—she leaned forward as they both sat, her left thumb sweeping the skin beneath Tori's right eye—"would be some mighty big black circles that are making you look just like one of those stuffed raccoons Carter Johnson hangs from the wall as art."

A raccoon?

"Which isn't to say they're not understandable, dear, because they are. But even under the direst of circumstances you must always be prepared to meet a man." The woman sat back in her chair, gently clasping her hands in her lap. "Gold doesn't just fall in one's lap."

"I—uh." She stopped, sputtered a few nonsensical words, and then stopped again, her mouth at a total loss for words.

"Close your mouth, dear. Gaping it open like that is most unbecoming. It makes you look as if you've given up on a flyswatter and opted to collect those pesky creatures with your mouth instead."

She nibbled her lower lip inward, her mind reeling from the unexpected yet irrefutable impact that was Leona Elkin. There was so much she wanted to tell her, so much she wanted to vent to a willing pair of ears, yet the surge of loyalty toward Debbie prevented her from saying anything.

Sure, the actual unfriendliness at last night's circle had come from Rose and Georgina, but Leona had sat by and let it happen, her nose buried in her travel magazine. Did that kind of loyalty—or lack thereof—deserve answers?

"I feel just awful to know Debbie is suffering right now. And with two such young children to care for." Leona brushed her hands down the length of her pale pink skirt. "You'd think that sabotaging her business, ostracizing her children, and taunting her husband would have been enough."

"Then why didn't you say anything last night while Rose and Georgina were all but attacking her? Why did you just sit there and act as if it wasn't happening?" Tori stood, strode across the room toward her desk, and then leaned against it, her hands braced against the steel gray metal. "Do you have any idea how much they hurt her?"

Leona tilted her head downward, peered at Tori atop her glasses. "I do. But I also knew you'd take care of her—you two are much closer in age."

"Age? Being supportive is about age?" She knew her voice was rising to a level it shouldn't, but she let it go. "Oh . . . I'm sorry . . . the last I checked, being supportive is part of what it means to be a friend. Then again that's something you could use a refresher course on, isn't it?" Surprised by the vehemence behind her words, she looked down and swallowed, waited for the sound of the office door opening and Leona's footsteps as she left. But they never came. Slowly, she raised her head, met Leona's unreadable eyes. "I'm sorry, Leona, that was uncalled for. All I can say is I'm more than a little sleep deprived and absolutely heartsick about Colby."

A moment of silence ensued before the woman finally waved a manicured hand in the air. "No, you're right. I was lost in my own little world last night and by the time I caught up with what was going on, it was too late."

"Lost in your own little world?" she echoed.

"Yes, lost in my own little world."

"Was something wrong?"

"I was planning. And plotting," Leona explained.

"I'm not following." She rubbed her right hand over her right eye as she released a deep exhale.

"Have I not taught you anything about personal maintenance these past few months, dear? Never, ever rub the skin around your eyes. We want it to be firm yet supple. Rubbing removes the natural glow in your skin."

She stared at her friend. "You're worried about my skin?"

"As you should be. You have it until the day you die. Unless you opt to have a little nip and a little tuck." Turning her body ever so slightly in the chair, Leona crossed her legs at the ankles and straightened her back. "Just make sure if you go that route that you find a reputable doctor to do it and not some backwoods quack."

On any other day, Tori would have laughed at the absurdity of the conversation playing out in her office. Never in her wildest imagination could she have anticipated receiving plastic surgery advice before she was officially thirty. Then again, she'd never known someone like Leona Elkin before, either.

"Anyway . . . where was I? Oh yes, while Rose was being her normally charming—and may I point out—spinster self, I was deciding the most appropriate way to meet William Clayton Wilder."

She felt her mouth gape open. "The magazine guy?"

Leona waggled her finger back and forth until Tori clamped her mouth shut. "The wealthy and widowed publishing genius."

"You're not serious. . . . Okay, wait. You are." Pulling her hands from the edge of the desk, Tori dropped her head into them. "Can't you just be in the kitchen when Margaret Louise meets him next?"

"And run the risk he thinks I cook?"

She laughed as she slid her hands down her face. "Um, Leona? He runs a culinary magazine. Don't you think he has an interest in . . . I don't know . . . maybe cooking?"

"Well, I sew, shouldn't that count for anything?" Leona asked with a sniff.

"You sew? Since when?" Suddenly the tension that had knotted itself throughout her body began to ease as she allowed herself to enjoy the easy repartee she'd enjoyed with this woman since the first day they met.

Leona's chin jutted in the air in defiance. "I've worked with buttons . . ."

"Worked with buttons?"

"Yes."

"You've worked with buttons, Leona? Hmmm . . . I remember buttons . . . and I remember you . . . but I don't recall you ever touching them, let alone sewing them."

"Semantics, dear. Semantics."

"Oh, is that what they call it in the south?" Tori pushed off the desk and walked over to the window, her face instinctively tilting toward the sunlight. "What is it about men that makes you shut down on your friends?"

"My friends don't wine and dine me, dear. And they don't have that stubble on their chins in the morning."

She turned toward her friend, eyebrow cocked. "Stubble?"

Leona nodded, a knowing glint in her eye. "Don't tell me you don't think it feels wonderful in the morning against your bare skin."

"Leona!"

"Thou doth protest too much, dear."

Shaking her head, Tori stepped out of the path of the sun, the warm rays doing little to offset the sudden heat in her cheeks. "You're going to quote Shakespeare now?"

"Who else?"

"How about this one . . . men come and go but friends stay forever."

"Touché." Leona uncrossed her ankles and rose from the chair, her short yet shapely legs lessening the distance between them. "What can I do?"

"Do, Leona?"

The woman rolled her eyes in dramatic fashion. "To help Debbie."

"I'm sorry, my ears must not be working. Could you say that again, please?"

"Vic-tor-ia . . ."

"I'm sorry, I was just yanking your chain."

"Yanking what?"

Tori waved a dismissive hand in the air before resting her forehead against the warm glass. "I'm not sure what we can do for Debbie. Maybe help out with the kids when she returns to work?" She stopped, stole a sidelong glance at Leona. "Okay, scratch that one. I know how you are about kids."

"You're a fast learner, dear."

"Maybe find ways to help her keep things as normal as possible?"

"I could patronize her little shop," Leona chimed in.

"But you said women must always be mindful of their figures, remember? Debbie owns a bakery in case you've forgotten . . ."

"I could stop by and gush over her cakes. Help her drum up business that way."

"Let's leave that to Ella May, shall we?" Tori took two steps back from the window and plopped into her office chair, swiveling it so she was, once again, in the path of the sun. "I think the most important thing we can do for Debbie is simply be there to listen and—"

"What does Ella May have to do with cakes and Debbie?"

At the risk of being tarred and feathered, Tori rubbed her hands across her eyes, the nearly sleepless night finally taking its toll. "She's hiring Debbie to make her wedding cake."

A sharp intake of air made her look up—mid-eye rub—just in time to watch the color drain from Leona's face.

"Ella May is getting married?"

"That's right."

"Sir Billy is about to become Mr. Ella May Vetter?" Leona raised up her forearm just long enough to tap the face of her sterling silver link watch with her perfectly polished fingernail. "Oh dear, would you look at the time? I really must be getting back to the shop."

"It's Tuesday, Leona. Elkin Antiques and Collectibles is only open on Friday, Saturday, and Sunday, remember?"

"I-uh . . . need to help my sister . . ."

"Doesn't Margaret Louise look after Melissa's brood on Tuesday mornings? So Melissa can attend a mom and me swim class with Sally?" she asked as the corners of her mouth turned upward in amusement. "Surely you wouldn't stop by a home with six children in it, would you? Unless, of course, you're preparing for your upcoming babysitting job?"

"Rose said something about needing help . . ."

"Rose visits the nursing home on Tuesday mornings, Leona. And you'd be sooner caught dead than go there."

Stamping her foot, Leona turned toward the office door. "I have something I have to do, Victoria. Something I'd rather not discuss."

"You have gossip to spread, don't you?"

Leona reached for the doorknob then looked over her shoulder and smiled ever so sweetly in Tori's direction. "It is my duty, as a good southern neighbor—one who realizes the importance of friendship—to gather together the women of this town in celebration of Ella May's wonderful news."

"To spread gossip, you mean."

With a ladylike shrug, Leona yanked open the door and stepped in the hall, a smile lighting her face from the depths of her soul. "As Margaret Louise would say . . . you're darn tootin'."

Chapter 7

Lowering her sandwich to her lap, Tori leaned back against the brick exterior of the Sweet Briar Public Library and lifted her face to the noon sun.

"Do you remember what you said the other day . . . at the festival? About the loyalty in this town being a good thing so long as it's in your favor?" She turned her face to the left and studied the man who'd become such a bright part of her daily life. A man who'd stood by her through thick and thin during the investigation into Tiffany Ann Gilbert's murder and stayed by her side even after it was all over.

Milo took a bite of his ham and cheese sandwich and nodded, his gaze focused somewhere in the distance.

"You were right. It can really get ugly when it's not, can't it?"

"I think you probably know that better than anyone." Wiping his mouth with one of the paper napkins he brought to accompany their impromptu picnic lunch, he, too, leaned his head against the brick wall.

"But I was an outsider, a newbie. Someone like Debbie Calhoun has lived here her entire life. She was born here, went to school here, was married here, is raising her family here, has opened a business here. Shouldn't the loyalty extend a little deeper and a little truer for someone like that?" It was a question that had nagged at her from the moment the woman had shared tales of the backlash her family had endured on the heels of Colby's article in the Sunday edition of the *Sweet Briar Times*. Backlash that had not only extended to Colby as the author, but to Debbie and her young children as well.

He shrugged, his strong capable frame rising ever so slightly. "It seems like it should, doesn't it? But the loyalty isn't for any one person. It's for the town . . . the image." Balling his sandwich wrapper in his left hand, he tossed it into the empty paper sack beside his thigh. "The image is what matters most."

"More than people?"

"More than people," he confirmed as he hoisted a bright red apple to his lips and clamped his teeth down.

She looked down at her own food—at the sandwich with little more than a bite taken out, at the untouched apple, at the still wrapped candy bar Milo had included specifically for her sweet tooth—and felt her stomach churn with repulsion. The overwhelming hunger she'd experienced when he first walked through the door twenty minutes earlier was nowhere to be found, a casualty of the worry and fear she couldn't seem to shake.

"I'm sorry, Milo." She set her sandwich back in the paper wrapper, sealed it shut, and then returned it to her own sack along with the apple and candy bar. "This was such a sweet idea, it really was. But"—she stopped, swallowed, and tried again—"I just can't get Debbie's face out of my mind."

Tossing his half-eaten apple into the bag, Milo scooted over on the sidewalk, draping his arm across her shoulder as he drew closer. “I’m glad she had you with her. I’m sure that was a comfort.”

“Her husband is gone.” She swallowed again as she rested her head in the crook of his shoulder. “I’m not sure what can comfort something like that.”

“Colby may be a soft-spoken guy, he may spend a large amount of his time behind a computer, but that guy is in shape. He’s not going down without a fight.”

She closed her eyes against the image of the bedroom he shared with his wife, a bedroom that backed up Milo’s words to a point. But in the end, Colby Calhoun was still missing. And there were still blood smears on the wall and droplets across the kitchen floor. She said as much to Milo.

“So maybe you’re right. Maybe he lost the fight. I don’t know. But whoever did it didn’t think things through very well.”

“What do you mean?”

“Well, the town’s image is still destroyed. There’s no way to get Colby to recant his story if he’s dead.”

“Recant his . . . wait.” She pushed off the wall and swiveled her body so she could meet Milo’s eyes. “You think whoever did this should have had him recant his article before killing him?”

He shrugged. “If they were thinking they would have.”

“You almost sound as if you think that’s the bigger issue here. That the town’s image is more important than a man’s life.”

“No. Killing a man is wrong under any circumstances. And justice must be served. But finding the culprit in this equation is going to be mighty difficult.”

“Why?”

“Because Colby set himself up as a target for a whole lot of folks. In fact, I’d be willing to say the list of people who despise Colby Calhoun after Sunday’s article is far longer than the list of people who don’t.”

She felt her mouth drop open. "You can't be serious?"

"Oh yes I can." Pushing off the ground, he gathered up their paper sacks and tossed them into a nearby trash can before reaching for her hand. "C'mon, let's take a little walk."

"I can't. Nina needs me," she said as she flashed an apologetic smile. "Besides my lunch break is—"

"Still in full swing." He turned his wrist so she could see the face of his watch. "We've only been out here for less than twenty-five minutes. You take forty-five, don't you?"

"I do, normally. But I've been worthless so far today. Between my too-long conversation with Leona this morning and the funk I've been in since I got here, I really need to step it up."

"And you will. When your break is over." He closed his hand over top of hers and gently tugged her down the stone steps of the library. "We won't go far, just around the building a few times. It'll give you a chance to vent some of this stuff out."

"Remind me what I did to deserve you?" she asked as she fell in step beside him, the warmth of the sun permeating her body and chasing away the chill she'd harbored all morning.

"You stole my question." He lifted her hand to his mouth and kissed it gently, his eyes looking down at her with a mixture of admiration and worry. "So what do you want to do about all this?"

"Do?"

"I haven't known you long Tori Sinclair, but I've known you long enough to know you can't sit idly by while your friends are hurting."

He was right. She couldn't. "I want to find Colby. Give Debbie and the kids some closure. It's hard to say goodbye when there is no body to bury."

"You're that sure he's dead?"

"I saw the blood, Milo."

For a moment he said nothing, his silence doing little to quiet the tension in her body. "And if you're right . . . and he really is dead . . . don't you think Chief Dallas is trying to find his body, too?"

She lifted her shoulders into the air and let them slide back down. "I suppose. But he's only one person and he's . . ." She stopped, considered the impact of her words on the man walking beside her, a man who claimed Sweet Briar as his birthplace as well. "Well, he can only be in so many places at one time. And if the suspect list is as big as you insinuated it could be, it might be difficult for him to cull through in quick fashion."

"What aren't you saying, Tori?"

Damn.

"I-I guess I'm just worried how the whole loyalty thing is going to play into the investigation." There, she said it. Inhaling slowly, she steeled herself for an argument that didn't come.

"Chief Dallas is a fair man. He may have spent the bulk of his life in this town but he also takes his job very seriously. He won't leave a single stone unturned in this investigation."

"But isn't it possible he might be a little hesitant in the stones he chooses to look under first?" She knew she was running the risk of offending him, but she simply couldn't leave the fears in her head unspoken. Not for anyone, including Milo Wentworth.

"I suppose. I mean, I know he's one of Carter Johnson's poker buddies and I know he goes fishing with Dirk Rogers every spring."

"See? That's all I'm worried about." She stopped, replayed his last sentence in her mind. "Wait. You think Carter and Dirk could be legitimate suspects in Colby's disappearance?"

They rounded the backside of the library, their feet leaving grass as they stepped onto the asphalt of the parking lot and continued walking. "I know Dirk was piping mad at the festival and you said Carter Johnson—"

"Threatened Colby with a rifle . . . you're right." She took stock of the near-empty parking lot, mentally calculating how many customers had left since she went on break. Milo was right, Nina would be fine for the remaining five or so minutes she had. "And then there's whoever wrote that letter, right? Assuming, of course, it wasn't written by Dirk or Carter."

"I doubt Dirk has ever seen a piece of stationery let alone written on one, so . . . although I'm no police detective . . . I think he can be ruled out as the author for now." They rounded the far side of the brick structure, their feet returning to grass and the occasional piece of scattered pine straw that served as landscape material around the moss trees that graced the grounds of the hundred-year-old building. "But, Tori, there are a lot of people in this town who are furious at Colby right now. Essentially everyone who calls Sweet Briar home could be a suspect."

"Except you, of course." The second the words were out of her mouth she could feel him stiffen beside her. Stopping, midstep, she tugged his hand until they were face to face. "Hey, I was only kidding."

"I guess." He ran his free hand through his burnished brown hair, leaving the top more than a little disheveled as he let a burst of air escape his lips. "Tori, I have to tell you that I'm not real happy with Colby right now either. He questioned my teaching in that article."

"He didn't call you out by name," she protested.

"He didn't have to. He said this supposed lie was taught in the classroom. Don't you see that statement calls all of the teachers at Sweet Briar Elementary liars?"

She stared at him, unsure of what to say in response to his growing anger.

"He had no right to do that, Tori."

She heard herself gasp, saw the hurt in his eyes as she removed her hand from his. "But if it's true . . ."

"What? That I'm a liar?" he asked through teeth that were suddenly clenched.

"I didn't say that!"

"You implied it. I mean, if the article is true—and I'm not saying it is—then that's what I am, isn't it?" He looked off into the distance, his jaw tight with anger. "C'mon, Tori . . . don't you find it even the slightest bit odd that we're just now hearing moonshine was to blame for the fire that leveled this town? Don't you think that would have leaked out along the way sometime over the past century or so?"

"Maybe." She pulled her hand to her face to shield the sun from her eyes as she absently watched an elderly man cross the grounds en route to the front door. "But if you were responsible for the mistake that destroyed a town, wouldn't you want to keep it hush-hush, too?"

"Drunks talk, Tori."

She met Milo's eyes once again, a sadness creeping over her body. "Just because someone makes moonshine doesn't mean he's a drunk. And just as some alcoholics have been known to talk, others have been known to be fiercely protective and more than a little cagey."

"That's a long line of cagey drunks then."

Realizing they weren't going to get anywhere on the topic at hand, she took a step backward and gestured toward the door. "I really better get back inside. It's time for Nina to take her lunch break."

She felt the wariness of his stare as she turned and headed toward the building. After a few feet she looked back over her shoulder and waved. "Thanks for lunch, it was very sweet."

Slowly, she climbed the same stone stairs she'd descended not more than ten minutes earlier, her hand now empty and her heart weighing heavily under a sadness she hadn't expected. Sure, all relationships hit their fair share of hurdles along the way, but this wasn't about a difference of opinion over what movie to see or whether floral curtains were too feminine. No, this one went much deeper—to a very basic belief system of what was right and what was wrong. And the realization that Milo Wentworth couldn't differentiate between the two when his pride was part of the equation.

As she pulled on the outer doors and walked into the branch's main room, Tori couldn't help but breathe a sigh of relief. In less than six months, Sweet Briar Public Library had become just as much her home as the tiny two bedroom cottage she rented. Here, she could be herself—a person who enjoyed sharing her love of books with people of all ages.

But at that moment it was more than just the love of books that brought her comfort. It was the knowledge that she was surrounded by truth, something she desperately needed.

"How was your lunch, Miss Sinclair?" Nina looked up from her place behind the information desk and flashed a quick, yet shy smile. "I sure wish Duwayne would show up out of the blue and bring me a picnic lunch one day."

"He sent you flowers just last week, didn't he?" she reminded, infusing as much cheer into her voice as possible. "I think that ranks right up there with a picnic lunch."

A slow blush worked its way up her assistant's neck as she covered her face with long dark fingers. "You're right."

"Now get out of here and get some lunch yourself." Tori looked around, mentally registered each patron scattered around the room. "Everything been okay?"

Nina nodded. "I'll take a short one."

"No, take your full break. It's gorgeous outside today."

She leaned against the counter as Nina retrieved her purse and headed toward the same door from which Tori, herself, had just come. There were so many thoughts swirling around in her head, thoughts she should set aside in favor of work. But she knew it was futile. She wasn't built that way. Never had been. Never would be.

When there was a problem at hand she needed to work through it—slowly, methodically. She wouldn't have any peace until she did.

The key, though, was where to start. Milo was right. Dirk Rogers and Carter Johnson were certainly worth exploring, especially in light of their friendship with the Sweet Briar police chief. But they were by no means the only two people in town who took offense to Colby's column.

There was Rose . . .

There was Georgina, the mayor of Sweet Briar . . .

And there was Milo—

She shook her head, willed her mind to skip forward to viable suspects—the kind of people who guarded Sweet Briar's history like it was the single largest piece of gold in the world. The kind of people who would take a secret to their grave if need be.

Clapping her right hand over her mouth, Tori grabbed the edge of the counter with her left.

The kind of people who would take a secret to their grave . . .

"A secret of monumental proportions," she muttered under her breath as she reached for the phone and punched in Margaret Louise's phone number.

"Hello?"

"Margaret Louise, it's Tori . . . I mean, Victoria."

"I knew that before you finished my name. You have a cute twangy way of sayin' *Louise*."

"I have a *twangy* way?" She tried not to laugh too loud as she held the phone to her ear and peered around the room. "Isn't that the pot calling the kettle black?"

"Do I speak with a twang?"

She couldn't help it. She laughed—a quick sound that brought more than a few looks as she soaked in the absurdity of the question and the sincerity with which it was spoken, the amusing exchange doing more to lighten her mood than anything else since Leona took off in search of a picket fence to hang over.

"Never mind. How's the recipe going?"

A long deep sigh filled her ear followed by something that sounded an awful lot like a cluck. "It's not. I'm tryin' to give it a uniquely southern twist and everything I come up with seems so, well, simple. Blah. I want to shake it up a little."

"You'll find it. Give it time."

"Bless your heart, Victoria. Aren't you a little ray of sunshine this afternoon."

A ray of sunshine? That's not quite the description she'd use for her present demeanor. But if it worked . . .

"I've tasted your cooking, Margaret Louise. You're a genius. That magazine should be begging you to be on their cover."

"Are you tryin' to sweet-talk me on my sister's behalf?"

She dropped onto the stool and rested her head on the countertop. "Why would I do that?"

"Because she hasn't even picked up a needle yet."

"How'd you know?"

"We're twins. I know everything about my dear sister."

"Have you seen her today?"

"No. But I've only been home a short while. Melissa took Sally to dinner after swim class."

Looking up, she noted the hands on the wall-mounted clock. "You mean lunch?"

"We call it dinner in the south. Hasn't Leona taught you that yet?"

"Then what do you call dinner?"

"I just said that. We call it lunch."

She shook her head. "No. I mean the meal the rest of the world refers to as dinner . . ."

"Supper."

Tori dropped her head back down to the counter with an audible groan.

"You'll catch on. Have faith. Now . . . what was that about Leona? Is she ready to concede the bet?"

Tori glanced up again, her eyes skirting the various reading chairs and research tables set up around the main room. "She has news. Ella May Vetter news."

She pulled the phone from her ear as Margaret Louise's shriek threatened to burst her eardrum. When the noise finally quieted down, she held it close once again.

"Really? What? What? Tell me!"

"And ruin Leona's fun? Never."

"Spoilsport."

"I actually called because I have a question. What's the name of that man who owns the moonshine distillery on the outskirts of town? The one you said gives samples?"

"Gabe Jameson."

She repeated the name as she reached for a pen and pad of paper. "Okay, thanks. I just—"

"I know last night had to be hard . . . and trust me, Victoria, I'm just as torn up 'bout Colby myself but . . . you sure you want to be nippin' at the bottle at this time of day?"

"I—"

"Cause if you are . . . I could use a little break myself. Jake Junior and the lot of them sure were wound up this mornin'," Margaret Louise rushed to add.

"No. It's not that. I just want to ask him a few questions. I mean, this column Colby wrote just blasted a long held Jameson family secret out of the water, you know?"

"You're investigatin' aren't you, Victoria?"

"No, I just—"

"You can't fool me. You're investigatin'."

She dropped the pen onto the counter, ripped the top piece of paper from the pad, and then shoved it into the small front pocket of her fitted summer jacket. "Okay, maybe just a little."

"I'm in."

"You're in what?"

"I'm in for investigatin'. And maybe a few . . ." The woman's voice trailed off into a mumble Tori couldn't quite decipher.

"I'm sorry, what was that?"

"I'm in for investigatin'."

"I heard that part. It was the part after that I didn't get."

The woman cleared her throat then continued on, her normally booming voice a bit more subdued. "And maybe a few samples, too. For quality control purposes, of course."

Chapter 8

She looked up from the notebook she'd been jotting thoughts in all afternoon as Margaret Louise's powder blue station wagon careened into the back parking lot and screeched to a stop just inches from where she stood.

Pulling the notebook to her chest, Tori leaned into the car through the open passenger side window. "Where's the fire?"

"Fire? There isn't any fire. My dear sweet sister drives like this all the time. Unless one of Jake's is in the car. Then she drives like a tortoise," Leona said with a groan as she closed her eyes and leaned against the vinyl backseat, her now red fingernails waving back and forth in front of her face.

"I'm surprised to see you, Leona. I didn't know—"

"Get in Victoria, time's a wastin'." Margaret Louise reached across, unlocked Tori's door, and then patted the empty passenger seat with her hand. "Leona just told me!"

"Told you what?" Tori yanked open the car door and

stepped inside, her hand barely reaching for the handle before Margaret Louise pressed down on the gas pedal. "Whoa! What's the rush?"

"We've got a stop to make before we head out to Gabe's place." The woman's short, pudgy hand turned the steering wheel sharply to the left, her maneuver barely clearing the line of massive moss trees that were as much a staple of the property as the library itself.

Dropping her notebook onto her lap, Tori reached over her right shoulder and pulled the seat belt forward, locking it into place.

"Smart girl," muttered Leona from the backseat. "I bet you hadn't entertained the idea of an untimely death when you left for work this morning."

She considered refuting her friend's weary words but opted to remain quiet. Talk of Colby and his fate would come soon enough. Ignoring Leona's continued mutterings, she cast a sidelong glance at Margaret Louise, the woman's face-splitting smile impossible to ignore.

"Where are we stopping?" she asked, the fingernails of her right hand digging into the gap between the window and the door as Margaret Louise peeled out of the parking lot and headed west.

Looking up into the rearview mirror as they sped along, Margaret Louise giggled with glee. "A little birdie informed me that we have a bride-to-be in our midst. And it's only proper that we stop by to offer our congratulations, don't you agree?"

Ahhh, yes, it made perfect sense now. Leona had finally tracked her sister down with the juiciest gossip to hit Sweet Briar since Colby blew the town's claim to fame right out of the water.

"So Leona told you?"

"Sure as day . . . didn't ya, Twin?" Looking into the rearview mirror once again, Margaret Louise winked at her sibling. "I have to say it was a surprise but sooner or later her fictitious man had to propose. Though it's goin' to be much harder for her to explain away his continued absence now."

"Perhaps she can hire a stand-in from time to time," quipped Leona in a voice that suggested her excitement hadn't waned much since hearing the news herself earlier that morning. "There are places like that . . . not that I'd have any reason to know, of course."

Tori shook her head as she looked over her shoulder. "You two just don't quit, do you? Why do you think Billy isn't real?"

"Billy? You know his name?" Margaret Louise pinned Tori with an amused stare as she blew through a four-way stop and turned north, her foot pressing more firmly on the gas pedal as they sped along. "It took years before she finally gave us a name. Before that it had always just been her man or her gentleman. Remember that, Twin?"

"I do, indeed. When I moved here nearly six years ago she was still being mum on his name. She'd say she didn't want to take a chance that sharing particulars might disturb the relationship." Leona leaned forward and rested her right forearm on Tori's seatback. "I think it took me all of about ten minutes to realize she was the one who was disturbed."

Tori glanced down at the black and white marbled notebook in her lap, recalled the list of potential suspects and motives she'd crafted in lieu of doing the work she should have been doing around the library. "If you both dislike her so much, why on earth are we stopping there? I'd really like to get out to this Gabe person's place as soon as possible. Debbie needs us."

"In the south, Victoria, we believe in celebratin' one another's triumphs as well as mournin' each other's tragedies." Margaret Louise let off the gas pedal long enough to make a wide turn onto Lantern Drive. "I want to help Debbie just as much as you do. And we will. But it would be right rude of us not to acknowledge Ella May's news and . . . offer our assistance."

"You mean your nosiness?" she asked as the corners of her mouth drifted upward.

"Our assistance," Leona repeated firmly. "There is a difference, Victoria."

She laughed. "Oh yes. Give me a moment. *Nosiness* means sticking your nose where it doesn't belong. *Assistance*—or, rather, assistance according to the two of you—means getting permission for your nosiness under the guise of being helpful." Glancing from Margaret Louise to Leona and back again, she cocked an eyebrow in their direction. "Am I right?"

Leona sat back against her seat in dramatic style, her fingers once again fanning her face as the car slowed to a crawl. "My work here is nearly done, Victoria. You really are getting the hang of southern ways in much quicker fashion than I could have imagined . . . especially in the beginning when you were so wholly inept."

"Wholly inept?" she repeated.

"Non-southern, dear." Leona glanced out the window as the car came to a complete stop, her nose crinkling at the mailbox beside them. "People who are not disturbed don't have black and white polka-dot mailboxes."

"With a big white weather-resistant bow on top," added Margaret Louise. With a quick turn of her hand, she removed the heavy key ring from the ignition and dropped it into her oversized purse. "Shall we?"

Tori held up her hand. "Wait. I'm curious. What kind of assistance are you planning on offering, Margaret Louise?" She felt her eyes narrow as she caught an exchange of curious looks between the sisters—looks that made the proverbial hair on the back of her neck snap to attention. "What?"

Leona cleared her throat daintily. "Assistance we're all offering, dear."

"We're offer—wait! Wait just a minute. I'm not going to be roped into your campaign to invade this poor woman's life."

Running her hands down her neck, Leona simply stared back at Tori. "Victoria, dear, don't you want to learn our ways? Don't you want to be a true member of this community rather than a constant outsider . . . from the north no less?"

Tori threw her hands into the air then glided them through her hair in frustration. "For the last time, I only lived in Chicago for eight years. Before that I lived all over. But I was born in *Florida*, Leona. Flor-i-da."

The woman snorted. "As I've told you before, dear, Florida does not count. It's the leech on southern society, an imposter."

She leaned her head against the seatback and looked out the front windshield, her gaze roaming across the lovingly shabby Victorian that was home to Ella May Vetter—a woman who simply valued her privacy, her fiancé, and, judging by the near-constant activity across her front yard, her bunnies. Her hundreds and hundreds of garden variety brown bunnies . . .

"Leona told me what you said about Ella May hirin' Debbie to gussy up her weddin' cake," Margaret Louise interjected. "We just want to find ways we can help with the special occasion as well. That's all, Victoria."

Setting the notebook on the empty expanse of seat between them, Tori crossed her arms in front of her chest. "What do you propose?"

"Well . . . Debbie can make the cake . . ."

"I'm thinking she probably has other things on her mind right now." She wasn't trying to rain on their parade, she really wasn't, but facts needed to be faced. The biggest of all being who killed Colby.

"Debbie will make the cake. I just plain refuse to believe Colby has been harmed." Margaret Louise cut her hand through the air, effectively ending that line of thinking for the moment. "So, like I said, Debbie'll make the cake, and I can cook the supper for the reception . . ."

"Who says she is going to have a reception? Maybe the two of them will simply have a quiet ceremony. With a wedding cake for two."

"Spoilsport." Leona huffed from the backseat.

"I can cook the supper for the reception," Margaret Louise continued, unfazed. "And you can find just the right poem to commemorate their special"—the woman looked at her sister through the rearview mirror once again and grinned—"love."

"And?"

"And what, Victoria?"

"And Leona? What will she offer to do?"

Margaret Louise's shoulders slumped. "We haven't come up with that yet."

"Perhaps an antique from my shop. You know, dear, something along the lines of a bunny trap from the 1800s?"

Tori rolled her eyes upward, her gaze resting momentarily on the spot where the ceiling fabric caved inward a smidge. Swiveling her body to the left so as to afford the most clear-cut view of the passenger in the backseat, Tori flashed a smile that made Leona shift in her seat. "I have an idea, Margaret Louise. It goes hand in hand with your bet. You know, the one about Leona learning to sew."

"Oooh, do tell." Margaret Louise rubbed her hands back and forth against each other.

"Well, you both know that famous saying about something old, something new, something borrowed, something blue . . . right?"

"Of course." A hearty laugh escaped Margaret Louise's mouth as she, too, turned to look over the seat separating them from Leona. "What do you have in mind?"

"I'm thinking that perhaps your sister, here, can make a

lace handkerchief for Ella May. It would be simple yet tasteful and more than a little appreciated . . . especially when Ella May learns how hard Leona worked on it."

The smartly dressed woman in the backseat simply stuck out her tongue and shook her head. "I wouldn't want to take the chance I'd ruin that portion of the famous tradition. It is, after all, supposed to be a perfect day for the bride."

"Memorable," corrected Margaret Louise as she reached for the door handle and pulled it up. "That's a splendid idea, Victoria. I don't know why I hadn't thought of it myself."

Following suit, Tori exited the car amid a string of protests from the one remaining occupant. "Think about it, Margaret Louise . . . long after Debbie's cake and your meal have been eaten . . . long after the words of my poem have faded into a distant memory . . . Leona's lace handkerchief will still be around . . . bringing such sweet joy to Ella May and Billy."

"Perhaps she could even put a small patch right in the middle of the lace. Something that symbolizes the happy couple's undyin' love." Margaret Louise didn't even attempt to bite back her smile as Leona stepped from the car. "Or maybe somethin' with special significance for the bride herself."

Tori clapped her hands together. "That's it, Margaret Louise! We could put a tiny bunny in the center of the fabric."

"I am not amused. Not in the slightest." Leona enunciated each syllable with the utmost clarity. "I believe an antique will be just—"

The sound of wood smacking wood make them all look up, the early evening sun temporarily blinding them. In simultaneous fashion, all three placed their hands over their eyes and looked toward the Victorian home that seemed more than a little ill-fitting among scads of bunny rabbits and countless placards boasting cutesy bunny sayings.

"It's her," Margaret Louise whispered from the side of her mouth. "It's Ella May."

"Well who else did you expect it to be?" Leona whispered back.

"We look ridiculous just standing here, ladies." Inhaling deeply, Tori wrapped one hand around each woman's upper arm and guided them forward until they were within speaking range of the woman who clamored down the front steps as quickly as possible, her body—decked out in a long dress with a tight fitting bodice and puffy floral sleeves—moving rapidly toward them. "Hi, Ella May!"

"Miss Sinclair. Ms. Elkin. Ms. Davis. Wh-what brings you by?" The woman looked down at her hands and then brushed them against the long skirt of her dress. "I-I wasn't expecting company."

She shot a glare at each of her friends, her initial reservation over the uninvited visit resurfacing with a vengeance. "We're sorry we didn't mean to—"

Margaret Louise stepped forward, her hand grabbing hold of Ella May's and pumping it up and down. "We heard the news. About you and Billy. We just wanted to stop by and offer our congratulations. He sure is a lucky fella."

Ella May blushed. "Thank you, but I'm the lucky one. I couldn't be any more blessed." Three small brown rabbits hopped across the dirt and gravel driveway and stopped at Ella May's feet, their little noses twitching in delight. The woman bent down and rubbed each one behind the ears, her voice taking on a singsong quality as she continued. "If Billy were here, he'd thank you himself. But—"

Leona's mouth twitched. "He's not here? Oh, what a shame."

Ella May reached into the pocket of her dress and extracted three tiny carrots, one for each bunny. "He's preparing for some important meetings. He's such a busy and important man that getting a few days for the ceremony and our honeymoon will take some doing."

"We have a few gifts for you . . . gifts to make your wedding more special but"—Margaret Louise waved her hands wildly in the air—"it's just so hot out here."

Tori rolled her eyes as her friend's motive became painfully clear. It wasn't enough just to stick her nose in Ella May's business, she wanted to stick her fanny smack-dab in the middle of it as well. "I have some water in the car," she hissed.

"No you don't," Leona offered.

"Yes. I. Do." As each word left her mouth, Tori supplemented it with a slight pinch on both women's arms.

"Ow . . . what did you do that for?" Margaret Louise howled. "I just said it was hot—"

With a second pinch, Tori took charge of the conversation. "Ella May, we'd like to offer our congratulations and our help. To make your day as special as possible."

Ella May looked up from her bunnies and smiled, a hint of a tear glistening in the corners of her eyes—a tear that tugged at Tori's heart and made her silently curse her friends' shallow motives. "That would be lovely."

"I know my way around a library pretty well," she offered, a lump forming in her throat at the notion she'd been coerced into playing along with Margaret Louise and Leona's gossip-gathering mission. "If you like poetry, and you give me an idea of the kind of sentiment you'd like to highlight, I could find a handful of poems for you to use during the ceremony."

Ella May squealed, a happy little sound that brought even more bunnies hopping in her direction. "Oh, Miss Sinclair, I would be honored."

"Please, call me Tori—"

"Actually, it's Victoria," Leona drawled.

"Victoria? That's such a lovely name. And yes, I'd be honored if you would find me some wonderful poetry . . . something that would celebrate the wonderful man who will share the rest of his life with me."

Tori shifted from foot to foot, torn between the desire to let her shoulders fall in relief and smacking Leona in the back of the head. "I'm glad. Just give it some thought and let me know if you have any ideas or themes you want me to work around."

"Ohhh. Ohhh. It's so very, very hot out here," Margaret Louise interjected with all the drama of an Oscar-winning actress. "I feel my legs getting just a bit wobbly. Perhaps I could sit down somewhere? Like maybe your kitchen table or your living room?"

"We only have two more things to tell Ella May and then you can rest your wobbly legs in the car." Tori changed the pinch to a grab, eliciting an even louder howl from her friend. "Go on, Margaret Louise, tell Ella May about your idea."

With a rare scowl, Leona's twin sister made a face at Tori before stepping forward, her sensibly clad feet kicking up a small dust cloud. "I don't know if you know it or not, Ella May, but I enjoy cookin'."

The woman reached into her pocket and extracted several more carrots, her fingers expertly wrapping around each one so as to feed more than one rabbit at a time. "Of course I know that. Your entries in the festival cook-offs are always the most delicious."

Tori raised an eyebrow at Margaret Louise as she rested her hands atop her hips.

"Well bless your heart, Ella May. You're just so sweet and good. Anyway I'd like to offer my services for your reception. You can even pick the menu." Gesturing toward the house, she took another step forward. "We could sit down . . . right now . . . and bat around ideas."

Ella May struggled to her feet, her hand shielding her eyes from the sun as she stood. "I don't think—"

"Margaret Louise, the walk to the house is much longer than the one back to the car. You really must consider your wobbly legs." Tori enunciated each word through clenched teeth, her hand finding her friend's arm once again. "Besides, we have another stop to make . . . remember?"

"The offer to cook for us is very touching. I know Billy will be pleased as well."

"Perhaps I could tell him myself . . ."

Tori's hip shot to the side, striking Margaret Louise in the stomach. "Oh, I'm sorry, did I hit you?"

"Yes. You did." Margaret Louise jutted her chin outward. "Why did you do that?"

"I had a cramp." Tori gestured toward the one woman who stood off to the side, her gaze soaking up everything. "Leona? It's your turn."

"Oh. Yes. Of course." Leona's eyes skirted across the yard, her nose crinkling in disgust over the gaggle of bunnies that continued to swarm Ella May. "I was thinking that perhaps you'd like to stop by the store and—"

Tori cleared her throat, a sound echoed by Margaret Louise. "Now Leona, don't be so shy. Tell Ella May about the present you'd like to make her . . . with your own two hands."

"I-I . . ."

"My sister, she's a modest one." Margaret Louise's mouth widened into a smile that rivaled the early evening sun. "What she's tryin' to say is that she'd like to make you somethin' new for your weddin'."

"Dear sweet sister," Leona bit back, "I think it's only natural that Ella May's gown will be the something new . . ."

"Actually, my gown will be the something blue."

"Blue?" Margaret Louise and Leona asked simultaneously—froth nearly forming at the corners of their mouths. "Have you been married before?"

Ella May shook her head as a dreamy look fell over her face. "No. I've been saving myself for just the right man—for my Billy."

"Then why blue?" Leona asked as her eyes narrowed in distaste.

"Because I think Billy will like my eyes best in a blue gown."

"Then that, right there, is a perfect reason." Tori looked at Leona and smiled. "So, see . . . your idea will work just fine, Leona."

"What idea?" Ella May asked.

"I-I—"

"My sister is learnin' to sew. She's workin' most diligently at it, as a matter of fact . . ." Tori's eyebrow rose once again as Margaret Louise continued to shovel on the lies. "And she would like to use this newly learned skill to make somethin' for your special day. Somethin' small you can tuck in a pocket or clutch."

Ella May brought her hands together, a gesture that brought even more bunnies in their direction. "How wonderful. Thank you, Ms. Elkin."

"Leona," Tori corrected gently. "But she prefers to go by Lee."

"No I—"

"Thank you, Lee. And thank you, too, Ms. Davis."

Margaret Louise stepped forward, pulling Ella May against her full polyester-clad bosom. "Call me Margaret Louise. I think it's high time we consider one another a friend, don't you? The kind of friends that stop by and stay for a glass of sweet tea."

Oh good grief . . .

"Would you look at the time?" Tori shoved her wrist in front of Margaret Louise's face. "We've got to get out to Gabe's before it gets too late. Besides, we've taken enough of Ella May's time, don't you think?"

"Well, no, not really. I think we've got plenty—"

Tori reached out, gently squeezed Ella May's forearm with her hand, and offered the woman a genuine smile. "I am so happy for you and Billy. It sounds as if the two of you have something truly special."

"We do. We really do. But you understand that, don't you?"

"Of course. One only has to see the way your face lights up to know you have something special," Tori said as she took her friends by the arms and turned toward the car.

"No, I mean you understand because you have the same thing . . . with Mr. Wentworth."

She closed her eyes as Ella May's words hit with a one-two punch to her stomach.

Like she and Milo had . . .

Chapter 9

She rested her forehead against the cool glass and watched the moss trees whiz past her window as Margaret Louise piloted them down Route 54. All afternoon she'd managed to downplay thoughts of Milo as she focused her attention on Colby and Debbie. But now, after what Ella May had said, the heaviness in her heart reemerged.

It wasn't that she didn't understand the disappointment the townspeople felt over the sudden change in their history, because she did. But disappointment aside, Colby had uncovered damning evidence that called into question a major piece of Sweet Briar history. How could that be his fault? Wouldn't it have been worse for him to discover the truth and then tuck it under a bed somewhere in favor of upholding a lie?

"Is something wrong, Victoria?" Margaret Louise slowed the car as it approached the intersection of Route 54 and Pike Road, her voice suddenly void of the mischievousness she'd displayed since the start of their trip. "If I upset you by draggin' you along to Ella May's, I'm sorry. I truly am. I didn't mean no harm. I just . . . well, I guess you could say I get a little tickled sometimes. And, Victoria, you have to understand we've been hearin' about Ella May's man for more years 'en Carter Johnson has been claimin' he uses real eggs at the diner."

She pulled away from the window and turned to look at her friend, the woman's troubled eyes bringing a lump to her throat. "I wish I could say that's all it is, but I can't."

"Did Nina put a cooking book in the American History section or a self-help book in with the mystery novels, dear?" Leona asked from the backseat.

"No."

"Did your great-grandmother's sewin' machine finally conk out?" Margaret Louise asked. "Because if it did, I'm sure Jake would take a look. It don't matter if it's a car engine or the motor in a vacuum cleaner . . . that boy has been fixin' things since I gave birth to him thirty-three years ago."

"No. Gram's machine is still going along fine." She looked down at the notebook in her lap, tried to focus on the reason for this car ride, but she couldn't. Milo Wentworth was front and center in her thoughts now. "Milo and I . . . we had—"

"Cover your ears, Margaret Louise," Leona cautioned as she sat forward, leaning her forearms across Tori's seatback once again. "You had what, dear?"

"We had a fight." Pulling the notebook to her chest, she hugged it closely, her eyes burning with unshed tears. "And I'm not sure it's something we're going to be able to work through."

Margaret Louise reached across the seat and gently patted Tori's leg. "Of course you'll be able to work through it. Fights happen sometimes, it's natural."

"And if you didn't fight, you couldn't make up." Leona

rested her head on her forearms. "That's the best part you know . . . the making up part."

"How would you know, Twin? You're never with anyone long enough to make up," Margaret Louise quipped.

She had to laugh. Not because she felt any better or held out a sudden hope that things would be right with Milo again, but because Leona and Margaret Louise just made life fun.

"Is that a laugh I heard?" Margaret Louise pulled her hand back and placed it on the steering wheel as Pike Road morphed into County Road 6. "See? Things are never as bad as they seem."

"I only wish that were true. Things are pretty awful right now for Debbie and the kids. I mean . . . someone broke into their home and took Colby, leaving his blood splattered everywhere." She set the notebook back in her lap and slowly fingered the cover's black and white pattern with her index finger, her thoughts replaying the previous night's tragedy. "It was just awful."

Tightening her hands on the steering wheel, Margaret Louise shook her head resolutely. "Now don't you talk like that, Victoria. Colby Calhoun is a good and decent man, an honorable husband, and an adorin' father. No one who values their life would dare hurt that man."

She looked at her friend in surprise. "You're not mad at him?"

The woman pulled her gaze from the road in front of them and fastened it on Tori's face. "Mad at Colby? Why, in good heaven, would you think I was mad at Colby?"

"Because everyone in Sweet Briar seems to have commissioned him as the town's most hated individual. So much so he received a death threat, Debbie had no business at the bakery other than Ella May, and the kids were taunted on the playground."

"Suzanna and Jackson were taunted?" Margaret Louise's foot pressed down on the gas, a motion that pulled Leona against the backseat with a resounding thud and a string of unladylike mutterings. "Who was mean to them? Was it that little Shelby Pruitt? That child is as nasty as her bleach blonde mama. Or was it Tucker West? That little good-for-nothin' has tried to make trouble for Lulu in the past . . . until I took to his face with a stare that child won't soon forget."

"I'm not sure. Debbie didn't say. But I know both were feeling much better Monday evening thanks to your grandchildren. They played all evening with each other." Tori rested a calming hand on Margaret Louise's shoulder until the woman eased up on the gas pedal once again. "I only wish the grown-ups had played as nicely that evening, because Debbie needed it almost as much as Suzanna and Jackson did."

Margaret Louise sighed, her ample chest rising only to fall once again. "I heard about that part. Melissa told me all 'bout it when I babysat for the kids this mornin'." The woman peered into the rearview mirror at her sister. "Leona, you wouldn't have been one of the ones who was rude to Debbie, were you?"

Tori looked over her shoulder in time to see Leona shifting in her seat as her face took on a pinkish hue. To Margaret Louise she said, "Leona didn't say anything. She was a little, um . . . preoccupied."

"About what? Wait. Don't say anything. My twin only gets preoccupied with one thing." Margaret Louise looked back at the road. "Now as for Debbie, we'll get her business back on track. Folks can't stay away from her bakery for long. And Colby? Do we know who sent that letter?"

Tori shook her head as her words rushed to confirm the action. "The killer I imagine. Though why he'd send a note beforehand seems a little strange."

"Did you get a chance to at least read it?"

She closed her eyes, the contents of the blood-spattered note cycling through her thoughts for the umpteenth time since it all happened. With as much accuracy as she could recall, she recited the threat aloud. "The people of Sweet Briar are most unhappy. Of that, you will soon see. Their beloved home you've made a laughingstock, an easy target for others to ridicule and mock. Revenge is, indeed, their battle cry. But I . . . I can't sit idly by. Article or not, I see who you are . . . and who you're not. And now . . . now it must stop."

"That's it?" Margaret Louise pulled her eyes from the road and fastened them on Tori. "That's the note?"

"As best I can recall, yes. Well, except for the last line."

"Wait. I remember that one," Leona interjected. "Debbie told it to us at the circle meeting. Something about Colby's life coming to an end . . . right?"

Tori nodded.

"I don't remember her saying it rhymed though."

She considered her friend's words. "I never really noticed that. I just knew it was oddly worded and that the crayon made it even worse."

"Crayon?"

Nodding, she pointed toward the road in an attempt to get Margaret Louise's attention back where it belonged. Before they all died. "Tougher to write with and thus easier to disguise, I guess. Anyway, I do know that two separate people were overheard making threatening statements about Colby and his article at the festival on Sunday."

"By whom?"

"Excuse me?" she asked as she peered across the seat at her friend.

"Who overheard these threats? Stories tend to get bigger 'n life in this town, Victoria."

"I heard one of them and Milo heard the other." She glanced out the window once again, the moss trees giving way to larger expanses of empty fields dotted with dilapidated farmhouses and various other outbuildings.

"We're almost there ladies, Gabe's place is right over

this hill." Margaret Louise let up on the gas pedal as the tires left pavement in favor of a gravely dirt road that wound around a grove of trees. "Who did you hear, Victoria?"

"Carter Johnson. He was furious after reading Colby's article. I overheard him telling his grandson that he ought to burn down the news tent."

"Brainless and ignorant and not the slightest bit out of character for ol' Carter Johnson, but that's not a threat to Colby outright."

She swung her gaze back to Margaret Louise as they followed the dirt road farther into the trees. "True. But the rifle he wanted to bring back with him sure was."

Margaret Louise slammed on the brakes, causing Leona to slide off her seat and add a few additional unladylike mutterings to her repertoire for the day. "Carter Johnson was going to take a rifle to Colby?" Leaning her head against the seatback, Margaret Louise let out a deep, hearty laugh. "Carter Johnson couldn't hit a target if it was two inches from his face. Unless, of course, it's a raccoon who happened to throw himself in front of the barrel . . . Mind you, Victoria, this is the man who serves carton eggs to his customers . . . *carton* eggs, Victoria."

"You didn't see him and you didn't hear him that day. He was mad."

Again the woman laughed. "Carter Johnson was mad? Victoria, that man is always mad. It's his ordinary face. The only variation is whether he's spittin' mad or just plain mad."

"He was spitting mad." Tori craned her neck forward, her gaze traveling down the remaining stretch of dirt road that extended beyond the car and coming to rest on the dilapidated gray clapboard shack with a rotting front porch and a series of skewed shutters. Beyond it stood an even larger building with the same colored exterior and barn-like doors—the type of place where it was easy to imagine a body stashed amongst the decay. *Could Colby be here?*

"And the other one?"

"The other what?" she asked distractedly as she continued to study Gabe Jameson's less than tidy property on the outskirts of Sweet Briar.

"Who was the other person who threatened Colby at the festival?" Margaret Louise kept her foot on the brake as she, too, scanned their surroundings. "Truvie Jameson—God, rest her soul—would be mortified if she saw what's become of this place."

"Yeah it's pretty bad." Tori scanned the grounds for any sign of life but saw nothing. "The other verbal threat was made by Dirk Rogers . . . you know, the guy who owns the garage out on—"

The car lurched forward only to stop on a dime as Margaret Louise's foot returned to the brake. "Did you say Dirk Rogers?"

"Whoa." She grabbed her stomach as a wave of nausea threatened to bring their little excursion to a halt. "Could you maybe watch the foot thing, please?"

"Yes, please," Leona groaned.

"Dirk threatened Colby?" Margaret Louise asked as she waved off her occupants' protests.

"All I know is what Milo said when we caught up by the news tent during the festival. Dirk was apparently furious over Colby's article."

Margaret Louise drummed her fingers against the top of the steering wheel. "That one's a loose cannon. Has been since he was a young-un in school with my Jake. He's sneaky and plays anythin' but fair."

Tori leaned over and grabbed her purse, her fingers instinctively finding the zipper and then a pen. As she shoved the purse back onto the floor of the station wagon, she flipped open her notebook and sought the page with Dirk Rogers's name. "So you think he could be a real threat?"

"Do I breathe?"

"Just because he might have stolen a few marbles from Jake on the playground twenty-five years ago doesn't mean he's capable of murder." Leona smoothed her pants with a practiced hand as her chin jutted upward. "I mean really, Margaret Louise, don't you think you're being a bit extreme?"

Margaret Louise reached upward, tilted the rearview mirror as to afford the best possible view of her twin. "Marbles were the start, Leona. His sneakiness extended well into adulthood. Why do you think Jake's garage hit that rough patch a few years ago? Why do you think he started workin' two extra jobs while Melissa was tryin' her best to keep up with five little ones and a newborn Sally?"

"Why?" Tori asked.

"Because Dirk Rogers started spreadin' rumors. He started questionin' Jake's business practices and leadin' people to believe he was chargin' for work he wasn't doin'." Margaret Louise's fingers encircled the steering wheel in a death grip. "And while I'm not the kind of mama to think my son is perfect, I do know a few things for sure. First and foremost I raised an honest boy."

"I—"

Cutting her sister off midsentence, Margaret Louise continued on, her fingers turning white against the chocolate brown steering wheel. "And then . . . when people started comin' back to Jake's garage because they realized he was fair, his buildin' was suddenly ransacked. Thousands of dollars in tools disappeared."

"You think Dirk Rogers took them?" Tori's pen-holding hand paused above the opened notebook.

"I don't think he did it himself. Oh no, Dirk Rogers likes to keep his hands clean. But I think he knows who did."

"Why wouldn't he say?"

Margaret Louise returned the mirror to its original position and then looked at Tori. "Because he wouldn't want the person who did it to point a finger at him."

"For what?" Tori asked.

"For hirin' him to do it."

She let her friend's words float around in her thoughts as she tried them on for size. If she'd learned anything about Margaret Louise over the past few months it was the woman's propensity for maintaining an open mind.

And being fair . . .

And good . . .

And a loyal and true friend. Qualities that were a little rarer than she'd originally thought.

"Then he's officially on our list of potential suspects." Tori underlined Dirk's name with three separate marks and then closed the notebook. "At least that gives us a good place to start. After this place, of course."

"Why, exactly, are we here again?" Leona drawled, boredom dripping from her voice. "Other than to give my dear sweet sister a reason to take a few nips from the bottle."

"Isn't that why you came, too?" Tori asked with a laugh as she tucked the notebook under her arm and hoisted her backpack purse back onto her lap.

"Me? Never." Leona shifted in her seat as a soft red glow sprang into her cheeks. "I'm here simply as moral support."

"*Moral support* my behind." Margaret Louise glided the car forward a hundred yards and then shifted into Park. Glancing at Tori, she gestured her head toward the shack that was home to Gabe Jameson. "You ready?"

She nodded, placed her hand on the door handle, and then looked back at Leona. "If Colby's facts are right, Sweet Briar didn't burn to the ground because of Yankees over a hundred and forty years ago. It burned to the ground because of moonshine made on this very property by Gabe

Jameson's kin. Which means if Colby is despised because he let the cat out of the bag, Gabe Jameson has to be hated every bit as much."

"And so why are we here? To offer him protection from the same lunatic who killed Colby?"

Margaret Louise's pudgy hands rose to her ears as her mouth started moving. "There is no reason to believe Colby is dead, Twin."

"Blood isn't a reason?" Leona asked as one of her perfectly tweezed eyebrows arched.

Margaret Louise slowly removed her hands, her mouth tugging downward in sadness. "I reckon."

Tori let go of the handle and swiveled her body to the left, her gaze moving between the woman in the backseat and the woman in the driver's seat. "We need answers, real answers—whether we like them or not. We owe that to Debbie and the kids."

"I agree," Margaret Louise said, her normally boisterous voice more than a little subdued. "But I know what answer I don't want."

Leona shrugged. "None of us want that answer, Margaret Louise. But there's something to be said for being realistic as well."

Ignoring the last comment, Tori took the helm of the conversation once again, her mind willing her heart to blot out Leona's words. "While it's true Gabe Jameson may need protection as much as Colby did, it's also true that Colby's article unveiled a truth that Gabe's own family has kept under wraps for well over a century."

"Ahhh," Leona said knowingly. "I get it now. As angry as most people are at Colby right now, Gabe has reason to be even angrier."

Tori nodded. "Absolutely. Because when talk of the article dies out, people won't remember who let the cat out of the bag any longer. They'll—"

"Remember whose cat it was," Margaret Louise finished in triumph. Pointing toward the building just beyond Gabe's home, she narrowed her eyes. "Should we split up? Maybe you and Leona go to the house while I check out the barn? You know, take advantage of Gabe bein' occupied by the two of you?"

Leona crossed her arms in front of her chest. "Do you think we just fell off one of your turnip trucks, Margaret Louise?"

She looked a question at the perfectly coiffed woman. "What are you talking about, Leona?"

The woman rolled her eyes upward and then settled them on the woman in the driver's seat. "Do you want to tell her or shall I?"

Margaret Louise's face reddened but she said nothing.

"Tell me what?" Tori demanded.

"Do you know what's in that barnlike shack, Victoria?" Leona posed.

"Answers, I hope."

"While that would be splendid, dear, I think there may be another reason my dear sweet sister has so generously offered to enter the danger zone."

"Why? What's in there—" She stopped as reality dawned. "That's where he makes the moonshine, isn't it?"

"Really?" Margaret Louise asked on the heels of a theatric gasp of surprise. "I had no idea."

Leona tilted her head a hairbreadth as she studied her sister angelically before grabbing for her antique clutch and snapping it open. Reaching inside she extracted a piece of folded white paper and handed it to Tori.

Wordlessly, Tori unfolded the paper, her gaze falling on a series of colorful doodles that filled the page. Doodles that resembled some sort of step-by-step process alongside a crude drawing of two squares—one big, one little. A smiley face filled the center of the big square. "What is this?" she asked as Margaret Louise tried to grab it from her hand.

"This is the moonshine making process from start to finish." Leona's index finger swept across the page as she briefly explained each doodle. "And these squares . . . are those buildings." The woman extended her hand down the middle of the front seat. "The blue square is Gabe's house . . . the building you and I are supposed to visit first. And the red square is the barn in the back . . . the one she wants to search on her own."

Tori pinned Leona's sister with a look of amusement. "Why'd you draw a yellow smiley face inside the red square, Margaret Louise?"

Ripping the paper from Tori's hand, Margaret Louise crammed it into the pocket of her polyester sweat suit and pushed her door open, her rounded form rising from the seat. "You can laugh all you want. But when Gabe hands you one of his samples . . . you'll be beggin' me for crayons so you can draw a few pictures of your own."

Chapter 10

For someone who'd been chomping at the bit to visit Gabe Jameson, the nervous flutter in her stomach as they approached the door was more than a little surprising.

But now that Tori was actually there, staring at the warped front door that hung precariously from its rusty hinges, all thoughts of securing answers for the Calhoun family had faded into the background. In their place were new thoughts. Unsettling thoughts.

What if the man who resided on the other side of the door really did abduct Colby Calhoun? Would they find Colby safe and sound as Margaret Louise was desperate to believe? Or would they be forced to bare the news she and Leona thought more likely—news that would forever destroy the lives of Debbie and her two children?

And if Gabe Jameson was behind it all, how far would he be willing to go to keep his actions hidden?

Casting a sidelong glance at Leona, Tori felt a surge of guilt wind through her heart. Just because she hadn't thought things through clearly didn't mean her friends should suffer. . . .

"Leona, if you don't want to do this . . . I understand. You could just go find Margaret Louise and wait in the car together."

Leona stopped, pointed at her dust-covered pumps, and sneered. "Perhaps that would have been an offer better made five minutes ago, dear?"

"I'm sorry, Leona. I wasn't thinking. I just wanted to find Colby and bring him home to Debbie . . . one way or the other." She looked from Leona, to her own dirty white heels, to Gabe's shacklike home that brought the notion of fixer-upper to a whole new level.

"That's changed now?" Leona carefully pulled one foot up and wiggled it back and forth in an effort to dislodge some of the dust. When it failed to achieve the outcome she sought, she set it back down and sighed.

"Huh?" Tori pulled her gaze from the front of Gabe's home and fixed it on her friend. "What's changed?"

Looking down at her off-white summer suit, Leona began furiously wiping dirt from the thin fabric, her face contorted in disgust. "You'd think people would be more considerate of others and clean up their homes."

"We're outside, Leona."

The woman stopped wiping at her clothes long enough to look up at the house in front of them. "And you think inside will be any different?"

Tori shook her head. "It doesn't matter."

"It does if you're no longer interested in finding Colby."

She turned her head, stared at the woman beside her. "Where on earth would you get the idea I don't want to find Colby? It's why we're here."

Resting her hands on her hips, Leona peered at Tori over the top of her glasses, her voice resembling that of a preschool teacher who'd hit her patience quota. "You just said I should go sit in the car . . . that you hadn't been thinking . . . you'd just wanted to bring Colby home one way or the other. Is this ringing any bells, Victoria?"

"I just meant I didn't want you in harm's way. That's all." She gestured toward the house as a sudden movement behind the front curtain—or was that a bedspread?—caught her attention. "Shhh. Someone's in there."

"Well, isn't that why we're here?" Leona elbowed her way past Tori and stepped onto the front porch—a slab of wood propped atop a series of bricks that ran the length of the Jameson home.

"Wait, Leona, we need to talk this thr—"

Without waiting for Tori to finish, Leona raised her fisted hand and knocked on the front door, her nose crinkling. "Good heavens, dear, what is that awful odor? It smells like something died right here on this-this front whatever-you-want-to-call-it."

Died?

Grabbing Leona by the wrist, Tori kept the woman from repeating her knock. "Do you really think it smells as if someone—"

"I said some*thing*, not someone." Leona pulled her arm free of Tori's grasp and knocked once again. "My money is on Gabe's supper not Colby Calhoun."

"Leona!" Tori hissed through clenched teeth.

"It's what you were thinking, dear." Leona's hands dropped to the sides of her skirt, smoothing away wrinkles from the dust-coated material as the door in front of them cracked open.

"Whudev' you sellin' lady, I'm not buying nothin'." A man of about seventy peeked his head between the wall and the door, his bushy gray eyebrows forming a *V* in the center of his forehead. "I gots everythin' I need."

Leona stamped her foot on the wood slab, the sound echoing outward as Tori simply stared, her gaze traveling over the man's head in an effort to see any sign of additional life inside.

Spreading her arms outward like wings, Leona narrowed her eyes at the man. "Is it necessary to be so rude? Do I really look like I'm selling anything?"

The man's dark brown eyes slowly made their way down Leona's trim body as a slight smile overtook the scowl that had graced his face just seconds earlier. "I might be inclined to change my mind on not buyin' nothin' if I thought you might be for sale, Ms. Elkin."

Tori's mouth gaped open as Leona paused momentarily to preen before striking the man over the head with her clutch. "Didn't your daddy teach you better manners than that, Mr. Jameson?"

"Wooo-eeee, I gots myself a real 'ive fireball on my front porch. I can see why my brother paraded you 'round town when you first came here. You're feisty and fancy all in one purty package." Slowly, the man's hand cracked the door open a bit more as his eyes left Leona and fixed on Tori. "And who might you be?"

"I-I'm Tori Sinclair." Stepping forward, Tori extended her hand to the man in the doorway, her gaze darting back and forth between him and the ever-widening interior view. "I've heard a lot about you."

His mouth widened into a bigger smile, revealing a few missing teeth and an assortment of crooked ones in the process. "Why, Ms. Elkin, have you been tootin' my horn 'round town again? People gonna talk if ya keep that up . . ."

Leona's finger shot outward, its tip barely grazing the man's nose. "There's nothing to toot, Mr. Jameson. And if there's talk, it has absolutely nothing to do with me."

A cloud passed across the man's face as Leona's words hit their mark. "Oh there's talk. Lots of it. Nasty letters, too."

Tori's ears hijacked her limited visual inspection. "Nasty letters?"

"Yes, ma'am. But that's not all—no sirree. There's been shootin', too."

"Someone's shot at you?" Tori asked as her mind raced to establish some sort of order for the questions begging to be asked. "Who? When? Where?"

"Don't know who. Though I've got me some ideas." The man's hand traveled upward to his chin, a day or two worth of stubble covering the sides of his face. "Happened just today. In this very spot. Can still see the marks."

"Where?" Tori stepped back, her visual inspection taking on a new stretch of territory that included the exterior boards of Gabe Jameson's home. "I don't see any holes."

"They weren't shootin' with rifles, ma'am. Near as I can tell it was tomatoes . . . or maybe cherries." Stepping onto the porch, the man made his way over to a series of red-stained boards to the right of his front window. "Now I'm not the best housekeeper—"

Leona sniffed, her arms delicately crossing in front of her body as her chin jutted in the air, the antique silver jewelry that graced her wrist and fingers glistening in the last of the sun's rays. "'Not the best' implies you try, Mr. Jameson."

"Leona!" Tori reprimanded from the corner of her mouth. "Now is not the time to be petty."

"Petty, dear?"

Amused, the man waved his hand in the air. "No need to worry none 'bout Ms. Elkin and me. My grandpappy used to say squabblin' between a man and a woman was a sign."

"A sign of what?" Leona asked as her hands found her hips.

"Feelins."

Tori laughed as Leona's mouth dropped open. "You know something, Mr. Jameson? I think my grandfather used to say the same thing." Resisting the urge to see her friend's reaction, Tori took control of the conversation, steering it away from Gabe's obvious interest in Leona and back toward the task at hand. "Any chance it was simply the work of teenagers bored with summer break?"

"Nope. It's the work of someone angry 'bout what's happened. 'Bout the truth comin' out." The man leaned against the house as he fixed his gaze on some distant point far beyond where they all stood. "Seems the truth ain't somethin' people want to hear when it ain't as pretty as the lie."

"You mean the fact that your family's moonshine burned Sweet Briar to the ground all those years ago instead of Yankees?" Tori asked, the need to peek inside the home all but gone.

"Yes, ma'am. Seems this town can only be proud of fixin' themselves up if the Yankees were the one to break 'em. Don't seem to matter none that bein' burnt to the ground is bein' burnt to the ground. An' buildin' up again is buildin' up again."

No matter how you sliced it, the man was right. Then again, she hadn't been raised in a town that celebrated its rebirth as an annual ritual complete with a festival and parade. If she had, maybe she'd feel differently.

Maybe.

Then again, some people were just born with certain qualities. Common sense was one of hers. And common sense couldn't dispute what Gabe Jameson had just said. Rebuilding—better than new—after complete incineration was noteworthy and cause for celebration regardless of what lit the fuse. It was the tenacity that mattered, not the act that called it into play. Why couldn't people see that?

She leaned against the side of the house, her hope of finding Colby Calhoun hidden somewhere on this man's property beginning to fade as reality dawned. Gabe Jameson was no more responsible for Colby's disappearance than she was, of that she was virtually certain. She slowly studied the man in front of her as he toed what remained of the tomato stains on his home, a sense of acceptance hovering over his actions. "It doesn't bother you that this secret is out, does it?"

He met her gaze with his own, his head shaking slowly from side to side. "Nope, can't say it does. If anythin' it's a blessin'. Carryin' a secret like that your whole life is rough. Real rough. That Calhoun fella showin' up at my door last week was a good thing in my book. Freein'."

"You didn't mind him showing up here and asking questions? Poking around at a secret your family's kept for generations?" She pushed the tips of her fingers through her hair in disappointment. Not because she wanted Gabe Jameson to be capable of abduction, but simply because she'd wanted to find Colby.

"Nah. He got right to the point. No pussyfootin' 'round. Can't hold nothin' 'gainst a man like that." Pulling a flat can from his back pocket, Gabe Jameson unscrewed the top and removed a hunk of chewing tobacco, which he shoved into a corner of his mouth. "I'm glad it's over. It is what it is. It's up to folks in town how they deal with it. Shame though, if they focus on the moonshine 'stead of the fixin' part. Real shame."

Leona's voice, quiet yet firm, cut through the silence that fell across the porch, her words reminding Tori that she and Gabe were not alone. "This secret . . . you don't seem upset about the fallout"—she gestured toward the red stains beside the man—"now or in the future."

The man shrugged, his mouth working the tobacco for a few moments before spitting some into the dirt just beyond the front of the porch. "It's not like a few red stains makes a diff'rence. It's not like I have a missus to protect unless"—his mouth parted revealing the gaps between his teeth—"you want to change that, Ms. Elkin . . ."

Leona straightened her stance, her shoulders rising majestically. "And break the hearts of so many women who want to fill that role? I wouldn't be able to sleep at night, Mr. Jameson."

"Now, Ms. Elkin. Are you tryin' to make me blush?" The man shifted from foot to foot, Leona's words bringing a rise to his chin and an endearing twinkle to his eyes.

Tori nodded ever so slightly at her friend. Leona Elkin could be a lot of things—some of which could be off-putting at times, but she was also a good egg.

"I imagine you do see all of this as freeing, Gabe. You really don't have all that much to lose by this secret coming out now." Peering over the top of her glasses at the shacklike house behind Gabe, Leona entwined the fingers of both her hands through the handle of her clutch. "But what about the person who stands to suffer a good deal because, unlike you, they do have something to lose . . . something they've worked long and hard to achieve despite considerable odds?"

Tori stared at Leona, her radar beginning to ping. What was Leona talking about?

"I didn't answer that Calhoun fella's questions to hurt Hank. I answer'd 'cause it was the truth."

"A truth that you have to know will hurt him."

"Whoa—wait. You two have officially lost me. Who is Hank? What did I miss?"

Gabe lifted his right foot and propped it on the wall behind him, his head shifting to the left long enough to spit out another round of tobacco. "Hank Joe, Hank Joe Jameson. He's my brother, not that that means nothin' to him anymore."

Gabe's brother?

Confused, she looked from Gabe to Leona and back again. "Okay . . ."

"Most folks don't know him as Hank and even more don't know he's a Jameson on account of his changin' his name to be somethin' he's not."

"He's accomplished a lot," Leona interjected, her right hand rising into the air as her index finger extended in Gabe's direction. "He made his choices and you made yours."

"Choices?" Tori asked.

"He was too good for this"—the man pushed off the side of the house and stepped off the front porch, his feet kicking up dust clouds as he walked forward a few feet only to turn back to them—"for the very land our daddy worked his whole life . . . and his daddy b'for him . . . and his daddy b'for that. But he's a Jameson. That's somethin' them fancy shoes, fancy clothes, and made-up last name ain't ever gonna change."

She watched Gabe as he continued to pace around, his feet shuffling through the dry dirt that seemed to surround his home for acres. Although she was out of the loop in terms of the sudden sparring match that had sprung up between the two, it was quite obvious it was a sore subject for both.

"You know Hank, Leona?"

"He goes by Harrison now, but yes, I know him. And so do you, dear."

"I don't know any Harr . . ." The words trailed from her mouth as her thoughts began to put two and two together, a picture emerging in her mind of a man wearing a dark blue suit, crisp white shirt, and a powder blue tie. A man who donated a number of law books to the library in honor of his career. In fact, if she remembered Nina's words correctly, Harrison James Law Practice was the most respected law firm in the entire county.

Not bad for someone who grew up alongside the man still pacing back and forth in the dirt, spitting tobacco into the distance and wiping his hands on his ill-fitting white sleeveless shirt.

"I wouldn't have known Mr. James was your brother," Tori stated matter-of-factly.

"Most people don't. 'Cept the folks who've lived in Sweet Briar most their lives. Hank prefers to keep it that way."

She looked over her shoulder at the shack Gabe called home, scanned the grounds to the left and right that boasted the absence of money and pride, imagined the barn behind the house where generations of the man's family made moonshine as their primary source of income and entertainment, and understood completely why Harrison James would want to keep his ties to this life hush-hush.

Who wouldn't? Especially if you were trying to build a career by earning people's trust and respect.

Suddenly she understood what Leona had been asking.

Sure, Colby's public revelation may have served as a breath of fresh air for a man like Gabe Jameson—a man who'd lived his entire life with the secret of what happened on his property over a century ago. But for a man like Harrison James, who wanted to distance himself from this place and its people in favor of a better life, the revelation of what happened here could blow everything he'd worked so hard to accomplish right out of the water.

She tucked her hand underneath Leona's arm and gently guided her off the porch and onto the dirt. "I think it's time we round up Margaret Louise and head back."

"Is everything okay, dear?"

"U-uh, yeah. It's fine. It's just getting a little late and we've taken enough of Mr. Jameson's time."

Gabe stopped pacing. "I didn't tell to hurt Hank. I really didn't."

Leona stopped, the bejeweled fingers of her right hand reaching out just long enough to offer the man a gentle pat on his bare arm. "I know you didn't."

And, strangely, Tori did, too. Gabe Jameson was an open book, it was something you just came to believe and know as you talked to him. But Leona was right. He didn't have too much to lose by telling the truth about Sweet Briar's incineration.

Harrison James, on the other hand, had everything to lose—his respectability, his character, his name, and the very life he'd worked so hard to create. Men killed for far less than that on a routine basis. The only question that remained was whether Harrison James was one of them.

Chapter 11

She pulled her knees to her chest and nestled back against the cushion, the crazy pace of her day finally loosening its grip as she took in the game of kickball that was winding down in front of her cottage. The workday had been a blur with a summer school field trip, a book club, and grant papers that had commanded her attention from the moment she'd walked into the library that morning until she'd closed the doors at seven.

The visit from the children had gone well, with most of the students eager to leave the confines of Sweet Briar Elementary in favor of something different. All twenty students had thrown themselves into the possibilities of the children's room, acting out various stories with the help of the costume trunk and the small stage that had been constructed for just that purpose. The monthly meeting of the branch's mystery book club had been a success as always, with many of its members flooding the shelves for the latest in their favorite genre before heading back home.

On any other day, Tori would have taken enormous pleasure in the large number of patrons and their intense enthusiasm for reading. It was, after all, everything she loved about her job. But no matter how much she'd tried to lose herself in the activity, her thoughts kept straying back to the same thing.

Colby Calhoun.

She hadn't realized just how certain she'd been about the whereabouts of his body until the moment Gabe Jameson had started speaking and all hope had faded away. And as hard as it was to realize she'd been wrong, she'd been glad, too. Gabe Jameson was no more capable of harming another human being than she was.

Leaning her head against the wicker back, Tori closed her eyes and lifted her face to the early evening breeze that stirred the tops of the trees. Summer in the south was rough, with its high humidity and even higher temperatures, a combination that made dusk the most tolerable part of the day.

"Miss Sinclair, are you okay?"

Smiling wide, Tori opened her eyes and focused on the little girl at the bottom of her porch steps—a little girl with long dark hair, big brown eyes, and a smile that had stolen her heart the moment they met.

"Hi, Lulu!" She dropped her legs to the ground and spread her arms wide. "How did you know I could use a Lulu hug tonight?"

The child's eyes sparkled as she hopped up the steps and skipped over to Tori. "Magic!"

"I like that kind of magic." Tori wrapped her arms around the little girl and inhaled deeply, a curious potpourri of sugar cookies, Play-Doh, and dandelions bringing a lump to her throat. She glanced over the top of the child's head and smiled at the woman lumbering up the steps with a covered casserole dish in one hand and a coloring book and crayons in the other. "You have no idea how much I needed this tonight, Margaret Louise."

"Sure I did." The woman stopped as she reached the top step, her breathing slightly labored. "I knew it yesterday . . . when we were in the car on the way to Gabe's and you mentioned—"

She shook her head softly as she held her hand in the air. She could talk about any number of things at that moment—books, sewing, her suspicions about Gabe's brother, dessert recipes, whatever. But Milo? No. Not yet. He'd popped in and out of her mind all day, her heart growing heavier with each passing hour that brought no contact.

Turning her attention back to Lulu, Tori tapped the child's nose softly. "Have you been reading this week?"

The little girl nodded as she hopped from foot to foot in front of Tori's chair. "I'm almost finished with a new Cam Jansen mystery and Mee-Maw is reading *On the Banks of Plum Creek* with me, too. Aren't you, Mee-Maw?"

Margaret Louise nodded. "We just finished reading about Laura and Mary's country party."

"Oooh. Wasn't that funny when Nellie got the leeches all over her?" she asked as she reached out and smoothed Lulu's hair from her face.

"Uh-huh." The child stopped hopping long enough to point at her grandmother before looking back at Tori. "Mee-Maw brought a coloring book for me to color while you talk. She even has some crayons for me, too!"

Casting a sidelong glance in Margaret Louise's direction, Tori nibbled back a grin. "Let me guess . . . blue, red, and yellow?"

Lulu's eyes widened in awe. "Wow! You could be a magician!"

"Or a distillery-map reader."

"What's that?" Lulu asked.

"That's Miss Sinclair's attempt at a funny, sweetie."

"Oh." Lulu pulled her gaze from her grandmother's face and fastened it back on Tori's. "Mee-Maw said if I color one real careful you might let me hang it on your refrigerator."

"I think that's a lovely idea." Tori stood, tucked Lulu's hand inside her own, and led the way into her cottage with Margaret Louise at their heels. "My kitchen table is the perfect spot for coloring."

Once Lulu was settled in the tiny kitchen with her crayons and coloring book, Tori joined Margaret Louise in the living room. "I can't tell you how much I needed that bright shiny little face tonight."

"You don't have to. Your face said it all." Margaret Louise pointed at the covered dish she'd set on the coffee table. "If you don't mind, could you grab a fork and a small plate and give this a taste? I need an opinion."

She leaned over the casserole and stared at two distinctly separate lumps of something mushy. "What is it?"

"My Sweet Potato Pie."

She clapped her hands together as a squeal left her lips. "Is this the one that caught the eye of that magazine guy?"

Margaret Louise nodded as she put a name to Tori's generalization. "William Clayton Wilder. And yes, it is."

"Why does it look like that?"

"He wants me to make it uniquely southern if he's goin' to feature it in his magazine. I've been swappin' things out and addin' new things one ingredient at a time since Sunday. I've tried so many different combinations that I'm not sure what I'm doin' anymore."

"So these are two different variations?" Tori asked.

Margaret Louise nodded once again.

"I'll be right back." She spun around and headed back into the kitchen. "How's it going in here, Lulu?" She peeked over the child's shoulder. "Oh, sweetie, that's wonderful."

"No looking, Miss Sinclair. It's a s'prise." Flipping the

coloring book over, Lulu looked up at Tori accusingly. "You can't see it 'til it's all done . . . okay?"

"Okay." She bent down, planted a soft kiss on the little girl's forehead, and then yanked open the silverware drawer. "Your Mee-Maw wants me to be her taste-tester. Do you know what that is?"

Lulu nodded. "I've already been one. Lots and lots and lots of times this week. Mee-Maw says I'm the best taste-tester ever."

"I'm not surprised." And she wasn't. While most eight-year-olds flitted from one thing to the next, Lulu Davis was the kind of kid who soaked up everything around her, remembering details most adults forgot. Reaching into a cabinet to the left of the stove, Tori extracted a small plate and started toward the doorway.

"Don't forget a cup of water," Lulu said as her foot thumped against the leg of her chair.

"Water?"

"Uh-huh. To clean your plate."

She laughed. "I'll clean it at the sink when I'm done."

"No, not your plate. Your"—the child's eyes rolled upward as she searched for the right word—"pa-late."

"You mean *palate*?"

"Yeah, that. Mee-Maw says you need to wipe your tongue's memory before you try something new."

"And, as usual, your Mee-Maw is absolutely right." She walked back to the cabinet, retrieved a small glass, and filled it with water from the tap. "Am I ready now, Lulu?"

"You're ready." The child nodded her head with absolute seriousness then flipped her coloring book over. "I have to get back to my work now."

"I'll leave you to it then." She looked over her shoulder one last time before rejoining her friend. "I love that child so much."

Margaret Louise dropped onto the love seat behind the coffee table. "I know you do, Victoria. And she loves you every bit as much." With a nod at the glass of water, she continued. "I see you've been a taste-tester before."

"No. You just have a brilliant granddaughter."

A loud hearty laugh filled the room as Margaret Louise leaned back into the sofa's cushions. "Of course. She takes after her Mee-Maw."

"I think—if your sister was here—she'd take this opportunity to point out that Lulu has some of her genes as well."

The woman rolled her eyes. "That'd be like sayin' she can sew because I do. And you and I both know that's a cotton-pickin' lie."

Tori perched on the edge of the armchair. "What are we going to do about that? She is more than a little reluctant—she's downright ornery."

Shrugging, Margaret Louise leaned forward and scooped a spoonful of sweet potatoes onto Tori's plate. "I'm too plumb busy plannin' where I'm goin' to take Melissa and Jake while she babysits."

Tori laughed. "Can you even imagine that? Those poor children would be locked in their rooms the entire time."

"Jake Junior is an expert lock picker. Now here . . . try a taste."

She took the plate from Margaret Louise's outstretched hand and extracted a generous forkful.

"Only put half of that in your mouth." Margaret Louise scooted over on the sofa, closing the gap between them with ease. "Savor it. Slowly."

She nodded at the directions and then slid the fork into her mouth, her lips closing over the halfway point of the fork. "Mmmm, wow. This is amazing . . ."

The woman beamed. "Good. Good."

Tori pointed at the casserole dish with her now empty fork. "Why are you trying anything else? It can't possibly be better than this."

"Just try it. This is one I just put together today. Lulu hasn't even tried this one."

She handed her plate back to the woman and watched as a second scoop of potatoes was heaped into the center. "How do you know what to try? I'd be so afraid of putting together a hideous combination."

"It's second nature, I guess. Like books are to you." Margaret Louise handed the plate to Tori once again. "Take a swallow of water first and swish it 'round your mouth a dab before you try this one."

"What inspired this one?" She took a sip of water and swished it around her mouth as she'd been told, Margaret Louise's cheeks turning a soft shade of red as she did. "What? What did I say?"

"Nothin'. Just try it."

"Margaret Louise, are you trying to poison me?"

"Just try it." The woman leaned closer as Tori slipped the fork into her mouth, her eyes closing as an explosion of taste made her groan. "Oh, Margaret Louise. This is mind-blowing."

"You rightly think so?"

She dug into the remaining lump on her plate and stuck a second forkful into her mouth, nodding as she did.

"Are you absolutely sure?"

She nodded again, the potatoes sliding down her throat as she turned her fork onto its side and chased every remaining remnant around the plate. "What did you put in this one? It's . . . well, mind-blowing doesn't even do it justice."

Margaret Louise flopped against the back of the sofa, the back of her hand covering her forehead. "It hit me while I was"—she clamped her mouth shut only to open it again a few seconds later. "Anyway . . . cover story here I come."

Tori set the plate on the coffee table and settled back into her own chair. "What's this Wilder guy like?"

"Willy?" The woman sat up, repositioned her plump form on the sofa, and then nestled into its soft cushions. "Famous. A little full of himself—you know, one of those men who thinks the world exists just to hear him crow."

"Which explains Leona's interest . . ." she muttered under her breath only to feel guilty the second the words were out. "Margaret Louise, I'm sorry. I didn't mean that the way it sounded."

"No, you're right. My sister is hankerin' for wealth and importance. Which is fine, I'll do my part to help."

"Your part?" Tori reached for the glass and took a small sip.

Margaret Louise nodded, her gaze straying to the casserole dish as a mischievous smile stretched across her face. "When he comes back to try this"—she pointed at the sweet potatoes—"I'll arrange to have Leona there as my assistant."

Tori coughed as a second sip of water hit her throat at the same time Margaret Louise's words registered in her mind.

Jumping up, Margaret Louise pushed Tori forward and began smacking her back. "Arms up in the air, Victoria."

She shook her head but did as she was told, the coughing subsiding almost as quickly as it had begun. "Th-thanks." Tori looked up at her friend as she swallowed once again. "You're going to make Leona your assistant? In the kitchen?"

"It'll be pretend, Victoria. Like one of those poor things at those car shows that travel 'round the country. They don't know any more 'bout cars than Leona knows about cookin'."

"True."

"If it makes Leona happy, I'll do it. That's what sisters are for." Margaret Louise walked over to the alcove that doubled as Tori's sewing room. Lifting the sample gift bag from the top of her sewing table, she spun around. "What's this?"

Tori stood, closing the gap between them in mere seconds. "It's an idea I have. I'd like to make about thirty of these and use them to fill book orders from the nursing home. That way, instead of just handing them a book, they get something cheerful looking, too."

"What a wonderful idea." Margaret Louise turned the bag over in her left hand as the fingers of her right played across the stitching. "This would be a great project for the circle."

"I was hoping it would be."

"Do you have the fabric?"

Tori yanked open a drawer and pulled out a stack of fabric in varying designs and colors. "These I already had. But I'm sure we can get more."

"Could you handle having all of us here on Friday night?"

"Friday night? Our next meeting is Monday . . . at Rose's house."

Margaret Louise set the bag down on the desk. "Group projects call for a special meetin'."

She warmed to the idea quickly. "Okay. Should I call everyone tonight?"

"I'll take care of it. How 'bout we say seven?"

"Seven works." She looked down at her hands and then back up at her friend. "Do you think Debbie would come? It might get her mind off things for a little while."

"I think that's a wonderful idea." Margaret Louise gestured toward the open window. "She might be more easily persuaded if we billed it as a way to get Suzanna and Jackson out of the house, too."

"Could you ask Melissa to bring Lulu and the others?"

"I'll have her bring Jake, too. He can watch them outside . . . keep 'em out of our hair."

"You don't think he'd mind?" Tori heard Lulu skip into the room and turned to smile at the child. "Hey, sweetie, did you finish?"

The little girl nodded, dimples forming in her cheeks. "I did. Wanna see it?"

"There's nothing I'd rather do." She tucked her left arm through Margaret Louise's, took hold of Lulu's hand with her right. To her friend she said, "You know . . . I think getting everyone together to work on these bags is a great idea. Debbie could really use the distraction."

"And so can you."

Tori blinked back the sudden moisture in her eyes, her mouth unable to find the right words.

"Everything will be alright, Victoria. I just know it." Margaret Louise brought her mouth close to Tori's ear as they headed toward the kitchen and Lulu's completed coloring page. "It's like Ella May said yesterday. You and Milo have somethin' special just like she has with Willy—I mean, Billy . . ." Her voice trailed off as they both sucked in their breath simultaneously.

"Wait . . . You don't think it's the same person, do you?"

Margaret Louise giggled with glee, a sound that ricocheted around Tori's cottage. "She said he's famous, right? That's he's travelin' all the time with his job."

"But she calls him Billy."

"Billy, Willy . . . it's the same, ain't it?"

"Jefferson changes his name on the playground when he's being a superhero," Lulu piped in as they rounded the corner into the kitchen. "He calls himself Jeff when he's got powers. But we all know it's still him."

Tori looked at Margaret Louise, saw the confirmation in her pale brown eyes. "He was here on Sunday for the festival and she was looking at wedding cakes with Debbie on Monday . . ."

"Victoria, I think we've just gone and solved the mystery of Ella May's man."

"I'm good at solving mysteries, too, Mee-Maw." Lulu stopped beside the table, her tiny hand sweeping across the carefully colored picture of Cinderella and her prince. "Even Miss Sinclair thinks so, don't you?"

Tori nodded as she bent over the picture, her eyes memorizing every detail. "Oh, Lulu, you did a wonderful job. I can't wait to see everyone's face when they see it hanging on my refrigerator on Friday night."

Lulu squealed with pleasure then skipped off into the living room as her grandmother leaned her stout frame against the kitchen counter. "And me? I can't wait to see the look on my sister's face when she realizes the wealthy bachelor she's schemin' to meet is plain taken . . . by Ella May Vetter."

Chapter 12

There were a lot of things about Sweet Briar, South Carolina, she didn't understand. Mostly because she hadn't grown up in the close-knit town the way so many others had. But still, she had Leona to guide her along, making sure she had the lowdown on southern expressions, proper southern etiquette, and who was and wasn't available from a dating perspective.

That was the easy stuff.

It was the unwritten stuff that seemed to change with the wind that made Tori want to pull her hair out. Stuff like who the important people were and who the *really* important people were. And why loyalty to one another only ran so deep.

She slowed her pace as she approached Debbie's Bakery, the constant foot traffic to and from its front door a not too distant memory that tugged at her heart. While there was a part of her that agreed with Debbie's mom in insisting she close down for a few weeks, there was another side that felt it would do her friend good to keep busy. At least until Colby's body was found and they could give him a proper burial.

But, then again, she could only imagine what Debbie and the kids were going through. Losing a loved one in such a sudden and violent manner was horrific enough; being robbed of a final good-bye was nothing short of unfathomable.

Glancing down at the documents she'd pulled together the night before, Tori inhaled deeply. She might be going about the notion of helping Debbie in the wrong way, but at least it was something. How the people in this supposedly unified town could continue to sit idly by, while one of their own suffered, was something she'd never understand. Where were the search parties through the woods? Where were the flyers on the telephone poles? Where were the door-to-door searches? Weren't they the kinds of things that friends did at times like these? Or were scenes like those simply part of big-budget movies?

She knew Chief Dallas was investigating the crime as she'd seen him around town talking to the likes of Carter Johnson and Dirk Rogers. Yet no arrest had taken place and no body had been found.

Which meant one thing. He needed more help in the investigation—help she intended to give whether he liked it or not. Talking with Gabe Jameson had been step one. Her meeting in five minutes was step two.

The creamy white shingle swayed back and forth above the door with a rare noontime breeze, the name it sported tough to make out around the motion. But that was okay because she knew what it said. She just hadn't realized—until three days earlier—that the name had been altered in an attempt to gain respect.

Tucking the stack of documents under one arm, Tori tugged the hem of her summer jacket down around her hips, took a deep breath, and then pushed her way through the front door, a sudden surge of adrenaline and determination guiding her forward.

"Can I help you?" A woman in her early twenties peeked her head around a computer monitor and smiled brightly.

"Yes, hi. I'm Tori Sinclair, I have an appointment with Mr. James at eleven thirty."

As the woman swiveled away from her computer to consult a calendar on her desk, Tori took a moment to study the room. The waiting area was cozy enough with khaki and navy upholstered armchairs grouped around a mahogany coffee table covered with a variety of reading material. The secretary's adjacent office space was small but ample with a number of filing cabinets lining the wall to the side of the woman's desk. A hallway to the left led to a closed door with a narrow yet prominent nameplate—a shiny gold sign that bore the same moniker as the various diplomas and recognitions proudly framed and scattered throughout the office.

"You can go on back, Mr. James is expecting you." The woman raised her long slender hand into the air and pointed down the very hallway Tori had just been eyeing. "Would you like a cup of coffee or a glass of water?"

"No, I'm fine. But thank you." She tugged her jacket down one last time and then headed in the direction the secretary indicated, the door at the end of the hallway swinging open as she approached.

She'd seen Harrison James a handful of times over the past six months, but other than engaging in occasional short-lived chitchat over his latest round of donated law books, she hadn't paid much attention beyond the basics—late fifties, thinning salt-and-pepper hair, wire-rimmed glasses. But today was different. Harrison James was no longer some nice man who supported his local library. He was Harrison James, formerly known as Hank Jameson—a man who just had his carefully spit-shined life turned upside down by Debbie's husband.

"Victoria, it's so nice to see you again. How are things at the library?" The man extended his hand outward, his grip surprisingly firm for a man who projected intelligence but not necessarily physical strength. "Did Tina offer you something to drink before she left for lunch?"

"Tina?"

"My secretary." He released her hand and gestured toward the chair in front of his desk.

"Oh, yes. Yes she did. But I'm fine." Tori perched on the chair the attorney indicated and crossed her legs at the knees. "Thank you for seeing me today, Mr. James."

With a shove of his hand, Harrison James closed his office door and strode around the desk, dropping into the high-backed muted red leather chair that looked as if it had been purchased fairly recently. "Call me Harrison, please." He placed his elbows on the leather armrests and tented his fingers beneath his chin. "So what brings you to my office, Victoria?"

"U-uh, well, I think I'd like to write up a will." Forcing her words to remain calm and steady, Tori pulled the stack of documents from beneath her arm and set them on the man's desk. "I don't have very much . . . just a car . . . and about ten thousand dollars in a savings account . . . but I was thinking that perhaps I should make sure it goes where I want it to go in the event something happens to me."

He nodded then rolled his chair back just enough to open a drawer on the right-hand side of his desk from which he extracted a yellow legal pad and silver pen. "That's very forward thinking on your part, Victoria. So many people shy away from drafting a will out of fear, superstition, and even a strange sense of immortality."

"Trust me, Mr. James—I mean, Harrison—I've been guilty of those same things. It's why I didn't come in sooner." She shrugged, her gaze playing across his face. "But now . . . after what's happened . . . I can't help but think that way, you know?"

His chin bobbed ever so slightly atop his fingertips as his left eyebrow lowered with concern. "Are you sick?"

"Sick?" she repeated, the word sounding foreign to her lips as much as her ears. "No, no nothing like that. I'm fine. Fit as a fiddle as my great-grandmother used to say."

Lowering his hands to his armrests, he rolled forward in his chair then spun to the left, drawing the ankle of his right leg across his left knee as his hands knitted together to cup the back of his head. "Then I'm not sure what you mean, Victoria. What's happened?"

Tucking a strand of hair behind her ear, Tori shrugged, her gaze still resting on his. "Midthirties isn't much older than I am. And while society tends to equate death with the elderly, it does happen at a younger age."

She knew she was leading him on, drawing out her answer as long as possible, but she had to know. She had to see if there was a reaction—a twitch, a movement to his jaw, a fisting of his hand . . . anything.

"Yes," he prompted in what was becoming a bored voice.

"Not that it's normal for someone in their midthirties to die"—she shot her hands out, palms down—"because I know it's not. But illnesses happen, accidents happen, and . . . well . . . apparently bad things happen as well."

"I'm not following." He unclasped his hands and brought them to his lap as his right leg returned to the floor with a thump. "Did something happen to a friend of yours?"

She nodded. "To one of yours, too. At least I imagine so. I can't imagine anyone not being friends with someone as kind and gentle and giving as . . . as Colby Calhoun."

Like clockwork, the man's relaxed—albeit bored—demeanor disappeared as a storm cloud rolled across his face tightening his lips and jawline. Pushing his chair back, Harrison James jumped to his feet and paced across the room, whirling around as he reached the window that stood open to the day's breeze. "You can't imagine anyone not being friends with Colby Calhoun?" he thundered.

"No, I-I can't." She watched as his hands fisted at his sides and his face reddened with anger. She'd pressed his buttons and he'd reacted exactly as she'd hoped. Only now that he had, she couldn't help but feel a little nervous, a little vulnerable.

Then again, the man's secretary was just down the—

Scratch that. Perky Tina was at lunch . . .

She swallowed. And waited.

"Do you know what your kind and gentle and giving Colby Calhoun has done to m-my town?"

Inhaling deeply, Tori forged ahead. She was, after all, already in a closed office in the middle of an empty building with this man. "Don't you mean what he's done to you, Mr. James?"

He stared at her, his teeth obviously clenching behind his closed lips.

"Or . . . should I say, Mr. Jameson?"

His jaw slacked open. "You know?"

"I didn't. Until Tuesday. But really, what difference does it make?" She pulled the stack of documents back onto her lap and straightened her shoulders.

"What difference does it make? What difference does it make?" His voice grew hoarse as he continued, his left eye developing a slight tic. "It's the difference between being taken seriously and being a laughingstock . . . it's the difference between living well and living like my brother . . . it's the difference between making something of myself and settling for status quo."

"So you alter your name, go off to college and then law school, only to come back to the same town you grew up in? That doesn't make any sense to me, Mr. James."

He leaned his head against the wall, his body slumping wearily at his shoulders. "I know it doesn't. You're not the first one to make that point and you most certainly won't be the last. But Sweet Briar is my home. It was the one consistently normal part of my childhood."

"But people knew who you were when you came back, didn't they?" She uncrossed her legs and leaned forward in her seat, wished she could pull the answers she sought right out of his mouth. "So why change your name and pretend you were someone other than who you are?"

"I wanted a fresh start in a place that meant something to me. And the people who'd known me since I was a little boy seemed willing to give me that chance. They knew my family and the way things were and they understood. There's not a person in this town who would have willingly traded their family for mine. I came from a pack of losers . . . moonshine guzzling losers who thought life was one big drunken night. They didn't have any aspirations. They didn't have any dreams. They didn't care if the house fell down around their heads so long as the moonshine was okay. But I did. I had aspirations. I had dreams. And the folks around here were willing to let me be my own person with my own present and future." He raked a hand through his thinning hair, his eyes darkening once again. "And they did. Until that damn Colby Calhoun started nosing around in something that wasn't any of his concern."

"The truth is everyone's concern, Mr. James."

"Not when that truth threatens to destroy everything I've built. Not when that truth makes everyone around here remember who I am and where I came from." Harrison James pushed off the wall with a firm foot and strode over to the door. Yanking it open, he turned back to Tori, his eyes narrowing as he addressed her with venom in his voice. "I think it's time for you to leave. If you're truly inclined to create a will I suggest you find someone else to do it."

She rose to her feet, her legs firmly planted in front of her chair. "It's quite obvious you're angry, Mr. James. Furious, even."

"Very astute observation, Miss Sinclair," he hissed as his knuckles whitened around the door.

Gathering her purse and papers, Tori walked past the man and into the hallway, her hands trembling as she spun around to face him once again. "Colby Calhoun's death doesn't make the truth go away. You have to know that, especially in your profession."

"In my profession, Miss Sinclair, all that matters is getting justice for the little guy."

"And that isn't Colby Calhoun?" she asked as he readied his hand to slam the door.

"Hell no. That justice was mine. All mine."

Chapter 13

One by one, each member of the Sweet Briar Ladies Society Sewing Circle descended on Tori's cottage, armed and ready to stitch away the hours on a project that would benefit the town's nursing home residents.

Rose Winters was the first to arrive in her drab colored housecoat and trademark cotton button-down sweater. Gone was the tension and hostility the retired schoolteacher had worn like a badge of honor just four nights earlier, in its place a weariness that sagged her frail and bony shoulders with an invisible weight.

Next, was Georgina Hayes, the tall and lanky mayor who looked as if she'd aged ten years over and above the ten she'd added when her husband was tried and convicted of the town's first murder just six months earlier. Slowly but surely her perfectly honed handshake had grown less enthusiastic, her loosened grip symbolic of her hold on life.

British nanny Beatrice Tharrington, the youngest of the group, was quieter than usual, her gaze skirting direct eye contact with everyone and anyone in favor of a spool of thread and a needle.

Dixie Dunn, the retired former town librarian, claimed one of the two chairs Tori had dragged inside for the evening, the woman's infamous sharp-tongued motormouth all but silent as she nodded a greeting at Leona, who held court in the plaid armchair that was everyone's favorite.

For a group of women who normally spoke from arrival to departure, the swollen silence that blanketed Tori's living room was nothing short of suffocating, the initial greetings between members fading away as the crickets beyond the open windows took center stage.

"Beautiful weather we're having," Tori said as she shifted from foot to foot. "The breeze we've been getting lately has been so nice, don't you think?"

"Yes," Rose muttered under her breath as Beatrice shrugged in agreement.

"Miss Anna at the market said a breeze at this time of year is almost unheard of." She knew she sounded like an idiot, chattering away like some bimbo, but she didn't care. Mindless chatter was preferable to the kind of morbid silence that hung around them like a black storm cloud. "She said these kinds of breezes usually happen in—" Tori looked over her shoulder in relief as the screen door smacked against its wooden frame, bringing an end to any additional—and relatively ignored—babbling on her part.

"We're here . . . we're here." Margaret Louise, in a charcoal gray polyester warm-up suit, strode into the cottage with a covered plate in her hand and her daughter-in-law at her heels. "We waited until the last possible moment just in case Debbie changed her mind and Jake needed to come along and supervise the brood . . . but no such luck."

"I know. I'd been hoping just as hard on this end, too." Tori spun around, covering the distance between them in two long strides. "Mmmm. Is there chocolate in there?" she asked Margaret Louise.

The woman's eyes sparkled as she headed toward the treat-laden kitchen table in favor of answering.

"Well . . . is it?" She pulled Melissa in for a hug, her words dropping to a whisper. "I'm glad you two showed up. Trying to get a conversation going in this room tonight is akin to torture."

"A repeat of Monday night, huh?" Melissa stepped back as the embrace ended, her words still a whisper as she continued. "You'd think by now . . . after everything that's happened . . . they'd give it a rest."

She peered around the room, her gaze taking in each and every member of the circle. "It's different tonight. There's no anger, no fight waiting to be unleashed. They're just sad."

"That we can work with." Melissa squeezed Tori's hand and then breezed into the living room, her long dirty blonde hair skimming her back as she carried her sewing bag to an empty folding chair to the left of Jake's aunt. "So I hear you may be babysitting my crew one night soon, Aunt Leona."

Leona's eyebrow shot up as she flipped the page of her magazine and peered over the top of her glasses. "Only if I don't learn how to sew." Margaret Louise's twin turned her head ever so slightly and smiled sweetly at Tori. "But I'm learning. Isn't that right, dear?"

Tori coughed. "You are?"

Leona's eyebrow rose even higher as her smile disappeared. "I'm learning about buttons, dear. Don't you remember?"

"Um, uh, we looked at buttons . . ."

"And we spread them on the table and I was instructed in how to thread a needle," Leona finished with a triumphant swish to her head. "One must start with the basics as you all know."

"I instructed, Leona, but you—"

The woman waved Tori's words aside, her fast-on-her-feet reply intended to garner sympathy from the older members of the circle. "Sometimes it's hard to see through that little hole at the top of the needle. But I'm trying"—she sighed dramatically—"desperately. I so want to learn to sew as beautifully as the rest of you."

"Oh cut the crap, Leona." Rose crossed her ankles and straightened the hem of her housecoat around her knees. "You have no more interest in learning to sew than I have in that garbage you read."

Leona's mouth gaped open as Melissa turned and winked at Tori. "See, sadness is workable. Anger is not."

Seizing the opportunity to get a meaningful dialogue off the ground, Tori dropped into the lone folding chair to the right of Rose. "I imagine we're all very aware that Debbie is not with us tonight. She is suffering the kind of loss none of us can even begin to imagine. She's lost her husband in a horrific and senseless act and doesn't even have the benefit of the kind of closure a funeral might bring."

"Chief Dallas is working day and night to find Colby and the person who did this to him. And the council will see to it that he has all of the resources he needs to that end," Georgina said as she pulled her straw hat from her head and placed it on her lap. "It doesn't matter what happened those last few days. Sweet Briar has rebounded from tough times before and we will again. Debbie has been a member of this town since she was born. If for no other reason than that, we'll find him and bring him home so his wife and children can give him a proper funeral."

It wasn't exactly the sentiment Tori had hoped for, but she'd take it. For now. If all she could get from the circle at the moment was support for Debbie and the kids, it would be enough. The apologies for their behavior toward Colby could come later.

"So what are we going to do? For Debbie and the kids?" Tori looked from one circle member to the next, her gaze coming to rest on her former nemesis, Dixie Dunn. "Dixie? Any ideas?"

The seventy-something woman with the short crop of white hair nodded slowly, the excitement she got from being front and center of any occasion shining forth in her eyes. "I think we should each make a point of stopping by her home over the weekend and offering our sympathy."

Margaret Louise perched on the armrest of her twin's chair, her head shaking side to side. "She's not stayin' there. Her mama insisted she and the children come out to her place . . . in case whoever hurt Colby feels there's more work to be done."

Rose gasped. "Surely she doesn't think anyone would hurt Debbie and those children?"

Margaret Louise shrugged. "Why wouldn't she? Whoever did this to Colby ain't someone who's in their right mind to begin with. Sane people—no matter how angry they may be—don't waltz into innocent people's homes and destroy lives."

Heads nodded around the room, the effect similar to that of a spectator-induced wave around a packed stadium of excited fans.

"So do we call on Joyce's then? And do as Dixie suggested?" Beatrice looked up from her lap long enough to wage the inquiry before looking back down, her soft British accent a stark contrast in a room of southerners.

A few heads nodded, but most remained noncommittal, as if the change in Debbie's residency prevented them from thinking or forming an opinion. After several long moments, Margaret Louise finally spoke, her loud boisterous voice quieting the crickets. "I say we get her business back on track. Colby bein' gone is somethin' we can't fix no matter how much any of us wish we could . . . and I'm quite certain"—she glanced slowly around the room, her eyes making direct contact with each and every member of the circle including Beatrice—"we all wish that, don't we?"

More heads nodded grudgingly as Margaret Louise continued, "But standin' by, day after day, as her once thrivin' business remains closed is simply inexcusable. We've been friends for years now. We've seen Debbie and Melissa through births, Tori and Georgina through the aftereffects of Tiffany Ann Gilbert's murder, Rose through her cataract operation, and Dixie through the adjustment of retirement. Why should runnin' Debbie's Bakery while she's mournin' be any different?" The woman reached up and unzipped her charcoal gray lightweight jacket to reveal a tired white T-shirt below. "I already help Debbie with much of the bakin' anyway, so I'd just continue doin' what I do. And I know that Emily, our part-time girl, is chompin' at the bit to get back to work, too. We'd just need a little help, which is where all of you could come in. Those of you who aren't workin' . . . like Rose and Dixie and Leona—"

"I work!" Leona interjected. "Have you forgotten about the little matter of the antique shop I own?"

"It's only open three days a week, Twin. I'm referring to the other four." Margaret Louise wiggled out of her jacket and draped it over the back of the love seat. "The point I'm tryin' to make is that we can all find some time to help."

Tori jumped up from her chair. "And I could help out on my days off from the library. Oh, Margaret Louise, I think it's a wonderful idea."

"So do I." Rose's voice, frail but firm, filled the room with an unmistakable show of support. "It's what friends do."

"True honest-to-goodness friends?" Beatrice asked quietly as she peered up at the group through her thick lashes. "Or the kind of friends who treat each other dreadfully when the wind shifts direction?"

Rose lowered her chin to her chest. Georgina followed suit.

"I held my tongue the other night but I've not seen a group of women treat a so-called friend in quite the way you all did Monday night. I rather felt as if I was at a lynching." The young girl's face flushed pink as she dropped her head back down, her honest and audible assertion surprising even her.

For a moment no one spoke, Beatrice's words hanging in the middle of the room, namelessly shaming those who'd earned them.

Rose was the first to speak, her admission of guilt honest and forthright. "You're right, Beatrice. I've taken issue with Leona for her lack of loyalty to Victoria when she needed it most. Yet here I am, just as guilty as she was. Only instead of forsaking Debbie for a man, I forsake her for pride . . . the town's pride."

Leona's chin jutted into the air only to lower just as fast as she swiped at a tear behind her glasses—a tear that seemed to be shared by just about everyone in the room.

Swallowing over the lump in her throat, Tori clapped her hands. "Then it's settled. We'll get Debbie's Bakery up and running until she's ready to take it over again. Margaret Louise, can you make up a schedule for us?"

"I most certainly can." The woman pushed off Leona's armrest and gestured toward the kitchen. "I have some powder-topped chocolate bars I'd like everyone to try before we get to the reason for this extra circle meeting. I noticed Tori has plates and cups set out so go on."

As everyone filed into the kitchen, Margaret Louise took hold of Tori's arm and tugged her into the sewing alcove on the opposite side of the living room. "How'd it go?"

She pulled her gaze from the stack of fabric squares she'd set out beside the sample gift bag and looked a question at her friend.

"I saw his card on your counter. You reckon he's involved?"

"Wh-what?" And then she knew. She'd stopped by the cottage after her appointment with Harrison James, her nerves too frayed to go straight back to work. She leaned against the sewing table as Dixie and Rose returned to the room, their china dessert plates—borrowed from Leona for the occasion—brimming with an assortment of treats guaranteed to elevate their sugar level into dangerous numbers. "He's angry, Margaret Louise . . . really, really angry. But I don't know if it was just the angry display of someone with a hot temper, or if it was the angry display of a guilty man."

"We'll keep an eye on him. I've always wanted to tail someone like they do in the movies," Margaret Louise said as she rubbed her hands back and forth against each other. "He probably wouldn't recognize your car since you walk almost everywhere you go."

Tori nodded. The woman had a point. But still, Harrison James was one of several suspects. Carter Johnson and Dirk Rogers were in need of some investigating as well. By someone who didn't go on fishing trips with them. . . .

"What are you two talking about over there?" Rose asked, her voice a playful accusation.

"Can I tell 'em?" Margaret Louise asked.

"Tell us what?" Dixie asked as she reclaimed the same wicker chair she'd had from the start. "What's going on?

Tori felt the corners of her mouth inching upward. "First things first. When everyone's had a chance to get their treats, I want to tell you my idea for a group project."

Leona pointed at her sister as she, too, rejoined the group, one small cookie on her plate. "That look on my sister's face is not because of some project. She looks like she's going to burst in two . . . and she only looks like that when Melissa is pregnant . . ."

All eyes turned to Margaret Louise's daughter-in-law

who shot her hands in the air and shook her head emphatically. "Oh no. Seven's enough."

"Well, if that's not it, then she's got news," Leona said. "So let's have it."

Margaret Louise nearly skipped back to her spot on the edge of Leona's chair, her teeth clamped down on the smile that threatened to rival the trio of sixty-watt bulbs that lit Tori's living room. "Civic duty first, ladies. Civic duty first. So tell us, Victoria . . . how can our circle help?"

Leona rolled her eyes before taking a dainty bite of her oatmeal cookie. "Yes, dear, please do."

Shaking her head, Tori grabbed hold of the fabric with one hand and the gift bag with the other. "Have any of you been out to the nursing home recently?"

Each and every head in the room shook in reply.

"Well, I have, and their on-site library is simply inadequate."

"People donate what they can," Dixie offered before taking a bite of Margaret Louise's powder-topped chocolate bar. "If I remember correctly, they have almost an entire wall of shelving filled with donated books in their common area. Has that changed?"

"No. It's still there. But as you pointed out, Dixie, those are books that have been donated, mostly by people looking to clear a spot in their personal inventory." Tori sat on the edge of an empty folding chair and set everything on her lap. "Which means old books. And if you're an avid reader as we all are in this room, you know that there are some amazing titles that have hit the stands in the past decade—in all genres across the board."

Dixie nodded. "True enough."

"But unless the nursing home residents happen to receive one of those books as a gift from a family member, they simply have no access to them. It's either read the same book they've already read fifteen times or don't read at all."

"Crying shame the way we forget our elderly," Rose grumbled as she set her plate on the coffee table in disgust. "Lock them away where you don't have to deal with them. . . that seems to be this generation's motto."

"So how can we help?" Melissa interjected as she pushed a strand of hair behind her ear. "Do you want to raise funds to buy newer titles?"

"No. We've got the titles in the library. I just want to make them more easily accessible to the residents in the nursing home." Tori set the pile of fabric at her feet and shook out the sample bag, holding it up for everyone to see. "What I'd like to do is comprise a list of some of our latest titles—by genre—and make it available to the nursing home. Once a week I'll stop and pick up any requests, bring them back to the library to fill, and then deliver them to the nursing home. But rather than simply hand them a book, I thought we could deliver it in a homemade bag to make it a little more personal . . . a little more special."

"Victoria, that's a wonderful idea!" Dixie beamed from ear to ear as she met Tori's gaze head-on, a reaction she hadn't expected quite so fast from a woman who still saw Tori as the reason she'd been all but forced into retirement from her position as Sweet Briar's head librarian. "We could make sacks that would be attractive to the male residents and sacks that would be attractive to the female residents."

"Excellent idea, Dixie." She handed the sample bag to Beatrice. "As you'll all get to see, as it's passed around, these bags are relatively simple. We can make big ones with a slightly sturdier fabric for those residents who request a title that may only be available in hardcover. And we can use smaller, more pliable bags for mass market and trade paperback books."

"These are wonderful and yet so simple," Georgina said as she took the bag from Beatrice's outstretched hand and examined it closely. "Maybe we could even make a few smaller ones around the holidays and fill them with little treats that could accompany the larger sack of books."

"Oooh, I like that idea," Melissa said as she peered over Georgina's shoulder. "For Valentine's Day we could get fabric with a heart design and fill it with sugar-free treats. Or around Christmas we could use red and green fabric and stuff them with a tiny homemade ornament or bookmark."

Rose waited patiently as the sample bag made its way around the room, a small smile carving dimples in her cheeks. "First, the children's room at the library, and now this? Victoria, you have such lovely ideas. Your great-grandmother would be very proud of you."

"Thank you, Rose." It was all she could manage around the lump that threatened to stop her speech completely. This was what she'd loved about this group of women from the moment she'd met them. They were fun loving and kooky and generous to a fault. And despite the occasional misstep, their loyalty for one another eventually shone through—whether in their hands-on support for an idea such as the bags, or in their emotional support for one another like she'd needed not too long ago and like Debbie so desperately needed now.

"So is everyone in?" Margaret Louise asked the group.

"Yes!" Rose said, her sentiment quickly echoed by everyone in the room.

She bent down, scooped up the fabric and set it on the table. "I've got lots of different fabrics already, but we can still use anything you'd be willing to donate at Monday night's meeting, too." Reclaiming the sample bag from Rose, Tori turned it inside out and held it up. "As you can see, it's quite simple to make but there's a lot we can do with them. I hadn't even thought of the holiday twist Melissa just mentioned but I love it."

As everyone grabbed some fabric and coordinated it with a thread color from their personal supply, Margaret

Louise took to her feet, glancing over her shoulder at Tori as she did. "Now?"

She laughed, her head nodding simultaneously. "Go ahead."

Spreading her arms out to her sides, Margaret Louise rocked back and forth on her sneakers, her teeth unleashing the smile she'd worked so hard to keep under control during Tori's pitch.

"Spill it, Margaret Louise," droned Leona as she nodded at Beatrice's fabric choice before switching her plate for the magazine she'd set on the coffee table. "What do you know?"

"What would you say if I told you I've finally figured out who Ella May's man is?"

Squeals of excitement broke out around the circle as needles stilled in their hands.

"Who?" Georgina asked with excitement, putting words to the question on the tip of everyone's tongue. "Who is it?"

Margaret Louise looked over at Tori and winked. "Well . . . he's famous like she said. And, sure enough, he does have the kind of job that would limit his time in Sweet Briar . . ."

"Go on," Beatrice prompted in breathless fashion.

"And his name is Billy, although that's a variation of the name he gives everyone." Margaret Louise paused dramatically before continuing, the eyes of everyone in the circle fixed on her face. "He was here just this past weekend, which explains the engagement we all know about by now."

Leona set her elbow down on the armrest of her chair and made a rolling motion with her index finger as she leaned forward. "Can we get to the name anytime soon?"

Margaret Louise stopped in her tracks and spun around, her smile even wider than it had been at the beginning as she rested the tips of her fingers at the base of her throat in theatric fashion. "I'm sorry . . . are you all waitin' for an actual name?"

Rose leaned over, snatched a cookie from her plate, and threw it at Margaret Louise. "Unless you want to be the reason we muss up Victoria's home, I suggest you get to the point."

Margaret Louise nodded and sighed. "If I must . . ."

Tori laughed, a sound she quickly stifled under Rose's reproachful eye.

"Ella May Vetter has indeed landed quite the catch with her Billy. Especially considering the fact he is the president and CEO of Lions Publishing."

Several mouths dropped open as others remained closed due to total oblivion.

"That's right, my friends . . . Sweet Briar's one and only Bunny Lady is about to become Mrs. William Clayton Wilder."

Leona's gasp echoed throughout the room as all color drained from her face. "M-m-my William Clayton Wilder?"

"Oh no, Twin. That would be *Ella May's* William Clayton Wilder." Margaret Louise strutted back to her spot beside Leona. "Which means you have a choice of patches for the middle of that pale blue handkerchief you're making for the bride. Unless, of course, you can find a patch with both a bunny *and* a book."

Chapter 14

She couldn't help but grin as she looked across the table at her friend, the woman's gaze scanning the menu in front of her with as much care as if she were hunting for a hidden picture worth millions.

"Anything new?" Tori prompted as she leaned against the cushioned seat and traced her finger along the simplistic design of the flatware the waitress had left behind. "Any sign of real eggs on the menu?"

Margaret Louise snorted. "The same day Carter Johnson cracks a real egg in favor of using a carton will be the same day my twin wears one of her own creations."

"Your twin can't even thread a needle yet."

"Exactly." Margaret Louise set her menu on the table between them and spun it around so Tori could see. "See this French toast? The way they say it's made with vanilla and cinnamon"—she pointed at the top item under the breakfast category—"I'd bet you a thousand dollars that's mine. Harriet was at a church breakfast with me last year where

I made this and she asked for the recipe . . . said she wanted to make it for Carter one mornin'."

"Maybe it is," Tori said with a shrug as she looked around the diner before meeting Margaret Louise's gaze head-on. "But like my great-grandmother always used to say, imitation is the sincerest form of flattery."

"Not if that man is makin' my recipe with carton eggs." With one swift push, Margaret Louise shoved the laminated menu to the side, her chubby cheeks deflating as she exhaled slowly. "So, do you think I handled the whole Ella May and Billy thing okay last night?"

"I think the way you hustled to keep your sister from toppling over the side of her chair was quite heroic, actually," she said with a laugh as her thoughts immediately returned to the moment Margaret Louise broke the news. "I mean, really, she could have broken a hip if you hadn't moved as fast as you did."

"I did move fast, didn't I?" The woman shifted in the booth, the brief showing of a mischievous smile disappearing just as quickly. "Rose pulled me aside when I was leavin' and told me I'd been mean to tell Leona in the way I did."

Tori's mouth dropped open. "Rose was defending Leona?"

Margaret Louise simply nodded, her mouth set in an uncharacteristically straight line.

"Did Leona yell at you for it on the ride home from my place?"

The woman shook her head as her hand swept at imaginary crumbs on the table.

"Did she say anything?" Tori asked.

Again, the woman shook her head. "Just that she couldn't believe Ella May would land a man who has traveled so extensively and—"

"Is so wealthy." Tori rested her elbows on the edge of the table and looked around the diner one more time, her thoughts registering names to faces even as she continued her conversation with Margaret Louise. "My guess is Leona is fine. Is she shocked? Of course she is—we were too, remember? But if she thought you'd been out of line she'd have called you on it."

"So what can I get you ladies?" Fran, a gum-chewing, big-haired forty-year-old, appeared beside their table in a pale blue knee-length button-down dress with an apron tied at her waist.

"I'd like the French toast with a side of bacon and a glass of orange juice," Tori said before gesturing to her breakfast companion. "Margaret Louise?"

"A slice of ham and a biscuit. Oh, and a glass of milk, please."

"Would you like eggs with that?" Fran asked, as she scribbled their order on a thick pad of paper.

"Do you have eggs?" Margaret Louise turned her head, pinned the waitress with her eyes.

The woman's brow furrowed. "Of course we have eggs, sugar." She leaned over the table and flipped over one of their menus, her index finger finding the egg options in short fashion. "See?"

Margaret Louise moved her own finger to the menu, tapped it up and down on the asterisk beside the word egg. "When your boss starts crackin' genuine eggs back there in that kitchen of his, I'll order eggs. Until then I'll simply stick with my ham and biscuits."

The woman's mouth gaped open as she stopped chewing long enough to stare at Margaret Louise. "Are you serious, sugar?"

"You're darn tootin', I'm serious." Straightening in her seat, Margaret Louise grinned at Tori as Fran walked away mumbling under her breath. "So I thought last night was a peach, don't you?"

"I do, too. I was glad to see everyone get so excited about making the book bags."

"I have one already." Margaret Louise swiveled her body

to the left, rummaged around in a large straw bag she'd carried into the diner with them, and extracted a khaki colored bag with a fishing design. "I went with a more casual look for this one, assumin' it would be better suited for a man. See"—she laid the bag across the center of the table—"I used pinkin' shears along the top edge to give it a more casual look . . . which should cut down on the likelihood of the fabric unravelin' over time."

"Oh, Margaret Louise, it's perfect." Tori took in the coordinating drawstring the woman had added at the top. "Oooh and I like the way you put this in . . . do you think it will hold up okay?"

"I reckon it will."

She leaned against the seatback as Fran returned to their table, a tray of drinks and food in her hands. Setting the tray on the edge of the table, the waitress expertly doled out the correct plates and drinks. "Need anythin' else?"

"Everything looks great, thanks." Tori looked down at her French toast, her stomach gurgling in hunger. "It looks delicious."

"Remind me to make you mine sometime . . . with real eggs. Then you'll know what delicious really is." Margaret Louise reached for the bottle of ketchup and squirted some onto the plate that held her ham. "I was mighty tickled with the way everyone was so willin' to help out at the bakery. I'll work on the schedule later today and we'll get things up and runnin' first thing Monday mornin'."

Tori stopped midcut, her knife and fork poised above her plate. "I can take an evening shift. And once in a while I even have a Saturday off just like I do today."

"I know. But us retired hens are off all the time." Margaret Louise slipped a piece of ham into her mouth and closed her eyes briefly. "Mmmm. Not bad."

She stared down at her own plate, at the now bite-sized pieces of French toast. "I like the way everyone agreed to help at the bakery . . . to come together to support Debbie. But"—she pulled her gaze upward, scanned it around the busy diner before looking back at her friend—"what about Colby? Shouldn't people be looking for him?"

"That's why we're here, isn't it?" Margaret Louise laid her fork beside her plate and leaned forward. "I mean, aren't we here to pump Carter with some questions if he gets a second?"

Tori nodded as she pushed her plate of untouched food to the side. "But why aren't people forming those big human chains and walking through the woods? Why isn't Chief Dallas going door-to-door?"

The woman shrugged before reaching for her biscuit and breaking it into two pieces. "From what I've heard from Georgina, the chief is lookin'. He's been out in the field behind Dirk Rogers's garage more 'n a few times this week. No one knows what he's doin' out there exactly, but most folks reckon he's searchin' for Colby's body."

Tori reached for her orange juice glass and pulled it closer, her index finger finding the rim and tracing it slowly. "It's so hard to know what to hope for."

"What do you mean?"

"Well, on one hand I want the chief to find Colby's body so Debbie and the kids can at least have that. But"—she glanced up at Margaret Louise—"on the other hand, by not finding his body it doesn't seem quite so real."

The woman reached across the table and patted the top of Tori's hand. "I know what you mean, Victoria. I feel exactly the same way. I think everyone does."

She shook her head. "No. I think most people don't care. If they did, wouldn't they be offering to help? Colby is one of their own, you know . . ."

"No. Colby was part of this town because of Debbie." Margaret Louise pulled her hand back and sliced another piece of ham. "Sure, he fit in well . . . as well as someone that good-lookin' and that intelligent can fit in in a place like Sweet Briar, South Carolina . . . but he's not one of their own. Especially not after what he wrote."

"He wrote the truth, Margaret Louise," she protested.

The woman held up her hands. "You're preachin' to the choir, Victoria. I know that. And you know that. And most folks would probably tell you that if you asked them in private."

"Then where are those people? Why aren't they looking for Colby?"

"Because they don't want to face the wrath of folks like"—the woman looked over her shoulder, pointing out the target of her words—"Carter Johnson, who thinks he and his kin before him are the heart and soul of this town."

"Shhh, he's coming this way," Tori whispered before sitting up tall and addressing the diner's owner with a welcoming smile.

"How is everything, ladies?" Carter Johnson gestured toward Tori's plate, his face growing stern. "Is something wrong with the French toast?"

"What?" Tori looked at the plate she'd shoved to the side and pulled it closer. "Oh . . . no . . . it looks wonderful. I'd just lost my appetite momentarily. Talking about everything that's going on around here kind of got to me, I guess."

"You mean with that rubbish in the paper last weekend?" The man took a napkin from his belt loop and dusted away a few crumbs from their table. "Don't pay that no mind. It's rubbish. Plain and simple."

"And the fact that Colby Calhoun is missin' and presumed dead? What's that?" Margaret Louise asked as she dropped the remaining piece of biscuit onto her plate and took another bite of ham.

The man snapped his hand back, twisted the napkin between his hands as Milo Wentworth appeared over his right shoulder. "That's what happens when people write rubbish."

Ignoring the rapid beat to her heart at her first Milo

sighting in four days, Tori kept her eyes trained on Carter Johnson. "Are you willing to tell that to Suzanna and Jackson Calhoun?"

"We-well, no. I don't think that's my place."

"Nor is it your place to be judge and jury of a man who did nothing more than share a piece of information he felt the town had a right to know." Tori's fist hit the table as the words poured from her mouth of their own volition. "That will never justify what's happened to him. Nor will it justify the way everyone is sitting around as if nothing has happened instead of combing this town seeking closure for this man's wife and children. That, Mr. Johnson, is the true meaning of rubbish."

"Hear, hear," Margaret Louise echoed as a smattering of applause broke out around the diner.

Realizing she'd spoken much too loudly, Tori quieted her voice as her cheeks grew warm. "I'm sorry, Mr. Johnson. I really am. But that needed to be said. Sweet Briar is the charming town it is because of the people who live here now. That's whom we should be fighting for . . . not some slightly mistold story about how we got to where we are now. The *how* isn't what matters. It's the *did* that counts."

"I couldn't have said it better myself." Chief Dallas approached the table, his shoulder grazing Milo's as he stopped just inches from Carter Johnson. "A member of our community was taken forcibly from his home. Had it happened an hour earlier, we might be looking for four bodies instead of just one."

A shiver ran down Tori's spine as the meaning of the chief's words hovered in the air surrounding their table. Blinking back a sudden tear, Tori glanced at Margaret Louise, saw the same reaction in her friend's face.

Carter Johnson sat on the bench beside Tori, the pallor of his skin chalky white. "I hadn't thought of that. I guess all I saw was the end to a story I'd grown up on . . ." The man's voice trailed off as he propped his elbow on the table and rested his forehead in his hand.

"We need to work together. To help Debbie and the kids. And Colby, too." Margaret Louise reached for her milk glass and took a big gulp, wiping her mouth with her napkin when she finished. "Come Monday the bakery will be open again. We need word to get out and we need everyone to come back. Debbie and the kids need that income."

"We'll get the word out." Carter pulled his head up and dropped his forearm in front of him. "And Chief, if you need some searchers, I'll get that word out, too."

The Sweet Briar police chief nodded as he looped his thumbs inside his belt. "The more eyes we have out there, the more apt we are to find what we're looking for."

"Count me in, Chief," Milo said before locking gazes with Tori. "I should have volunteered long before now."

She mouthed a thank-you over the lump in her throat, her eyes stinging with unshed tears as Carter shifted in the seat beside her.

"I'll be there, too." Carter Johnson rose to his feet, looking back over his shoulder at Tori as he did. "You've been quite an asset to this town, Miss Sinclair."

"Yes she has," Milo echoed as he heeded Margaret Louise's urging and slid onto the bench beside the heavyset woman. "Anyone who thinks otherwise needs his head examined."

"Just let me know, Chief." Carter Johnson patted his poker buddy on the shoulder before turning back to Tori and Margaret Louise's table one last time. "Breakfast is on the house this morning, ladies."

As he headed toward the kitchen with the chief on his heels, Margaret Louise leaned forward across the table, her voice barely above a whisper. "I guess I should've ordered the eggs after all, huh?"

Tori rested her head on the seatback and laughed. "But they'd still be from a carton . . ."

"True." With a quick wink at Tori, Margaret Louise turned to Milo. "So how are you, stranger?"

"Embarrassed."

"Embarrassed?" Margaret Louise repeated as a smile spread across her face like wildfire.

"Humbled."

"Humbled?"

"Willing to admit I was a close-minded jerk."

"I'm sorry, can you say that again?"

"Margaret Louise, stop. You heard what he said." Tori lifted her head forward and began fiddling with the flatware once again, her thoughts zigzagging from one thing to the other—Colby's disappearance, Debbie's pain, Milo's willingness to put pride in front of truth . . .

"Did *you*?" Milo asked.

"Did I what?" She looked up from the flatware long enough to feel his intense gaze on hers.

"Hear what I said. About being willing to admit I was a close-minded jerk . . ."

She shrugged. "I heard it. I just wish it hadn't happened to begin with."

"Victoria! He's trying to say he's—"

Milo held up his hands then scooted his way out of their booth. "It's okay, Margaret Louise. Tori is right. Showing up at your table just now wasn't the way to handle this." He stepped over to her side of the table, brushed a strand of her hair behind her ear with a gentle hand. "But you'll see. I was wrong and I know that. And I'm going to make it right. But first I have to make it right for Debbie."

And then he was gone, his back disappearing down the steps and toward the front door of the diner, parents of his former students waving as he passed.

"It's not very often you find a man who can admit his mistakes, Victoria." Margaret Louise reached across the table and removed the flatware from Tori's reach.

She shrugged as she watched him disappear through the door. "That may be true. But saying and doing can be two very different things. I'd prefer to wait and see if the doing actually happens."

"Suit yourself." Margaret Louise took another gulp of her milk and then set the empty glass near the edge of the table. "Are you ready?"

"Yeah. I'm just not hungry anymore." Tori pointed at the book bag Margaret Louise had moved to the far side of the table when the food arrived. "Thank you. For supporting my crazy ideas with such zeal."

"My pleasure." The woman folded the cloth sack and placed it back inside her straw bag before leaning across the table once again, a renewed sparkle in her brown eyes. "Did I tell you he's coming back next week? To try the new version?"

"Who? Oh, wait. You mean the magazine guy?"

Margaret Louise nodded excitedly. "One and the same."

Tori clapped her hands together. "Does that mean you're going with the one I tried the other evening?"

"Everyone who has taste-tested it had the same reaction. So I reckon that's the one I should try on him, too."

"Does it give it a southern twist?" Tori asked.

Margaret Louise's face reddened slightly as she grabbed her straw bag and slid out from behind the table. "You could say that."

"Can you tell me?" she asked as she joined her friend and headed toward the door.

"A cook never shares her secret."

"But won't you have to if he gives you the cover spot on an upcoming issue of his magazine?"

The woman leaned her full frame against the door, pushing her way into the sunlit morning with Tori just steps behind. "Oh . . . if this goes the way I think it will, these sweet potatoes will be getting more than a cover spot on *Taste of the South*."

"Ten thousand dollars sounds like a pretty nice more to me."

"True. But there'll be even more."

She stopped beside Margaret Louise's car, watched as the woman reached inside the open window and inserted the key into the ignition. "Like what?"

"You'll know when it's time."

"Oh, c'mon, how about a hint? A teeny tiny little hint?"

"You want a hint?" The woman yanked open the car door and tossed her straw bag inside. "Hmmm. Okay, this is all I'll say so don't be askin' no follow-up questions."

"Yes . . ." Tori prompted.

"One man's rags are another man's riches."

"Uh, oooo-kay. Translation, please?"

"I said no follow-up questions, Victoria." Dropping into the front seat of her wagon with a loud *umph*, Margaret Louise pulled the door shut and started the engine.

"I didn't ask a question. Not a real one, anyway. I just asked for clarification," she pleaded, cocking her head to the side in angelic fashion. "There's a difference."

"Don't give me those eyes, Victoria. You forget I'm a grandmother who sees those eyes all the time." Readying her hand on the steering wheel, Margaret Louise popped her head out the open window and smiled. "But I'll oblige by sayin' it one more time . . . slower so you can follow."

Tori righted her head and stuck out her tongue instead.

Margaret Louise laughed. "That doesn't work either, Victoria. Now follow along this time . . . One. Man's. Rags. Are. Another. Man's. Riches." Slipping the gearshift into Drive, Tori's friend pulled her head back inside the car only to stick it out once again. "Oh, and Victoria?"

"Uh-huh?"

"Give Milo a chance." And with that, the woman was gone, her powder blue station wagon disappearing out of the parking lot like a shot, a cloud of dust rising in its wake as Tori turned and headed toward the sidewalk.

Chapter 15

Tori flipped on the radio and settled into her seat, the wind through the driver's side window sending errant strands of her light brown hair in every direction as she accelerated on the wide-open road. She'd passed Dirk Rogers's garage any number of times since moving to Sweet Briar yet she'd never been inside, preferring instead to use Jake Davis whenever her car needed a little routine maintenance.

But that was about to change.

Dirk Rogers was a person of interest in Colby's disappearance as far as she was concerned. He'd been livid after reading Colby's expose on the wartime fire that had annihilated Sweet Briar, he had a reputation—at least in Margaret Louise's eyes—for being deceptive and sneaky, and Police Chief Dallas had reportedly made a few trips into the woods behind his garage since Monday night. Whether any of that added up to his involvement in the death of Debbie's husband remained to be seen.

Had she told Margaret Louise what she was up to when

they'd met for breakfast, Tori wouldn't be making the drive alone. But she hadn't and so she was.

She'd intended to ask Margaret Louise to join her on this leg of her investigation, but after the brief and unexpected Milo sighting midway through breakfast she'd realized she simply needed time alone. To think.

Back in Chicago, when she'd been engaged to Jeff, she'd believed in the man he was . . . his principles, his views, his goals. Yet, in the time span of about thirty seconds, she'd watched those beliefs self-destruct before her very eyes when she'd found him in a coat closet with another woman.

From that moment forward, Tori had been determined to keep her eyes wide-open in all future relationships. Milo's early reactions to Colby's desire for truth had sent off warning bells—loud ones. Were they as glaring as the ones Jeff had set off in the coat closet of the hall where their engagement party was being held? Of course not. But she didn't intend to be the recipient of a blinding sucker punch ever again.

As she rounded a curve on Route 6 and turned onto Lantern Drive, she let up on the gas, loose strands of hair falling limp against her head. Sighing, she twisted the knob of the radio to the left and pulled into the parking lot of Dirk's garage. Disappointment over the presence of other cars in the lot turned to relief as she realized they were ownerless—the kind of vehicles that people dumped off at a garage in the hopes of earning a little money from harvested parts.

She pulled up to an open car bay and shifted into Park, the final few notes of the song she'd just switched off echoing through the garage.

She smiled to herself as she turned the key and stepped out of the car. As cued in to Dirk Rogers as Margaret Louise seemed to be, Tori didn't know very much about the man other than the fact that he'd never stepped foot in the library in the six months she'd been working there as head librarian.

"How can I help you, young lady?" A deep voice caught her off guard and she spun around, the rapid movement upsetting her balance. "Whoa there, didn't mean to scare you."

"You didn't . . . I-I just didn't see you." She shifted from one wedge-heeled foot to the other as she watched the man's gaze play across her face before moving slowly down her body, taking in her pale pink halter top and white denim jeans. "Do you know where I might find Dirk Rogers?"

A soft whistle escaped his lips as his eyes traveled back up her body and settled on hers. "I'm Dirk Rogers. What can I do for you, Miss . . . I'm sorry, I don't know your name."

Swallowing quickly, she extended her hand in his direction. "I'm Tori. Tori Sinclair."

His hand, thick and strong, closed over hers, a shot of warmth spreading from the tips of her fingers to the tips of her toes. "Tori. Now that sure is a pretty name. You from around here?"

Willing her mind to focus on the task at hand rather than the rugged yet incredibly handsome man in front of her, Tori nodded. "I moved to Sweet Briar about six months ago."

"Wait! I know you . . . you were the one everyone was pointing at for Tiffany Ann Gilbert's murder. Wow, now that you're standing right here, in front of me, I don't know how anyone could think you were guilty of anything besides sending a guy's heart pumping."

She felt her face flush at the unexpected compliment. Good grief, what was wrong with her? She was here for one reason and one reason only—to find answers about Colby.

And to get an oil change she didn't really need . . .

"Thank you." Extricating her hand from his lingering

grasp, Tori tucked her fingers around the shoulder strap of her backpack purse. "I was hoping to get my oil changed if you're not busy. I haven't kept up with it the way I should since moving here."

"Then let's take a look, shall we?" He reached around her and into the open window, pulling the release for the hood. "Wow, you sure smell good. Lilac, right?"

"Uhhh, yeah, actually it is." She followed him as he lifted the hood and gestured her over.

"Do you check your oil from time to time?" he asked as he reached for a black cap and began twisting his hand to the left.

"No. I'm not sure how to do that." She tucked her right hand behind her back and crossed her fingers as she continued. "I'm not even sure where the oil box is."

He laughed, a hearty sound that started somewhere deep in his muscular chest. "It's an oil pan, Miss Sinclair."

"I didn't know that." She pulled her left hand behind her back as well as she crossed additional fingers.

Slowly, he lowered the dipstick into a long tube and pulled it back out, his eyebrows furrowing as he examined the results in the light.

"You sure you haven't changed your oil recently?"

"I'm sure."

He dipped the stick again, the second reading doing nothing to dispel the downward turn to his lips. "It sure looks clean and full to me."

"Could you change it anyway? I'm considering a somewhat lengthy road trip in the next few weeks and I want everything to be running right."

"Where are you going?" he asked as he closed the cap and wiped his hands on a cloth he kept stuffed in his jeans pocket.

"Where am I going?" she repeated.

"That was my question." Dirk Rogers leaned against

her car and flashed a smile that surely charmed his way into more women's beds than she could ever hope to count.

"I-I'm thinking about heading up to Chicago for a few days. To visit with some friends."

Where on earth had that come from? The last thing in the world she wanted to do was run the risk of seeing Jeff ever again.

"Chicago, eh? I've never been there, myself. I bet it's got some great nightlife, huh?"

She nodded.

"Man, I'd kill to get out of here for a few days." He cast a sly look in her direction. "Got room for one more? I could cover the gas both ways. And maybe"—he raked a hand through his blondish brown hair—"we could go in on a place to stay . . ."

She considered squashing his hopes like a bug but she resisted. Until she had what she needed from this man, she needed to play nice. And if nice meant flirting, she needed to keep up pretenses for Debbie's sake.

Using her best theatrical skills, Tori dipped her head and giggled. "I don't know what to say."

"I bet we can come up with something when I'm done with your car." Dirk tossed the cloth to the ground and reached for a long black tool box that sat on the floor not far from her car. "This won't take me too long. Why don't you have a seat in my office and I'll come get you when I'm done."

"Your office?"

"Yeah, sure. The owner always has his own office." Inhaling deeply, Dirk puffed his chest outward then pointed toward an open door on the far side of the garage. "It's right there. Make yourself at home."

"I will, thank you." Cocking her head ever so slightly to the right, she flashed a slow, sensual smile at the man. "Thank you, Dirk. For being so sweet."

"Mmmm. It's my pleasure, Miss—it is Miss, right?"

She batted her eyelashes slowly. "Yes. But, please, call me Tori."

He looked at her for a long moment, his charm-filled eyes taking on a slightly different edge—one of a more predatory nature that set her nerves on edge. Stepping backward, she hoisted her purse higher on her shoulder and pointed at his office door, her mind making mental calculations as to how quickly she could pull her cell phone from her back pocket if needed. "I'll just wait inside."

Willing herself not to run, Tori crossed the wide concrete garage floor and stopped just inside the doorway of the office, her mouth gaping open. For a man who played with grease for a living, Dirk Rogers was a certifiable neat freak. The large metal desk that stood in the center of the room was void of anything except a blotter-style calendar, a wooden pencil box, and a computer. Across from the desk stood a metal folding chair she assumed was for customers to utilize while filling out paperwork for their cars. A lone three-drawer filing cabinet stood in a far corner, a framed photograph of an old-fashioned car perched atop its dark gray metal surface.

She took a step farther into the room, scanned the certificates and various mechanic licenses hung with careful precision on each and every wall. A small window, designed to offer a view into the car bays, was covered by a set of wood paneled mini blinds that had been left in the closed position.

Peering quickly over her shoulder to confirm the garage owner's whereabouts, Tori examined the room once again, her attention coming to rest on a door slightly recessed into the back wall. Did it lead to a bathroom? A storage closet? The outdoors?

"There's only one way to find out," she mumbled under her breath as she rounded the corner of the desk and grabbed hold of the recently polished silver knob, twisting her hand to the right as she pulled. She stepped back and peered up at the series of shelves that ran from top to bottom—shelves filled with auto supply boxes and tools she couldn't identify. A second set of shelves on the bottom housed various office supplies—paper, pens, pencils, paper clips, Sharpies, and a plastic bin with crayons and colored pencils. Shrugging her shoulders, she reached for the door again, her eyes scanning their way up its interior side.

"Oh my G—" She clamped her mouth shut as a wave of nausea racked her body. There, just inches from her face, was a picture of Colby Calhoun—the same glossy black and white author photograph she'd seen countless times since moving to Sweet Briar. Only instead of the unobstructed view of Colby's dark brown hair, smoldering gray eyes, and disarming smile that she was used to, this version was chock full of holes—hundreds of holes that covered every inch of the man's handsome face.

"What do you think you're doing?"

Tori jumped backward, her hand instinctively slamming the closet door as she spun around to face a very angry Dirk Rogers. "I-I had to go to the bathroom. I figured that's where this led." She knew the words sounded pathetic, feared he'd see right through them, but she had to try. "I wasn't trying to—"

"Snoop?"

Planting her hands on her hips, Tori forced a scowl. "Of course not. Why on earth would I be snooping around a garage?"

"I don't know. How about you tell me," he thundered as he kicked the door shut behind him. "Your car no more needs an oil change than you were looking for a bathroom. So what gives? Who are you?"

Squaring her shoulders, she inhaled deeply, willed herself to remain calm and in control. "I'm Tori Sinclair, just as I said."

"Why are you here?"

She ignored his question, opting instead to reopen the closet door. Pointing at the photograph, she matched his intimidating tone with one of her own. "I think the better question is this . . . why are you using a picture of Colby Calhoun as your personal dartboard?"

Clenching his teeth as his lower jaw jutted left, Dirk stepped around the desk, closing the gap between Tori and himself with a threatening presence. "It seemed fitting under the circumstances."

"Circumstances?" she asked as she backed into the doorframe. "What kind of circumstances could possibly justify mutilating someone's picture like that?"

"What kind of circumstances?" He propped the heel of his left palm on the wall as he leaned his face mere inches from hers. "What kind of circumstances? How about his high-and-mighty attitude, his I'm-famous-you're-not strut for starters."

With a burst of energy she ducked out from beneath the man's outstretched arm. "Colby Calhoun has never lorded his fame in anyone's face."

He turned around, his breath playing across her bare shoulders as his gaze inventoried her body once again. "That's because you're probably one of those women who fall for it hook, line, and sinker."

"On the contrary sir, it's because I believe it." She gestured toward the dartboard once again. "So basic male jealousy made you do that?"

The man snorted. "Jealous of a blowfish like Calhoun? Puh-lease."

"Then why?" she persisted despite the little voice in her head jockeying for an escape route rather than answers.

"Because he ruined everything. He stuck his nose where it didn't belong and fixed it so everyone who's ever taken pride in this town's history is nothing short of a laughingstock now."

"Oh c'mon. You can't really believe anyone outside the

town limits of Sweet Briar gives a hoot whether this town was burned by Yankees or a moonshine mishap, can you?"

"I can't, huh?" He yanked open the top drawer of his desk and extracted a brick with white lettering spray painted on each side. "Then how do you explain this?"

"What is it?"

"Why don't you take a look for yourself?" He extended his hand, placed the reddish brown brick in between hers as his voice took on a taunting quality. "Still think no one cares?"

She stared down at the brick, turned it over in her hands as she read each side . . .

SWEET BRIAR

HOME OF DRUNKIN

FOOLS TOO STUPID

TO USE A HOSE

"How did you get this?" she asked as she reread each side once again.

"Right through the middle window of my garage door, that's how."

"When?"

"Sunday night. After everyone within a day's radius knew about that piece of trash Calhoun wrote." Leaning over the top of his desk, Dirk pulled a dart from his pencil box and hurled it at the dartboard, the point hitting his intended target with the same accuracy he'd obviously maintained for quite some time. "I swear I—" The man clamped his mouth shut midsentence, opting instead to kick the leg of his desk.

"You'd what, Dirk?"

Reaching a grease-stained finger outward, the man let it trail down Tori's shoulder as he slid his tongue across his upper lip. "How about you stick around for a while. I'm pretty sure a few minutes alone with me would make you rethink a guy like Calhoun. Not that it matters much now . . ."

"Oh it matters. To his wife. To his children. To his friends. And to the police chief." Wrapping her hand around the strap of her backpack purse, Tori backed up around the desk.

"You mean Robbie?"

"Who?"

"Robbie . . . or—for the rest of the folks in town—Robert. Dallas. The chief." He followed her toward the door to the garage, his gaze fixed on hers with an intensity that made her hands tremble.

"You call him Robbie?" she asked, her voice growing shrill.

"Sure do. We've been buddies for years." He raised his arm to the door as she bumped into it, loosely trapping her once again. "Good, good buddies. The kind that are loyal to the end. No matter what."

Summoning every ounce of courage she could find, Tori leveled an index finger at the man's chest, poking him hard with each word she spoke until he backed up enough to allow her escape. "I don't care who your buddies are. No amount of loyalty can keep the truth down for long."

Chapter 16

Driven from her bed well before dawn, Tori sought refuge at the one place she seemed most equipped to deal with life's curveballs. Yet hours later, she was still roaming around the library with no real intent or purpose. She'd replayed her conversation with Dirk Rogers over and over throughout the night, the dartboard and the man's cockiness making sleep an unattainable goal. Sure, he'd frightened her on a personal level, but it was more than that. Much more.

Dirk Rogers's anger over Colby's article ran well beyond that of the average Sweet Briar resident who may have shaken a head once or twice or expressed a few choice words over the subject. Colby's picture was proof of that.

But something about the garage owner's actions in his office the day before had gnawed at her subconscious ever since, leaving her mind to torture itself with the kind of questions she simply couldn't answer.

Was Chief Dallas's integrity in this case truly compromised because of his long-standing friendship with Dirk Rogers?

Was a man who mutilated a picture of another human being capable of murdering that same person?

"Ugh," she mumbled under her breath as she flopped onto the stool behind the information desk and dropped her head into her hands. "Ugh. Ugh. Ugh."

There'd been so many times over the past few hours that she'd reached for the phone, ready to call Milo. But she'd stopped. If she was going to reach out to someone with the information she'd gathered, it wasn't going to be someone who was battling his own misguided feelings about Colby Calhoun.

Lifting her head, she peered around the darkened room, the only hint of light streaming through the hallway from her office playing across a small handful of shelves and a few reading chairs. There was so much about Dirk Rogers that raised the hair on the back of her neck and sent her internal radar pinging. But he wasn't the only one. Harrison James was every bit as angry at Colby as Dirk was, and he had a far stronger motive than simply being seen as a laughingstock.

"A laughingstock," she said aloud, the sound of the word through her own lips making her sit up tall. "Why does that sound so familiar?"

And then she remembered.

". . . it was kind of written in a rambling . . . whimsical way, bemoaning Colby for making Sweet Briar the laughingstock of the south . . ."

Debbie's words filtered through her mind with startling clarity, the woman's voice repeating the sentence again and again as if she were sitting behind the information desk at that very moment.

Was it a clue? Or simply an oddly timed coincidence?

Shaking her head, Tori grabbed the first few book request sheets the nursing home had faxed over the day before and willed herself to focus on work. Her great-grandmother had been a big believer in the watched-pot-never-boils way of thinking, and perhaps she'd been right. The more Tori tried to examine the possible suspects in Colby's death, thc more confused she became. Maybe concentrating on something else would be enough to bring her subconscious thoughts to the foreground where they belonged.

She looked down at the top sheet, her willpower deflating as she scanned Eunice Weatherby's initial wish list . . .

1. *A Cry in the Night* by Mary Higgins Clark
2. *In a Split Second* by Colby William Calhoun
3. *To Kill a Mockingbird* by Harper Lee

"Oh Colby, I'm so sorry," she whispered as the list blurred before her eyes. "So very, very sorry."

Pushing the list to the side, Tori stood and wandered back to her office, the early morning sun ushering in waves of natural light that played across the tiny room. She stood in front of the window that spanned the east wall and stared out into the empty grounds of the library.

As much as she loved seeing the library brimming with readers, there was something special about the building when it was quiet, void of nothing but books—those that existed purely for entertainment and those designed to further people's knowledge.

She leaned forward, rested her forehead against the cool glass. It wouldn't be long before the sidewalks of Sweet Briar sprung to life with people walking to church, shopping for groceries, stopping for a book. Glancing over her shoulder she eyed the small digital clock.

8:45.

In a little over three hours, Nina would be unlocking the front door in honor of yet another day at the Sweet Briar Public Library. If Tori stayed, the busyness of work might quiet the bothersome voices in her head. But if she did that, she'd be forgoing the first full weekend she'd had off in six months.

A weekend she'd originally planned to spend with Milo . . .

"Ugh. Ugh. Ugh." She returned her forehead to the glass and closed her eyes, reveled in the momentary feel of calm that came with the sun's warmth on her face.

Tink. Tink. Tink.

Tori's eyes flew open just as a woman's well-dressed body darted behind a large bush just outside the window.

Raising her hand to the glass, Tori thumped back with a bent finger. The figure re-emerged.

Leona.

Holding her index finger upward at her friend, Tori jogged out of her office and down the hallway to the employee entrance in the rear. With a quick turn of her wrist, she unlocked the metal door and pushed it open, her head peeking around the corner. "Leona? What are you doing out here?"

"Shhh. Be quiet." A red-faced Leona appeared from the side of the building, her hands clutching a large straw bag in front of her as if she were carrying something fragile.

"Why? What's wrong? What are you doing out here hiding behind a bush and tapping at my office window?"

"Never mind that, dear. I have a problem."

"C'mon. Come inside. Are you okay?" she asked, concern for her friend chasing all other thoughts away.

The woman shook her head, her normally salon-styled hair showing rare movement. "Isn't there a policy about no animals in the library?"

"Animals? What are you talking about?" Tori's gaze traveled to the bag in her friend's hands. "Oh no . . . don't tell me you have an animal in there. I really don't want a pet, Leona. Not yet."

Scowling, the woman shook her head again. "It's not for you."

"Then who—"

Looking one by one over each shoulder, Leona lowered her voice to a near whisper. "It's one of Ella May's bunnies."

"What?"

"Shhh!" Leona hissed through clenched teeth. "You heard me, dear. It's one of Ella May's precious bunnies."

Holding her hands in the air, Tori took a step back into the still open doorway. "Oh no. No, no, no. Please don't tell me this is some sort of weird revenge on the woman for marrying a man you'd hoped to snag for yourself . . ."

"I don't snag men, dear. I hook them, make them squirm with anticipation and desire, and then I let them go."

Tori rolled her eyes. "Whatever. But is that why you have one of Ella May's"—she reached out, wedged open a corner of the woman's straw bag—"bunnies?"

"Don't be silly. I don't need to resort to things like revenge. I'm above that." Leona's chin jutted into the air, revealing a smudge of dirt.

"Uh, do you know you have dirt on your chin, Leona?"

"I do? Where? Good heavens, dear, where is your compact?"

"I don't have one."

The woman gasped. "You don't have a compact in your purse . . . for quick touch-ups of your nose and lips?"

"Nope." Tori shook her head, the disgust in Leona's face making her laugh out loud, the straw bag wiggling in response.

"Well then we must add that to the list of things I still need to teach you."

She shrugged. "Sure thing. Right after you learn how to sew."

The woman stared at her. "You never give up, do you?"

"Nope."

"I don't have time for this, dear. I have a bunny to take care of . . . or return."

Stepping out from behind the door, Tori let it shut behind her as she claimed a seat on the concrete step. "Tell me, how did one of Ella May's bunnies get into your purse?"

"He hopped in."

"He hopped in?" she repeated, the corners of her mouth twitching upward.

"Yes. He hopped in."

She pointed at the bag. "I've known you for what . . . six months now? And never, in all that time, have I ever seen you carry a bag like that. Margaret Louise? Sure. You? No way."

"The binoculars wouldn't fit in my clutch." Leona looked at the ground, toed a small rock with her sensible yet stylish white pumps.

"Binoculars?"

"That's what I said."

"Why would you need—wait. Don't tell me. You were spying on Ella May, weren't you?" She stared at her friend, saw the way her cheeks grew still redder. "Leona! What on earth were you thinking?"

"I just wanted to see them with my own two eyes." Leona looked around the employee entrance with a trace of disgust before finally resigning herself to a spot on the steps, the straw bag–encased bunny on her lap.

"Them?"

"Ella May and William Clayton Wilder, who else?"

Tori reached for the bag and transferred it to the patch of concrete between them, her fingers reaching through the top to stroke the soft animal. "You know he's not here often, so why drag yourself out of bed at some ungodly hour to see someone who probably isn't even there?"

"Because today, of all days, he should be. He's got the perfect excuse if anyone happens to see him."

"What kind of excuse?" She glanced up at Leona only to look back at the snatch of brown fur she could see through the top of the bag as her fingers continued to stroke its back.

"My sister. She's baking her new Sweet Potato Pie for him today."

"Ahhh, I get it now." She pulled her hand from the bag and rested it behind her body. "So, was he there?"

"No!" Leona muttered a string of unladylike words beneath her breath before addressing Tori once again. "I stood out there, waiting, for nothing. Well"—the woman leaned forward, peeked inside the bag—"nothing except for him . . . or her."

"When you realized he was in there, why didn't you just set the bag down and let him hop right out?"

"I heard a noise. And I didn't want to take the chance Ella May might come around a corner and see me standing there with binoculars in hand."

It made sense. Sorta. "So why'd you bring him all the way here instead of dropping him off along the way?"

Leona peered at Tori over the top of her glasses. "Would you drop off someone's dog any old place?"

"No. But that's different."

"They're still her pets, dear. And I didn't have the heart to dump him off where he might become a shooting target for Carter Johnson or any of those other gun-toting crazies."

Tori's lips inched upward as Leona's true meaning hit home. "Why, Leona . . . if I didn't know any better I'd think you've gone all soft in the head over this little guy in here." She lifted the bag off the step and set it back in Leona's lap.

Leona opened her mouth to speak then closed it without saying a word.

"Bunny got your tongue, Leona?" she teased.

Peering over her glasses once again, Leona stared at Tori. "Has anyone told you how positively awful you look this morning? Have you given up on Milo altogether?"

Tori gasped. "What does my appearance have to do with Milo?"

Leona smoothed the lines of her pale pink skirt. "Everything, dear. Men don't come crawling back to women who, well, look as if they haven't slept in a week."

"That's because I haven't, Leona. I have a lot of things on my mind right now. And as for Milo"—she turned her head and gazed out across the empty parking lot as the man's face flashed before her eyes, tugging at her heart—"I'm not looking for Milo or anyone else to come crawling back. Unlike you, I don't need a man to make me feel good about myself. And I don't change what I believe to please anyone else."

"I don't date men to feel good about myself, dear. I date men who will pick up the tab for a nice dinner and who will lap at my heels until I'm tired of them." Leona slid off the step and stood.

"Isn't that basically the same thing?" Tori asked.

"I don't think so." Leona peeked inside the bag. "You wouldn't happen to have an organic carrot inside, would you?"

"Oh darn, I knew I forgot something at the market the other day." Tori rose to her feet as well, her momentary irritation toward her friend disappearing as quickly as it had come. "But I could probably find something at my place if you want to tag along."

"Can we drive out to Ella May's after dark and return him?" Leona shifted from foot to foot, the bag in her hands beginning to wiggle.

"Sure. Under one condition." It was a crazy notion in light of everything that was going on, but it made sense, too. The only way she was going to be able to think through the Colby situation with any clarity was to get some sleep. And the only way she was going to get a decent night's sleep was to relax. Sewing served that purpose . . .

The bag wiggled harder.

"What's he doing?" Leona asked as she held the bag outward, confusion etching lines around her eyes. "Why's he moving like that?"

"He's probably pooping."

Leona's eyes widened as her upper lip rose on one side. "Pooping? In the bag?"

"That's my guess." Tori stifled a giggle as she watched panic balloon across her friend's face. "So . . . are you in for my one condition in order to get that bunny back where he belongs?"

"Yes! Here"—Leona shoved the bag into Tori's hand—"hold this."

"Was that a real yes?" she asked as the bag settled down once again.

Leona nodded.

"No matter what the condition is?"

"Yes!" Reality dawned across the woman's face as her eyes narrowed at Tori. "You're going to make me sew, aren't you?"

Tori handed the bag back to Leona and smiled. "Trust me, Leona, bunny poop is nothing compared to babies in diapers."

Leona grabbed hold of the bag, furrowing her brows in a silent question.

"If you don't learn, you lose your bet with Margaret Louise. And if you lose, you'll be watching seven children."

"Yes?"

"At least one of those seven is in diapers."

Chapter 17

"Is he okay? Does he have enough water?" Leona stepped away from the front window just as Tori strode into the living room. "Did you find carrots for him? Or some lettuce? Does he seem sad?"

"Sad?" Tori stopped beside the coffee table and studied her friend closely. "Why would he be sad?"

"Because he misses his mama?"

"Leona, I must say, this softer side of you is very endearing." Tori dropped onto the love seat and patted the cushion to her left. "As for everything else, he's fine. I have him in one of the moving boxes I hung onto and he has a plate of freshly sliced carrots and a bowl of water to keep him company."

"And the bag?" Leona perched on the edge of the armchair instead, her legs bent gracefully to the side. "Was it . . . was it what you thought?"

"It was. And trust me, it's nothing compared to what baby Molly will produce."

Leona waved her hand in the air before bringing it back to her lap. "I'm here, aren't I? Must you really continue with the scare tactics?"

Tori laughed. "Scare tactics? Oh, Leona, you truly don't have a clue, do you?"

"Nor do I want to, dear. So let's get on with it." Leona looked around the small cottage. "Where do we start?"

She knew she should be running for the sewing alcove and gathering up every piece of paraphernalia she could get her hands on before Leona changed her mind, but she didn't. Not yet, anyway.

Inhaling deeply, Tori followed a thread that had been flapping around in the back of her mind all morning. "Leona, what can you tell me about Harrison James?"

The woman's shoulders rose a hairbreadth only to sink back down as she nestled into the plaid armchair. "What would you like to know?"

"What's he like? Does he have a hobby? Does he have a girlfriend? Does he have a relationship with his brother or anyone else in the family? Does he drink like the rest of them? Does he have a temper?"

Setting her elbow on the armrest of her chair, Leona propped her chin on the backside of her bent hand. "He likes to golf, although I'm not sure whether he's any good at it or not. I suspect he likes the club atmosphere of playing more than the actual sport."

"Okay . . ."

"He doesn't seem to actively seek the companionship of women. Not since he and I dated a few times about a year ago."

"You think you ruined him for everyone else, huh?" Tori teased.

"I tend to have that effect." Leona looked up at the ceiling for a moment before continuing. "Now what else? Oh, yes. He seems to prefer keeping his brother at arm's length.

And, after seeing Gabe with your own two eyes, I'm sure you can understand that, dear."

Tori shrugged. She pulled her legs up onto the couch and tucked them underneath her body, her hand instinctively reaching for a nearby throw pillow and hoisting it onto her lap. "I liked Gabe. Sure, he's a little rough around the edges, but I thought he was sweet."

"Well, he's not the type to travel in the same circles as an attorney."

"Do they see one another at all?" she asked.

"If they do, it's not by Harrison's choice." Leona lowered her arm then clasped her hands inside her lap. "The only drinking I ever saw was wine with dinner. At the club. If he drinks anything stronger I'm not aware of what it might be or how often he does. And as for your last question, why would you ask about a temper?"

Slowly, Tori relayed her visit to Harrison James's law office, leaving nothing out. When she was done, she hugged the pillow to her chest and waited for her friend's response.

But there was only silence.

"Leona?"

Still nothing.

"Leona? Did I say something wrong?"

Finally, the woman spoke, her voice soft yet firm. "So you suspect Harrison could be behind Colby Calhoun's murder?"

"Yes."

"And you think this because . . ."

"Because he's furious at Colby for telling the entire town that it was Harrison's family—not bloodthirsty Yankees as everyone's been raised to believe—who burned Sweet Briar to the ground over a century ago."

"Go on," Leona prompted.

Tori looked down at the pillow then back up at Leona.

"Suddenly, those who were willing to give Harrison a chance to forge his own path in life remember who he really is, thus jeopardizing his career and his new lifestyle in the process. Think about it, Leona, do you really think the people at his club are going to be excited to see him show up for dinner and drinks now? He—Harrison James—the great-great whatever of the man who accidentally torched the town with moonshine?"

Leona nodded. "Moonshine is considered backwoods liquor."

"Exactly."

"You may have a point. But, dear"—she dipped her head downward, peered at Tori over the top of her glasses—"I still don't see Harrison as the killing type. He-he's kind of"—she scrunched her nose—"wimpy if you know what I mean."

"No. Tell me."

"Harrison was the type to walk proudly until someone of a larger stature entered the room. He was the type to feel good about his clothing until someone better dressed walked in the room. He wouldn't get nasty or sulky, he'd simply shrink into himself like a wounded flower."

She tried Leona's description on for size, saw where the woman was taking it, and realized she was still without the crucial answer she needed. "Okay, so maybe Colby could overpower him . . ." she said, her voice trailing off only to regain its necessary momentum. "But Colby was also under the influence of sleeping pills that night."

"Sleeping pills or not, Colby Calhoun is the closest thing this town has to a celebrity. That fact alone would make Harrison lean toward timid."

She rested the side of her head against the seatback as she traveled back to Harrison James's office, her stomach tightening at the memory.

". . . the folks around here were willing to let me be my own person with my own present and future. And they did.

Until that damn Colby Calhoun started nosing around in something that wasn't any of his concern . . ."

A shiver ran down her spine at the memory.

"Victoria?"

"I'm here. It's just . . . I hear what you're saying, Leona. I really do. But the man I saw was anything but timid."

"What was he?"

"Angry at Colby. Bitter over the potential threat the article posed to his new life and—" She stopped, her eyes widening as another snatch of their conversation floated through her mind. . . .

". . . It's the difference between being taken seriously and being a laughingstock . . ."

Laughingstock.

There was that word again . . .

Coincidence? Or something more?

"And what, dear?"

"Huh?" She looked at her friend, saw the question in her eyes. "Oh, yeah, sorry. He was angry. Bitter. And vengeful."

"Vengeful?"

"Toward Colby."

After a moment of silence, Leona scooted forward in her chair, turning her entire body toward Tori. "Then it appears it's time for another date with Harrison, doesn't it?"

Tori's head shot up. "You'd do that?"

"Of course, dear. Why wouldn't I? Debbie is my friend as well."

She released the pillow from her arms and sat up straight. "Leona, if you could find out anything it would be a big help."

"I failed to stand by you during the Tiffany Ann Gilbert incident. It's why I allowed myself to even entertain the idea of learning to"—her nose scrunched again—"*sew*. As a sort of peace offering. To you, dear. But I learned a lesson from that experience and I need to do things differently this time."

Feeling a familiar burn behind her eyes, Tori pushed off the couch and made her way over to the sewing table in the alcove, her hands finding the wooden sewing box in record time. "Hearing you say that means a lot to me, Leona. But I'm still going to hold you to the sewing."

She turned around just in time to see Leona's shoulders slump. "Oh."

"I truly think you'll like it if you'll just try. And beyond that, there's that bet with your sister."

"Don't remind me," the woman grumbled as she covered her eyes with her forearm momentarily before jutting her chin upward in defiance. "Okay, let's do it. Let's prove to my dear sweet sister that I'm not the hopeless woman she thinks I am."

"You won't regret it, I promise." Tori set the sewing box on the coffee table and lifted its lid.

"I already do."

"Don't." She sat on the love seat once again. "Look at it this way. If you learn to sew, you make me happy . . . if you learn to sew, you win your bet with your sister and get a home cooked meal delivered to your door every night for a month . . . and if you learn to sew, you—"

"No, that's it."

Tori shook her head. "There's one more thing."

"What's that, dear?" Leona met Tori's gaze with unadulterated boredom.

"If you learn how to sew, you make Ella May's blue handkerchief . . ."

"I'm not following, dear."

"You'll have to give it to her, won't you?"

Leona rolled her eyes in response.

"Which means you won't need a pair of binoculars."

"You mean . . ." The woman stopped, scooted her body

upright and leaned forward in her chair. "Where do we start?"

She leaned over Leona's shoulder as the woman's manicured fingers held the piece of pale blue fabric in place beneath the machine. "There you go. See? I knew you could do—"

A loud knock at the door made her turn. "Okay, hold on. Why don't you stop right there for a moment and let me see who's at the door."

A sigh of relief escaped Leona's mouth as she pulled her arms into her lap. "By all means, let's stop."

She made a face at her friend. "You're doing fine, Leona."

"Fine doesn't mean fun." Leona slid out of the chair and wandered over to the window that faced the front porch while Tori crossed the living room and headed toward the front hallway. "Perhaps that's about to change, though."

Pulling the door open, Tori stepped back. "Margaret Louise, what a nice surprise!"

"Or maybe not," mumbled Leona under her breath as she returned to the plaid armchair.

"He loved it. Absolutely loved it," Margaret Louise gushed as she breezed into the cottage and spun around to face Tori. "He said they were the best he's ever had!"

"Who's he?" she asked as she pushed the door shut.

"William Clayton Wilder!"

"Oh, that's right. Oh, Margaret Louise, I'm so sorry. I completely blanked there for a moment." Grabbing her friend's hands, she squeezed them inside her own. "I knew he'd like them."

Margaret Louise jogged her pudgy legs in place, her hands squeezing Tori's back. "He loved them. Which means I'm going to be on the cover of *Taste of the South*!"

"Do you hear this, Leona? Your sister is going to be

famous." Tori felt Margaret Louise's grip loosen as they both turned and looked at Leona. "She's going to be the face of southern sweet potatoes."

"Sweet Briar's Sweet Potato Pie," Margaret Louise corrected with a sparkle in her eye.

"It's the same thing, right?" Tori gestured toward the living room. "C'mon in, sit down."

"Actually you're right in that they're southern, that was the main requirement Mr. Wilder had. But I took it a step further and made it specific to . . ." The woman's words petered out as she stopped, midstep, and looked from Leona to the sewing alcove and back again. "Have you been sewing, Twin?"

"Maybe." Leona's chin jutted upward as she folded her arms daintily across her white eyelet sweater.

Margaret Louise stepped closer, her index finger pointing down at the floor. "Is that dirt on your white pumps, Leona?"

Leona pulled her feet backward against the armchair. "So what if it is?"

"Did you go out to Gabe's again?" Margaret Louise accused.

"I most certainly did not." Leona waved the suggestion aside as if it were utter nonsense. "I went for an early morning walk is all."

Thump. Thump.

Thump.

Thump. Thump.

"What was that?"

Leona's face paled as she shot a look at Tori. "I didn't hear anything. Did you, dear?"

"I-I . . ."

Margaret Louise set her hands on her hips and looked from one guilty face to the other. "What have you two gone and done?"

Backing up, Tori held her hands out. "I haven't done anything."

"Twin?" Margaret Louise narrowed her eyes at her sister only to stop as she scrunched her nose in distaste. "What's that smell?"

Leona squirmed in her chair.

"Twin?"

"Your bag."

"My bag?" Margaret Louise repeated.

Leona nodded. "The straw one I borrowed the other night."

The woman's eyes narrowed once again. "What did you do to it?"

"I didn't do anything to it. It's just that . . . well . . ."

"What?" Margaret Louise demanded.

Leona looked to Tori for help.

Tori shrugged in response.

"Well, it w-was," Leona stammered. "It was deflowered."

"Deflowered?" Margaret Louise repeated.

"Yes. Deflowered."

"I'm not followin'." Margaret Louise looked at Tori. "What's she talkin' 'bout, Victoria?"

"Well, one of Ella May's bunnies kind of . . ." She stopped and looked at Leona. "Leona?"

Margaret Louise's sister made a face. "It made a mess in your bag."

"What kind of a mess?" Margaret Louise's eyes narrowed to near slits.

Leona shifted in her seat, clasping and unclasping her hands in her lap. "I believe you call it a number two whenever you're talking with Melissa about the children."

Margaret Louise's mouth gaped open.

"But we cleaned it out," Leona insisted.

"We? We?" Tori asked. "I don't remember you doing anything except planting yourself on that very chair while

I cleaned the bag and found a temporary home for the bunny you-you bunny-napped out of Ella May's yard."

"You stole a bunny?" Margaret Louise asked.

"I didn't steal him. He hopped in when I wasn't looking." Leona rested her left hand at the base of her neck and fluttered her eyelashes. "You have to believe me."

"Save the eye flappin'. I'm not one of your male conquests, Twin."

"Why don't you tell your sister what you were doing when the bunny hopped into your—I mean, her—purse," Tori prodded sweetly.

"Do tell, Twin. I can hardly wait to hear this." Margaret Louise folded her arms across her ample chest.

"I was trying to catch a glimpse of true love."

Tori snorted. Margaret Louise rolled her eyes.

Leona's face turned red. "Okay, okay. I just wanted to see him with her. With my own two eyes. It just doesn't make any sense that someone of William Clayton Wilder's caliber would fall for someone so—"

"Weird?" Margaret Louise offered.

"Sweet!" Tori corrected.

"I was thinking more along the lines of plain. Simple. Boring."

Margaret Louise flounced onto the armrest of her sister's chair. "And? What'd you see?"

Tori felt her jaw slacken. She pointed at Leona, her eyes never leaving Margaret Louise's face. "You're going to let her get away with it? You're not going to lecture her for being nosey?"

"No. I'd rather hear what she found out." Margaret Louise glanced a grin at her sister. "Because after today, I'm more curious than ever."

Leona's eyebrow rose. "Today?"

"Today," Margaret Louise repeated.

"Why?" Tori asked, unable to resist the curiosity welling up inside her own mind.

"He showed nothin'. No reaction, no recognition, no nothin'."

"Who are we talking about now?"

Leona waved a dismissive hand in Tori's direction as she stared at her sister. "You said her name?"

Margaret Louise nodded. "I offered to put the Sweet Potato Pie on the menu for their wedding dinner."

"And he didn't say anything?" Tori asked, finally catching up with the conversation.

"Oh he said somethin'."

"What? What did he say?" Leona grabbed her sister's knee and squeezed. "What did he say?"

"When he didn't say anything, I said it again. And that's when he said it."

"What?" Tori and Leona asked in harmony.

"Actually, to be technical, he didn't say it. He asked it."

"Asked what?" Leona said, her nails digging into Margaret Louise's skin.

"Who."

Leona rolled her eyes in exasperation. "William Clayton Wilder, that's who. So, what did he ask?"

"Who," Margaret Louise stated. "He asked, who."

Leona gasped, her hand leaving her sister's leg in favor of her own mouth.

"He didn't know who Ella May was?" Tori asked, her thoughts racing to make sense of the verbal Ping-Pong match she'd unwittingly stepped into.

Margaret Louise shrugged, her head shaking as her shoulders rose and fell. "He didn't have a cotton'-pickin' clue."

Chapter 18

She methodically worked her way through the stack of books Tucker Wrenwick left behind, her hands instinctively sorting each title into separate piles based on where they were to be shelved around the library. A twice-weekly patron, the elderly man seemed to enjoy history books best—particularly ones packed with photographs.

"Mr. Wrenwick sure does like his books, doesn't he?" Nina returned from the Civil War section to grab a pile of Vietnam War titles. "Every once in a while I'll catch him peekin' his way through the middle pages of a romance novel, but mostly he stays true to his war books."

Tori nodded, her mind registering Nina's words on some level. "Uh-huh."

Pulling the war volumes to her chest, the assistant librarian bobbed her head to the side until Tori engaged eye contact. "Are you okay, Miss Sinclair? You seem mighty distracted this mornin'."

She stopped sorting, rolled her shoulders backward, and then dropped into the chair Tucker Wrenwick had vacated less than ten minutes earlier. "Yeah, I'm okay, I guess. It's just"—she traced her index finger down the spine of a stray book—"well, I can't believe it's been a week and still no sign of Colby's body. It must be just horrible for Debbie."

Nina leaned against the table, her sensibly clad feet extended outward. "I can't imagine what she's goin' through, Miss Sinclair. But at least they're lookin' now."

"Looking?"

"There was a whole pile of 'em walkin' through the woods on the west side of town on Saturday evenin' and again most of yesterday. Duwayne said they walked side by side like a human chain."

Swallowing over the sudden lump in her throat, Tori stared at the petite woman with the dark woven brown hair and the large sympathetic eyes. "Duwayne helped?"

"He sure did, Miss Sinclair. He said pretty much every man in town was there . . . 'cept a few." Nina set the books on the table beside her hip then wrapped her hands around the edge of the table. "He said some stayed for a short while and some stayed all day. He was pretty much in between."

She willed herself to focus on Nina's words as the woman launched into a list of people her husband had mentioned seeing during the search, but it was difficult. Just thinking about groups of men scouring the woods for the body of her friend's husband was enough to drive her mad. The whole thing—the town's anger at Colby, the mistreatment of his wife and children, and the violent way in which he'd been removed from his home—was just wrong. And the longer the person responsible was allowed to roam free, the more wrong it became.

". . . and of course Chief Dallas was runnin' the show . . ."

There were so many questions roaming through her head at any given minute, yet the answers remained just as elusive as ever.

". . . and Milo was there. Mr. Johnson, too . . ."

Milo?

She shook her head against the barrage of questions pestering her thoughts like a swarm of aggravating mosquitoes. "Milo was there?"

Nina nodded. "Duwayne said he was there when he arrived both days and still there when he left."

She waited for a sense of shock to engulf her, but it didn't. If anything, shock was the antithesis of what she felt at that moment. Because deep down inside, she knew Milo Wentworth was a good and decent man. A good and decent man who simply had a different way of looking at something. A good and decent man who'd resented being called out for something he hadn't done . . .

Margaret Louise had been right. Milo had gone out of his way to reach out to Tori at the diner on Saturday morning, his gesture given in the form of an active apology and a commitment to change. She, on the other hand, had brushed him off unfairly.

Pulling her fingers from their incessant tour of Tucker Wrenwick's final few unshelved books, Tori looked up at Nina, her mouth suddenly dry. "Hey, would you mind if I headed into my office for a few minutes? I really need to make a call . . . I owe someone an apology."

Nina nodded once again, a shy yet knowing smile starting on the right side of her face and spreading left. "I'll be fine, Miss Sinclair. Looks like we've hit our quiet time of the mornin'."

"Let me know if that changes, okay?" Tori stood and squeezed her assistant's shoulder as she headed toward the hallway. "Thank you, Nina."

When she reached her office, Tori shut the door, the momentary separation from the main room of the library providing the kind of privacy she needed to make her call. Her hands trembled as she slid her cell phone out of her purse and flipped it open. Would he talk to her? Would he hang up as soon as he heard her voice?

The questions were barely completed in her thoughts

before their answers came in a moment of absolute certainty.

Milo was different. He was kind. Compassionate. Understanding. And forgiving.

Scrolling through her contact list, Tori found his number and pressed the green button. She pulled the phone to her ear and listened as each subsequent ring went by, unanswered.

Her shoulders sagged as her mind raced ahead to the recorded voice mail message she'd long since memorized . . .

"Hello?"

She remembered the first time she'd heard his message, remembered the way she'd almost called back just to hear it again . . .

"Tori? Are you there?"

Tori?

Gripping the phone tightly, she cleared her throat, willed her voice to sound calm, steady. "Hi, Milo. How are you?"

"Better now."

She plopped down onto her desk chair and swiveled it around to face the window that overlooked the library's grounds. "Now? Have you been sick?"

"No. I just haven't heard your voice. I missed it. I missed you."

Blinking against the instant burn in her eyes, Tori nibbled her lower lip for a moment. "I-I . . . oh, Milo, I'm so sorry I got all high-and-mighty the other day. I was wrong to—"

"Hold on a second. You were standing on what was right. I was the one who was being blind and standing on something that really wasn't important in light of what Debbie was going through," he said, his voice deep. "I'm not sure what got into me."

She leaned her head against the seatback and closed her eyes, memories of Jeff juxtaposed against the realities that were Milo Wentworth. "You love Sweet Briar. And you take your job as a teacher very seriously. I can understand why Colby's article would have upset you."

"I love people more. Especially you."

Love? Did he just say love?

"I was a fool, Tori. Can you forgive me?"

A tear trickled down her left cheek as she held the phone still closer. "Done."

"Really?"

The pure hope in his voice made her laugh. "Really."

"Phhhew."

"I heard what you did over the weekend," she offered as she gazed out the window at the branches of the moss tree that swayed in the gentle breeze. "Thank you."

"You mean searching?"

"Yes."

"It was the right thing to do. We should have been doing it six days ago. I only wish we'd found something."

"There's a part of me that feels the same way. And a part of me that doesn't," she admitted, her voice cracking. "I want to believe that Dirk or Harrison or whoever pulled him from his home hasn't harmed him. But blood doesn't lie."

"No, it doesn't." A moment of silence filled her ear before Milo's voice returned. "But what's this about Dirk Rogers and Harrison James? Have you heard something to indicate either, or both of them, were involved?"

She shook her head.

"Tori? You still there?"

"What? Oh . . . sorry. No, I haven't heard anything official. I've just had private—and extremely heated—conversations with both men about Colby Calhoun. They both hate him for what he set in motion."

"*Hate*'s a strong word, Tori," Milo cautioned.

"You're right. And I stand by it."

"Tell me."

Just the willingness in the man's voice to listen—really

listen—was all it took for Tori to share everything that had happened at both Harrison James's law office and Dirk Rogers's garage. She shared every word that was spoken, every threat that was hurled, every innuendo that was made.

"He trapped you against a wall?" Milo bit out as she got to the part about Dirk.

"He was just trying to intimidate me," she said. "At no time was I truly trapped."

"Perhaps I need to pay him a visit . . ."

"No. Please. He's got a violent streak. But . . . Milo . . . do you think he's right? About Chief Dallas looking the other way because of their friendship?"

"Nope. Chief Dallas is a man of respect. Truth and justice are paramount for him."

She felt her shoulders relax just a bit. "Should I tell him about the dartboard? Let him check it out for himself?"

"Yeah, I think you should. But you said he threw one while you were there, right?"

She nodded, only to realize her mistake and put words to the unseen motion. "He threw it hard and with a whole lot of anger."

Silence greeted her statement.

"Milo?"

"Yeah, I'm here. I think you should tell the chief about the dartboard to be safe but . . . I don't know . . . I just think . . ."

"What?" she asked as she spun her chair toward the desk and leaned back, her eyes finding the digital clock. She really needed to get back out on the floor with Nina. . . .

"If Dirk was really involved, doesn't it seem strange he'd still be angry enough to throw that dart at Colby's picture? Wouldn't killing him be enough to rid him of that kind of intense hatred?"

She sat up straight, Milo's words tickling her own subconscious inquiry to the surface. It made sense. A lot of sense . . .

But if not Dirk, then who?

"I think it's something that definitely needs to be looked into, but I gotta say, from what you've told me, Harrison has one heckuva motive for harming Colby."

"I think so, too," she echoed. "Leona agreed to try and see what she could find out under the guise of a date-type situation but now . . . after last night . . . I'm not sure that's the man she's after any longer."

His heartfelt laugh filled her ear, made her smile in response. "Uh-oh. Who's the poor victim this time?"

"William Clayton Wilder."

"The magazine guy?"

"One and the same." She rose from her chair and made her way slowly toward the office door, her heart protesting the end to a conversation her head knew was necessary. "Now that he's not who we thought he was, Leona has him in her sights."

"Who you thought he was? What does that mean?"

She waved her hand in the air. "How about I fill you in on all that over dinner tomorrow. I'll make Italian."

"Sounds wonderful. Though tonight sounds even better."

"Tonight is our circle meeting."

"Oh, yeah. I forgot. Tomorrow sounds perfect then."

She inhaled deeply, the pleasure she derived from having Milo in her life flooding her body with a much needed sense of calm. The stress that remained would be navigated together. "I'll see you at six then. Have a great day, Milo."

"Your call made it great, Tori."

Snapping the phone closed in her hand, Tori slipped it into the front pocket of her off-white slacks and stepped back into the hallway, her feet turning toward the library's main room as if they were equipped with an autopilot feature. Fixing things with Milo didn't lessen the heartache over Debbie and the kids, but it did make her feel less alone. In fact, if she were honest with herself, his support served to reignite the strength she'd felt wilting the past few days—a strength that had been challenged by the inability to find answers.

But one thing was certain. A killer was out there. Somewhere. And it was only a matter of time until she put the pieces together . . .

She looked up from the computer as Nina returned from lunch. "Good break?"

"It was. I got a few errands taken care of for Duwayne. That'll make him real happy when he gets home from work." Nina came around the counter and set her purse on the ground beside the stool. "Did I miss anything?"

"Nope. Sally Colter was in here earlier with her triplets. Those boys are so well behaved. She's doing an amazing job with them." Tori looked back at the screen, her fingers tapping out the names of a few just-released paperback titles for the mystery shelves. "I'm almost done here and then I'm gonna get our first few orders together for the nursing home."

"Do you have any of your bags yet?"

"I do. Just three. All from Margaret Louise. But I'm sure I'll get a bunch tonight at circle." She closed out of the ordering screen and reached for the order slips she'd placed inside a small wicker basket under the counter. "It works though, because—as of right now—we only have two orders. One for Eunice Weatherby and one for"—she looked at the sheet of paper—"a man named Milton Gregory."

Nina extended her hand. "I could fill one if you'd like."

"Okay, sure. How about you do"—she looked down at

the two order forms in her hands, felt her throat constrict at the sight of Colby's name on Eunice's sheet—"Mr. Gregory. I already know Eunice's list. I read through it yesterday."

"I'm not sure I ever told you, but I think takin' these orders from the nursin' home is a neat idea." Nina looked down at the sheet in her hand. "My granddad was in a nursin' home 'fore he died and it was sad how many people there never had visitors, never got home baked treats, never got a present. And puttin' the books in special homemade bags just makes it even more special."

She tried to follow Nina's words but it was no use. Nothing seemed to stick in her mind for very long these days except thoughts of Colby Calhoun. A whole week had gone by since the night she and Debbie discovered he was gone. And still, there were no answers. As much as she hated to lower Dirk's position on her possible suspect list, Milo had had a point. If Dirk had harmed Colby, why would he still be throwing darts at the man's picture?

"I hate to see you so upset, Miss Sinclair."

Tori looked up, forced her mouth to turn upward in some semblance of a smile. "I'm okay, Nina. It's just . . ." She stopped, looked back at the list in front of her, her shoulders slumping of their own volition. "I don't know. I can't explain it, I guess."

Sliding her dark and slender arm behind Tori's back, Nina gave a gentle squeeze. "I can. You feel other people's hurt. I saw it the first time we met. Do you realize you look downright stricken every time a child cries in the library—not stricken because they're loud but because you want to fix things. And back when that whole mess with Tiffany Ann Gilbert was goin' on, you thought about me instead of yourself."

She set Eunice's list down and peered up at her assistant through long, thick lashes. "Thought about you?" she asked, her voice raspy and unsure.

Nina nodded. "Duwayne told me what happened."

"He did?" She shifted on the stool, unsure of what to say in the event they weren't on the same page.

Nina nodded again. "All those things that happened to you? Duwayne told me they were his fault. He told me he was just tryin' to help me get ahead. And he told me how you simply encouraged him to believe in me."

"Wow," she whispered. "That took a lot of courage for him to do. I hope you know that."

"I do. But it all just goes to show the kind of person you are. So it makes perfect sense why Mr. Calhoun's disappearance has upset you the way it has." Nina's hand dropped to her side as she looked down at the book order in her hand once again. "I also have faith you'll figure it out. I only wish I had half of your motivation."

Tori watched the petite woman exit the information desk area in favor of finding the first book on Milton Gregory's list. Her words, however, stayed right where she'd left them—in Tori's heart.

She looked back down at her own list, lingered her sights on Colby's name. "Nina's right you know," she whispered. "I will figure out what happened to you."

Shifting Dirk's name lower on her list was a minor setback in the grand scheme of things. Harrison James was still very much on the top.

Shaking her thoughts free of potential murder suspects and their motives, Tori headed toward the mystery section and Eunice Weatherby's first choice. *A Cry in the Night* was one of her favorite suspense novels as well.

Colby's novel brought her to the true crime section and the large display she'd assembled months earlier in honor of the local author. As she neared the face-out display, Tori's feet slowed. The static display featured four shelves, one for each of Colby's novels. With each successive book, the man's name had grown larger and larger on the cover. Yet no matter how big the font, his name had still failed to supersede the title in prominence. It was a goal she knew he'd been working toward . . .

A goal he'd never get to reach now.

Sighing heavily, she grabbed the copy the elderly woman had requested and simply held it, her fingers tracing the author's name as if it were lettered in gold.

"Colby," she muttered, as her fingers fanned out over the book's title and impressive cover art. Slowly, carefully, she turned the book over, examined the back cover, read the blurbs from fellow authors, scanned the Web site address of the pub—

She pulled the book closer to her face, her gaze reading and rereading the name in front of her.

Lions Publishing.

"Lions Publishing . . . Lions Publishing. That's"—she searched her memory bank for the correct name—"William Clayton Wilder's company."

"Miss Sinclair?"

Had he known one of his authors lived in Sweet Briar?

Nina popped around the end of the aisle. "Miss Sinclair, you okay?"

She held the book upward. "Did you know Colby's books were published by Lions Publishing?"

Her assistant shrugged. "I didn't 'fore last weekend. I guess I don't pay much mind to anything besides the title and author most times."

"What was last weekend?" She pulled the book back into her arms and studied the publisher's Web site address once again.

"Last week . . . on the mornin' of the festival . . . Mr. Calhoun was here with some man from Lions Publishin'."

She stared at the woman. "He was?"

"Yes, Miss Sinclair. Mr. Calhoun was showin' him the display you set up and the man was wavin' his hands 'round and talkin' 'bout the importance of promotion." Nina pointed at the tiered shelf and smiled proudly. "He said your display, Miss Sinclair, is what they needed everywhere—bookstores, too."

"Did you happen to hear the man's name?" she asked, the woman's words circling her thoughts wildly.

"Mr. Calhoun introduced me. It was some big long name and sounded very important."

Closing the gap between them, Tori stopped in front of Nina, her hands tightly gripping the books in her arms. "William Clayton Wilder?"

Nina clapped her hands together. "Yes, yes. That's exactly right, Miss Sinclair. Did you meet him, too?"

"No . . ." Her words trailed off as she strode past Nina and over to the information desk.

"Is somethin' wrong, Miss Sinclair? Should I have called you that day?"

She waved her hand in the air. "No, of course not." She replayed the woman's words again, words and a voice that morphed into Debbie's . . .

Only to be cut off by Georgina.

William Clayton Wilder hadn't simply been passing through Sweet Briar on the day of the festival. And he hadn't been there to see Ella May Vetter, either. He'd been there to meet with Colby.

Colby.

"Nina? How did Colby seem that morning?"

"Unhappy. Distracted. I'd thought maybe he didn't like that William Clayton fella. He was kind of pushy. I mean, I wasn't trying to listen, Miss Sinclair—I really wasn't. But he was houndin' Mr. Calhoun about doin' everything he could to be a household name from here to California."

"Well he got his way, didn't he? Colby's death has probably landed him on television sets across the entire . . ." She stopped, her mouth gaping open as a rush of thoughts flooded her mind simultaneously. Bit and pieces of ideas flitted to the foreground only to disappear before she could assemble them into some sort of order.

"Miss Sinclair?"

She held up her finger as she tried to keep up with the path her thoughts had chosen.

"*. . . William Clayton Wilder is single, Victoria. Single and wealthy . . .*"

"Rose?" she whispered as the elderly woman's words continued, their frail raspy quality echoing inside her ears . . .

"*. . . Though why she'd be interested is beyond me. That man has a reputation for being ruthless with everything from his handling of employees to his unethical publicity tactics . . .*"

She slapped her hand over her mouth as the enormity of the woman's words hit her with a one-two punch.

Was it possible? Was there a chance Colby's disappearance was nothing but a publicity stunt?

"Nina, I need you to hold down the fort." She ran around the desk, grabbed her purse from the ground beside Nina's, and headed toward the hallway, her heart slamming against her chest as a week's worth of torturous questions faded to the background in favor of one.

But was it really possible?

Chapter 19

Tori sat in her car and stared up at the Calhoun home—a home that was envied for the happiness and love it witnessed on a daily basis. Everything, from the wide front porch with the cluster of rockers to the swing that dangled from a moss tree in the front yard, screamed family. And closeness. Yet in a week's time, that happiness—that closeness—had all but faded into a memory as the present became inundated with unimaginable heartache.

On the drive over, she'd done everything she could to discount the thoughts running through her head. Tried to chalk them up to lack of sleep and increased self-pressure to bring at least a small sense of closure to Debbie and the children.

But try as she might, she couldn't shake the troubling picture that had assembled itself in her mind—the first few pieces forming at the library, the rest falling into place as she maneuvered the streets of Sweet Briar. The only saving grace, though, was the completed picture that emerged.

A picture she couldn't share with Debbie until she was absolutely certain of its reality.

Summoning up every ounce of courage she possessed, Tori pushed the car door open and stepped out onto the pavement, her legs uncharacteristically wobbly. There were so many things she needed to ask Debbie, little bits of information that could mean all the difference in the world.

The problem was whether she could glean what she needed without tipping her hand in the process—a mistake that could serve to reshatter an already broken heart.

Tori walked around her car and stepped onto the sidewalk, her feet instinctively stopping as she stared up at the house and swallowed. Her poker playing skills had always been atrocious thanks to the very thing Nina had pointed out that morning—Tori wore her heart on her sleeve.

A quality that was completely unacceptable at the moment.

Inhaling deeply, Tori willed her legs to follow the stairs that led to the Calhouns' front porch, her heart pounding with each step she took. As she reached the top, she stared at the door—the same door she and Debbie had found ajar just one week earlier.

She knocked, her tiny fist barely making a dent amid the afternoon sounds of a neighborhood teeming with children. She knocked again, louder.

A curtain to the left of the door inched aside, revealing Debbie's ashen face and red swollen eyes. Unsure of what else to do, Tori waved.

Seconds later, the sound of a lock disengaging echoed through the door just before Debbie's face peeked around its corner. "Victoria, how are you?"

She reached out, pulled her friend into an embrace. "How are you holding up?"

"Okay, I guess." Debbie stepped back and motioned Tori inside. "When I need to cry—like now—my mom takes the kids to her house. When I need to be strong, she brings them back."

"If now is a bad time, I-I could come back." She stopped just inside the front entryway and eyed her friend with concern. "I don't want to force a visit on you if you're not up to it."

Debbie pushed her hand through her unkempt hair and leaned against the wall. "I'm not sure there will ever be a good time again. For anything."

"I'm so sorry, Debbie. So very, very sorry." She knew the words were useless but it was all she could think to say, to do. "If there's anything at all I can do . . . you have to tell me."

The woman managed a wan smile as she pushed off the wall and gestured for Tori to follow her into the parlor. "It's nice to have someone who cares regardless of what they think of Colby."

Think of Colby?

"You haven't heard, have you?" she asked as she sat down on the chair Debbie indicated, a navy armchair that looked as if it could swallow her whole.

"I haven't heard anything. I haven't really wanted to," Debbie said, her voice cracking as she claimed the cream-colored sofa across from Tori. "Colby was my husband. He was a good husband, a good father, and a good man no matter what anyone in this town says."

"They've been looking for him. They spent the entire weekend searching." She studied her friend as the woman twisted her hands inside her lap, her shoulders hunched forward in sadness. "I think most of them realize they were wrong."

Debbie's hands stilled momentarily as she looked up through tear-filled eyes. "What are you talking about?"

"The residents. The men, really. They've been walking the woods. Knocking on doors." She leaned forward, engaging Debbie in eye contact. "They've been looking for Colby."

One by one, tears trickled down the woman's flawless skin. "Who?"

Rising to her feet, Tori walked around the coffee table in the center of the room and sat beside her friend, her hand pulling the woman's from her lap and holding it gently. "Pretty much everyone. Duwayne Morgan, Carter Johnson, Milo, Chief Dallas." She continued rattling off names as Debbie's tears fell more rapidly. "And that's not all. There are others who are determined to make amends as well . . . to help you and the kids."

Debbie swiped her cheeks with the back of her hand as she waited for Tori to continue.

"In fact, right now"—she glanced at her watch—"Margaret Louise and Rose should be greeting the after work crowd at the bakery and getting ready to turn things over to Emily so they can get ready for our sewing circle later this evening."

"Rose is helping at . . ." The woman's voice trailed off as sobs racked her athletic body—gut-wrenching sounds that brought tears to Tori's eyes.

"Yes. Rose. And Georgina's taking the afternoon shift tomorrow."

"B-b-but they w-w-were so ang-angry at Colby at the l-l-last meeting." Debbie spoke through the tears as she rested her head on Tori's shoulder.

"And they were wrong to put that on you the way that they did. They realize that now." Tori swiveled her body toward Debbie as the woman picked up her head. "They love you, Debbie. We all do. We want to help you."

"Then bring Colby home . . . alive," she whispered as the sobbing began again.

Seconds turned to minutes as Tori simply held her friend, her shirt growing wet against her shoulder. But it didn't matter. Being there, did.

When the crying finally stopped, Debbie leaned her head back against the couch, her nose red, and her eyes puffy. "I can't get it out of my mind. Not any of it. The letter. The blood. The knife. The mess in our room."

Tori nodded in understanding. "I know. I can't either."

"Thank you for being there with me that night." Debbie raked a hand through her hair and looked at Tori through eyes that were suddenly hooded. "I'm not sure what I would have done if you hadn't been there."

She patted the woman's hand. "I'm glad I was there, too."

"Chief Dallas doesn't seem to have any leads at all. The only prints on the knife were mine, which doesn't help, and the only prints on the letter were mine and Colby's."

"Are you serious?" She mulled over the information, tried it on for size. "Then doesn't that mean there's a good likelihood that whoever wrote the note was also the one who took Colby?"

Debbie lifted her shoulders only to let them fall downward once again. "Why would you say that?"

"No prints on the knife . . . no prints on the letter . . . seems to me the same smart person was responsible for both. Though why someone would bother to write a threatening note prior to killing someone is beyond me."

Unless the whole thing was a ruse from start to finish. To create a better story . . .

"I don't know what we're going to do, Victoria. I do okay at the bakery, but it's not enough to raise two children in"—she raised her hands into the air—"a home like this by myself."

"We'll figure it out."

"William has been so nice. He's checked in every day on the phone and he even stopped by yesterday after he met with Margaret Louise."

"You mean William Clayton Wilder? The publisher?"

Debbie nodded.

"He was here the day of the festival because of Colby, wasn't he?"

Again, Debbie nodded, the slight motion one of great effort for the distraught woman.

"What can you tell me about him? Why did he come to see Colby in the first place?"

"He was on his way from point A to point B and stopped here. They had a bit of a powwow regarding publicity and marketing."

"Is that normal for a publisher to do with an author of Colby's level?" She prayed the question didn't offend, as that wasn't her intent.

If Debbie noticed though, she said nothing. "Apparently the stop enabled William to write off a pleasure trip. You know, a moment of work amid a week of fun in the sun."

"How'd the meeting go?"

"I don't really know. By the time we met up after the festival, the fallout from the article had already started. His meeting with William was the least of our worries." Debbie stared at her hands, her words taking on an almost wooden quality. "You know what's funny?"

"What?"

"The publicity Colby is getting now . . . because of, well, because of this week . . . that's the kind of national exposure William wanted. Ironic, huh?"

Ironic *is one word for it . . .*

She willed her thoughts to stay with Debbie, right there in the present conversation rather than in the newly awakened conspiracy-theory corner of her brain.

"H-has Mr. Wilder been working hard to reassure you?" She hated putting the question out there, but it had to be asked. She only prayed Debbie didn't put much thought into the inquiry.

"Some, I guess. But the money part wasn't very reassuring."

"Money part?"

"About having to give Colby's advance back."

She stared at Debbie. "Give it back?"

"Colby was paid an advance for his next book. He never finished it." Debbie's voice grew weak as her body seemed to shrink into the sofa. "That money was given on good faith."

"Colby didn't know he was going to die!" She slammed her mouth shut as tears rolled down Debbie's cheeks once again. "Oh, Debbie, I'm so sorry . . . I just . . . I'm sorry."

"I-I-I have to get used to it, Victoria. Colby is dead. He's not coming home." Her voice eked out each word with a pain so tangible Tori could almost reach out and touch it. "And William is r-r-right. That money has to g-g-go back."

Tori fought the urge to scream, to vent her anger and frustration over the publisher's insensitivity at such a trying time. But as much as she wanted to scream, she wanted to cry, too.

The notion of paying back an advance shot a huge crack right through the middle of her latest theory—a theory that had Colby holed up in some four-star hotel room while the nation grew infatuated with his name. Because if she'd been right, there would have eventually been a book . . .

In the absence of any credible evidence to support her suspicion though, Colby was still dead. And Debbie was still heartbroken.

Damn.

Chapter 20

Margaret Louise's home was bright and colorful with alphabet letter magnets, a dollhouse, a bucket of miniature cars, and more finger painted pictures hanging on the wall than Tori had ever seen in one place.

But it fit. Perfectly.

For as wonderful a cook, sister, and friend as she was, everyone around Margaret Louise knew that her son and his family were her true pride and joy. She spoiled each of her seven grandchildren with love, yet respected Jake and Melissa's top role and number one standing in their lives.

Tori claimed a tan rattan chair positioned in the westernmost corner of the large sunporch, the last of the day's lingering rays making it one of the primo places to sit for that evening's circle meeting. The chair was set slightly back from the rest of the seating choices, yet still had access to an electrical outlet—a must if using one of the group's portable machines.

"Being antisocial this evening, Victoria?" Rose asked as she shuffled into the room wearing a soft gray housecoat with a thin white cotton sweater thrown over her shoulders. In her hand was a stack of fabric in varying color schemes and patterns.

She stood and walked over to her friend, their quick embrace revealing yet another drop in weight for the retired schoolteacher. Alarmed, Tori stepped back and studied the woman, her gaze playing across the deflated cheeks and bony hands. "Rose? Is everything okay?"

"Everything's fine, Victoria. I've just been fighting a cold is all and my appetite hasn't been very good." Rose patted her hand and then gestured toward a love seat not far from where Tori's chair was. "I think the sun on my body will do me some good though . . . ewww . . . that smell is awful."

"Smell?"

The woman's nose scrunched in disgust. "You don't smell that? It smells like a litter of pent-up cats."

Come to think of it, she had noticed a strange odor when she walked through the door, her nose instinctively chalking it up to the children that came and went all day long.

"One of the kids probably left a juice cup somewhere and forgot to tell their grandmother. Another day or two and she can't help but find it. Now here, let me help." She reached for the woman's pile of fabric only to get her hand smacked away.

"I'm not an invalid, Victoria, I can do it." The woman shuffled over to the sofa, aligned the back of her thighs with the cushion, and slowly lowered herself down, her voice dropping to a near whisper. "But thank you anyway."

She meandered over to her own chair aware of a sudden tightness in her throat. Although she'd only been in Sweet Briar a relatively short time, the women of the circle had become her family in many ways—people she relied on for opinions, advice, help, and friendship. The thought of one day losing one of them was a pain she hadn't considered.

Shaking her head free of the sad turn to her thoughts, Tori reclaimed her chair and pulled her tote bag onto her lap. As much as she was looking forward to the gossip-infused conversation that was synonymous with their circle meetings, she had a number of book bags to make. Just that afternoon alone, a representative from the nursing home had phoned in four more request lists from their residents—titles Nina had diligently set aside for the next day's first-ever book delivery.

"I made eight. Some bigger for hardcovers, some smaller for paperbacks." Rose's arm rose into the air, her sweater slipping down from her wrist and revealing an arm that had become much too frail. In her hand was the fabric Tori had tried to hold for the woman. "I made some for women and some for men."

"I made a few, too," Georgina Hayes said as she strode into the room with her trademark straw hat atop her dark brown hair. "The only fabric I could find, though, had sprigs of flowers on it . . . so mine would be better for women."

"I have some, too," Margaret Louise's voice boomed across the room from her position in the center of the doorway. "I'd hoped to get a few more done but things have been a little extra crazy lately with tryin' to perfect the recipe and gettin' the bakery back up and runnin' for Debbie."

Debbie.

Tori closed her eyes briefly as she thought back to her visit with Colby's widow that afternoon, the woman's swollen eyes and pink-tipped nose etched in her mind with startling clarity.

"And we ran it like two professionals if I must say so myself, didn't we, Margaret Louise?" Rose's eyes looked enormous behind her thick glasses as she nodded at her bakery cohort and the evening's host. "I dare say we would have made Debbie proud."

Margaret Louise nodded, her smile nearly splitting her face. "I agree."

Tori pulled her sewing box out of her tote and opened the lid, her hands intuitively finding the thread she needed to complete her latest bag. Removing the spool from the box, she set it on one of the small snack tables Margaret Louise had scattered throughout the room for the meeting. "I saw her today."

Georgina peered over her portable sewing machine as it zipped along the first side of her bag. "Saw who, Victoria?"

"Debbie."

Machines switched off, heads looked up.

"How is she?" Beatrice asked. "How are the children?"

Tori shrugged. "I didn't see Jackson and Suzanna, they were with Debbie's mom. But Debbie . . . well, she's doing as well as can be expected, I guess."

"Did you tell her what we're doing? With the bakery?" Rose's voice, shaky and quiet, forced more than a few of the circle members to lean forward in their chairs just to hear. "Did you tell her how badly we feel about last week's meeting?"

She offered the elderly woman what she hoped was a reassuring smile. "She was touched, of course."

"Did she tell you anything more about the investigation?" Dixie asked, from her spot beside Beatrice.

"Not much. Seems all the chief has shared with her is the fact that the only prints found on the letter and the knife belonged to her and to Colby. If there's anything else, he hasn't shared it with her." Tori set down her thread and sighed, heavily.

"There isn't much else to share," Georgina volunteered before turning her sewing machine back on. "Robert is following leads, but there aren't very many to follow. Besides the absence of prints on the knife and the letter, the only other peculiar thing is the missing pills."

"Missing pills?" Tori echoed.

Georgina nodded. "Debbie had given Colby sleeping pills that evening. The rest of the bottle hasn't been recovered."

Tori stared at Sweet Briar's mayor, a woman who'd had her world blown to smithereens just six months earlier when her newlywed husband had been thrown into prison on murder charges—charges she, Tori, had set in motion. "Isn't that rather odd?"

"I suppose. Though it's possible Debbie simply forgot what she did with them. She's not taking this whole affair very easily."

"I'm not happy about the news trucks that have infested this town like a pesky influx of mosquitoes. They're everywhere." Dixie's hands flailed wildly in the air as she continued, "You can't walk five feet downtown without some reporter asking you how you feel about the famous Colby Calhoun being snatched from his own home."

Heads nodded around the room followed by a few snorts of disgust.

"I think most of those reporters were former students of mine—the ones who showed absolutely no sign of remorse or compassion for anyone else." Rose leaned back against the sofa and crossed her legs at the ankles. "If they would turn even half of their energy from how everyone feels to investigating what happened we'd all be better off."

Tori looked down at the fabric in her lap, her desire to make more bags waning. "I've been trying to follow one thread—I mean, threat—at a time." She laughed in spite of the seriousness of her intended words. "Oh boy, it's official. Sewing has infiltrated my every thought."

"Perhaps it was a Freudian slip, Victoria, but it's also true."

She met Rose's eyes. "How do you mean?"

"Each piece of thread makes up a project . . . whether it's a skirt, a shirt, or"—the woman lifted one of her bags into the air—"a bag. Same goes for any truth."

"Just look at what happened with Thomas," Georgina interjected without a shred of emotion to indicate how she felt about her former husband. "Without following each and every thread, you never would have been able to hand the police such a perfect motive behind Tiffany Ann's murder."

Rose nodded. "That's right, Victoria. You've seen shoddy sewing. You know what happens when someone doesn't take care with each and every strand of thread."

What they said made perfect sense. And, in a way, it was what she'd been trying to do over the past week. She'd followed Carter Johnson's thread from start to finish, realized his verbal thrashing of Colby was nothing more than frustration and disappointment. She'd followed Gabe Jameson's potential culpability and discovered he was thrilled to be free of the weight of a lifelong secret. She'd followed his brother, Hank Jameson and—

She scanned the room. "Where's Leona?"

"Leona?"

"Yes, Leona. Your sister." Her eyes narrowed on Margaret Louise's reddening face.

"Uh, she's, uh, upstairs . . . taking care of somethin'. She'll be down in a few minutes."

"I'm sorry, but I have to ask. Margaret Louise, what is that stench?" Rose, who'd behaved herself long enough for any self-respecting seventy-nine-year-old, waved her hand in front of her face. "It's awful."

If Margaret Louise answered, Tori didn't hear. She was busy putting an equation together in her head that didn't include a sippy cup of juice. Pushing the fabric off her lap, she stood and headed into the hallway, Margaret Louise lapping at her heels. "Where are you goin', Victoria?"

Stopping just out of earshot of the others, Tori spun around, hands on her hips. "You never brought it back last night, did you?"

"It?" Margaret Louise asked as her head dipped forward.

"Ella May's bunny," she hissed before lifting her nose into the air and inhaling deeply. "It's in this house, isn't it?"

A thump from above the kitchen served as confirmation. She headed toward the front hallway and the wooden staircase that led to the second floor. "We tried to, we really did. It's just that he was really, really cute."

"It's not your bunny, Margaret Louise," she said over her shoulder as she took the steps two at a time, the co-bunny-napper panting a few steps behind. "You can't just decide to keep him because you think he's cute."

"She has so many," the woman protested.

Leona stepped into the hallway just as Tori hit the top step. "Hello, dear, what brings you up here?"

Pushing her way past bunny-napper number one, Tori stopped just inside the doorway of what appeared to be a spare bedroom, the moving box she'd used as a temporary home for the bunny on Sunday now equipped with blankets, carrots, water, and a stuffed animal.

"A teddy bear?" She snorted back a laugh in an effort to preserve even a shred of reproach to her voice. "What on earth does a bunny rabbit need with a teddy bear?"

"He has to sleep sometime, dear." Leona bent over the box and wiggled her fingers at the rabbit. "How's my little Paris?"

Her left eyebrow rose. "Your little Paris?"

"You don't want to know, Victoria. Trust me," Margaret Louise interjected from her spot as door sentry. "But do you see now why I agreed to keep him?"

"You mean steal him," Tori corrected.

"Semantics, Victoria."

"Leona! You stole this bunny."

"If you want to get technical about it, dear, he stole me, remember?"

She rolled her eyes upward. "That's a stretch."

Leona stamped her foot. "No it's not. He hopped into my bag."

"Actually, it was my bag," Margaret Louise reminded gently.

"Oh, shut up!" Leona gestured toward the bunny. "With me he gets the attention he deserves. With Ella May he's one of a hundred."

"More like a thousand." Margaret Louise looked back toward the staircase for a moment before reestablishing eye contact with Tori. "Do you see this"—the woman pointed at Leona, then the bunny, and then back again—"this rare burst of maternal instinct here? I've been waitin' to see this from my twin for years. How could I let that go unexplored?"

She returned her hands to her hips as she looked from one sister to the other. "He has to go back."

Leona's mouth moved in a perfect mimic of Tori's. Margaret Louise nodded in silent, albeit slow, agreement.

"Tonight," Tori repeated.

"Tomorrow," protested Leona. "Or Wednesday."

"Tonight, Leona."

"I need to prepare him. He's gotten attached."

Tori rolled her eyes again. "Wednesday—at the latest. Otherwise . . ." Tori's voice trailed off as she took one last look at the bunny before heading back into the hallway. "Do they know downstairs?"

"Rose? Georgina? Do they know? Good heavens no." Margaret Louise shut the door behind her sister who'd reluctantly accompanied them out of the room. "Leona would be the laughin'stock of the sewing circle."

Laughingstock.

"What is it with that word?" Tori asked in frustration. "In just the last few days I've heard it from Dirk, Harrison, Milo, and now you. And that's after it was used in the death threat Colby received."

Margaret Louise shrugged. "Common expression that is fittin' of a lot of things 'round this town lately."

She turned to Leona. "Any luck with Harrison?"

"No. But I have a date with William Clayton Wilder after the photo shoot on Friday."

"They're doing a photo shoot on Friday?" she asked Margaret Louise, who nodded proudly. "That's fabulous. Congratulations!" To Leona she said, "But you agreed to see what you could find on Harrison, remember? I need you for this part."

"I will. I will." Leona led the way down the staircase, her tan pumps hitting the wood planked foyer with a telltale staccato. "Though I still say he's much too wishy-washy to overpower a man like Colby Calhoun, sleeping pills or not."

"She has a point," Margaret Louise said as she trailed them back into the sewing room. Like clockwork, her voice rose to its normal booming octave as she addressed the entire circle. "How are things going in here?"

A chorus of "Goods" shot around the room.

"When will you start the deliveries to the nursing home, Victoria?" Dixie asked.

"Tomorrow. Nina and I filled two orders this morning and then a few more came in during the afternoon." Tori walked around the room slowly, stopping to look at everyone's work, excitement for her latest project building once again. "And when the residents see these beautiful bags, I suspect the orders will increase tenfold."

"I suspect you're right. It's a wonderful idea," Georgina said. "What made you think of it?"

Finding her way back to her own chair, Tori sat down,

pulling the fabric back onto her lap before situating one of the portable machines on the snack table. "Actually it came from Ella May Vetter."

"Ella May?" several voices said in unison.

"How on earth did Ella May give you the idea?" Dixie questioned.

"She called in a few books she wanted us to set aside. Nina gathered them up in less than a few minutes and they were waiting for her the next chance she had to stop by the library."

"And you should have seen the books she wanted. They were a mighty strange collection." Margaret Louise sat on the edge of the single step that led from the kitchen to the large sunporch where they were all assembled. "Not that strange is strange where Ella May is concerned. Get it"—she shot her elbow outward despite the absence of anyone sitting next to her—"not that strange is strange?"

Laughter erupted around the room.

"Did you know she's asked me to make her wedding dress?" Rose asked, her mouth twisted in a self-satisfied grin.

"I'm cookin' her weddin' dinner." Margaret Louise clapped her hands together with glee. "And Debbie's makin' the wedding cake . . . or, at least, she's been asked to."

"Are you doing anything, Victoria?" Beatrice asked quietly.

"I don't think—"

"Of course she is," Leona interrupted. "She's finding poetry that can be read during the ceremony."

"Leona is making something, too," Tori shot back, her lips twitching. "Isn't that right, Leona?"

The woman made a face at Tori much to the delight of the rest of the women in the room.

"What are you making, Leona?" Rose asked.

"Nothing."

"I'm sure Melissa and Jake will be happy to hear that,

Twin. They've been wantin' me to take them out to supper without the young-uns for a while now," Margaret Louise taunted.

"Leona is babysitting? For children?" Beatrice asked, the look of absolute horror on her face priceless. "You can't be serious . . ."

"Oh, I am." Margaret Louise pushed herself off the step and gestured toward the kitchen. "I think it's time for dessert, don't you?"

A few heads nodded, others remained stalwart. "But we want to hear what Leona is making," Georgina said, her machine still whirring along. "It's not polite to keep such secrets."

"She's making a lace-edged handkerchief for Ella May," Tori explained, as she scooted the snack table to the side in favor of a trip through the dessert line. "Isn't that—"

"You mean *buying*, right?" Rose interrupted.

Tori shook her head. "No. Making."

"C-can you make a lace-edged handkerchief with glue or Velcro?"

"Leona is sewing one, Beatrice." Tori stood and walked toward the doorway, her hand gently tapping Leona's shoulder as she passed. "And she's doing a fabulous job so far."

"Leona . . . sewing? And doing a fabulous job?" Rose struggled to her feet, pulling her sweater tighter to her body as she, too, made her way in the direction of the treats. "Everyone grab your blankets and coats, it's happening again."

"Happening?" Beatrice asked, her eyebrows furrowed in confusion as she joined the parade into the kitchen. "What's happening, Rose?"

"Hell. It's freezing over."

Chapter 21

She peeked inside the oven, her eyes instinctively closing as she inhaled the telltale aroma of pasta sauce and sausage. It had been months since she'd last made a baked ziti and her stomach wasn't crazy about the idea of waiting another thirty minutes until it was done.

But patience was a virtue, as her great-grandmother always used to say, although it was a virtue Tori didn't seem to have in bulk supply. Especially when so many other things around her were moving at a snail's pace . . .

Like solving the mystery around Colby Calhoun's disappearance. Like giving at least some semblance of closure to Debbie and her children.

"Tori?" Milo's deep voice startled her, the oven door slamming shut as her hand flew to her side. "Tori? Are you here?"

Bobbing her head to the left, Tori consulted her reflection in the microwave door then hurried out to greet her dinner guest. "Milo, hi."

A slow grin crossed the third-grade teacher's face as

his gaze roamed its way shyly down her body, taking in the pale yellow tank top and body-hugging jeans she'd opted to wear for their first date in a week. "I knocked. A few times. But you didn't answer. I hope you don't mind that I let myself in."

"Of course not, don't be silly." She strode across the living room and stopped beside the tall, lanky man. Rising up on tiptoe, she brushed a gentle kiss on his cheek. "I couldn't hear you over the gurgling of my stomach."

He laughed. "That hungry, huh?"

She poked her index finger into his chest and made a face. "I haven't had a baked ziti in much too long and the smell is driving me nuts."

"Then I guess I'll just have to take your mind off it until it's ready." Milo wrapped his arms around her back and pulled her in for an embrace. Resting his chin on the top of her head she could hear him inhale. "Mmmm. You smell good."

"I think that's the sausage."

"Nope. It's you." He held her for a long moment before finally releasing his hold and stepping back to tilt her face upward with his hand. "This past week without you really stunk."

She searched his eyes, saw the genuine remorse behind the sparkle she'd grown to love. "I know. I'm sorry I wasn't more understanding about your feelings. I just know that no matter what, Colby Calhoun is a good man."

He pulled his hand from beneath her chin and brushed her cheek. "And that should have been my top concern as well. But it is now."

Stepping back into his arms, Tori pressed her cheek to his chest, the frustration and the fear and the worry of the past week escaping through her mouth. "I just don't know what to think. At first I was so sure Carter Johnson was a viable suspect only to realize that, like you, his town pride was hurt and he had a knee-jerk angry reaction. And then I was sure Gabe Jameson was our man because Colby's article unleashed a secret his family had guarded for over a century. But he didn't care . . . in fact he's the one who verified Colby's suspicions."

Wordlessly, Milo released one of his arms from her back and guided her toward the love seat in the center of the living room, his body the first to sink into the cushions before pulling her down beside him. "Okay. And so where are you now?"

She pulled back just enough to search his eyes once again. "It doesn't bother you that I'm trying to solve this? That I'm sticking my nose into police business?"

He shook his head. "Why would it? You're not doing it to be a busybody. You're doing it because you love Debbie. How can I fault that?"

Swallowing over the sudden lump in her throat, Tori looked quickly down at her lap. "It's more than that, though."

"I know that, too."

She looked up at him once again, her head tilting to the side as her eyes narrowed on his expression. "What do you know?"

"That you don't have a lot of faith in our police." Pulling her into the crook of his arm, Milo raked his free hand through his hair. "And after the way things went down during Tiffany Ann's murder investigation I can't say as I blame you. But I do truly believe that Chief Dallas is looking at everyone and everything."

"Even his friends?"

His head nodded against her hair. "Even his friends." His nod turned to a nuzzle as his chin grazed her ear. "So come on, who else are you looking at?"

She shrugged. "Well then I was sure it was Dirk Rogers. You'd told me how furious he was at the festival, Margaret Louise told me about some of his underhanded ways, and then I saw the dartboard. And"—her voice dipped lower as another thought—one she'd missed until that moment—hit her like a ton of bricks—"the crayons . . ."

"Crayons?"

"In his supply closet . . . he had crayons," she whispered.

"So?"

"Don't you see?" she asked as she pushed back to see his face. "The death threat Colby received was written in crayon."

"I have crayons."

"You're a teacher, Milo."

"And Dirk is an uncle."

An uncle . . . It made sense.

Lots of people had crayons. Margaret Louise had some for the grandkids, she had some for the children at the library. . . .

She felt her shoulders slump along with her resolve. "I guess you're right. Besides, what you said about him still throwing darts at it has some merit. If you've killed someone, you wouldn't display anger like that in front of someone else. And it stands to reason that most of his anger toward Colby would have been satisfied by killing him."

"Okay . . ."

"Which leaves me with Harrison James—aka Hank Jameson. A man who is absolutely furious at Colby for reminding Sweet Briar who he really is . . . the offspring of moonshiners. Town-incinerating moonshiners."

Milo was quiet for a moment as he seemed to consider her words. When he finally spoke, his voice was gentle yet firm. "But have you seen Harrison?"

"I went to his office."

"He's not the killer type, Tori."

She sat up, swiveled her body to afford a better view of the handsome man. "What is the killer type, Milo?"

He spread his hands out, palms upward, and elevated them just above his lap. "Tough."

"What about furious? And vengeful? Don't those count?"

"If they're inside someone who's tough, yeah."

She considered his words, realized they meshed with Leona's almost perfectly. "I'm not ready to discount him, too."

"Then don't. But keep looking."

"I was. Especially earlier today."

His eyebrows furrowed. "What happened earlier today?"

She leaned back against his arm and sighed. "A dead end involving Colby's publisher."

"You thought William Clayton Wilder had killed Colby?"

She heard the disbelief in his voice, tried not to take it too personally. "No. For that brief shining moment I actually let myself believe Colby was still alive . . . that his disappearance was some sort of publicity stunt to put a little extra zip in his career."

His lips met her forehead, lingered there for a moment before moving in time with his words. "What made you ditch that theory?"

"He wants Colby's advance check back."

"Are you serious? The guy's been missing a week and that millionaire is already hassling Debbie for money?" Milo's head jerked back as his hand fisted at his free side. "What nerve."

She placed a calming hand on his thigh as a beep from the kitchen signaled the completion of the ziti. "Can we table this long enough to eat? Maybe try to catch up on other things we've missed this week?"

He raked a hand through his hair once again, his shoulders sagging just a little. "Yeah, that sounds good. Can I do anything to help?"

"Nope. Just take a seat at the table"—she gestured toward the small dining room table she'd carefully set with a white linen tablecloth and her great-grandmother's special china—"and make yourself comfortable. I'll be out in just a minute."

"Will do."

She felt his eyes on her as she strode toward the kitchen, a smile tugging at her lips. As much as she liked to think she was independent and completely fine without a man in her life, having Milo around just made things nicer. Lighter.

As her stomach had suspected, dinner was wonderful. The cheese had bubbled to perfection atop the noodles and bits of sausage bathed in homemade pasta sauce. The wine she'd chosen was a perfect complement to the meal as was the salad and bread she served as well. The best part of all though was the companionship, the easy camaraderie between two people who genuinely fit well together.

"So how was your circle meeting last night?" Milo lifted his wineglass to his lips and polished off the last sip.

Reaching for the bottle in the center of the table, she refilled his glass before pulling her napkin from her lap and setting it on the table beside her near-empty dinner plate. "It went well. I've decided to start a book delivery to the nursing home and I asked everyone to help make some homemade bags. In less than a week, I now have more bags than I could ever hope to fill."

Milo grinned. "Those ladies love you, Tori."

She felt her face warm. "I think they're just nice women who want to do their part."

"Oh, they're that, too. But they love you. Trust me."

Embarrassed by his praise, Tori searched for something to say. "I was going to make my first delivery today but opted to wait until tomorrow. Tuesday is apparently the day the doctor makes his rounds to all the residents. So I figured the books would be a treat better saved for another day."

"Good call." He scooted his chair back from the table just enough to allow the ankle of one leg to rest on the knee of his other. "So, what kind of books are the elderly of Sweet Briar reading these days?"

"Everything and anything. Nonfiction, romance, suspense, reference, women's fiction." She looked down at her napkin, her voice breaking as she continued. "One of the women even requested a Colby book."

"I'm sorry, Tori." In an instant, Milo was beside her chair, tugging her to her feet. "But you have to know that whoever did this to him will pay."

"I hope you're right. But from what Debbie told me earlier today, there aren't any real clues."

"You saw Debbie today?"

She nodded her head against his chest. "I wanted to see how she was."

"And?"

"She's struggling horribly."

They walked arm in arm back to the couch, dirty dishes taking a backseat to the topic neither could stay away from any longer. "And what do you mean by no clues? Surely they're looking for fingerprints and evidence around the house."

Tori shook her head as she sunk into the love seat beside Milo. "They cleared the house days ago. That's where I saw Debbie."

He stared at her. "There's nothing?"

"The knife had no fingerprints at all. Except for Colby's and hers. They'd used it that evening while preparing supper." She laced her fingers inside each other before setting them inside her lap. "And the only clue—if you want to call it that—is the fact that the sleeping pills Debbie gave him seem to be missing."

"That's weird," Milo said, echoing a sentiment Tori shared.

"All I know is that whoever dragged him out of there

had to be strong. I mean, have you ever seen the size of Colby's arms?"

Milo laughed. "They're the talk of many women in this town, Tori. And, quite frankly, every man in Sweet Briar knows about Colby Calhoun's arms, too."

"Oh."

"But I have to disagree on the notion the person had to be of some superhuman strength. He had taken sleeping pills that night, hadn't he?"

"Uhhh, yeah." She turned her head to the side, studied his face for some sort of clue as to where he was going with his comments. "Debbie said he only took two. She said one tended to do nothing for him, yet two were just enough to send him off into la-la land."

"And that's exactly what I'm saying. People in la-la land can be coaxed without really having a clue as to what they're—"

A knock interrupted his words. Shrugging her surprise at Milo, Tori stood and hurried toward the door, her hand pulling it open to reveal Leona Elkin standing on her front porch.

"Leona?"

Bobbing her head to the left to afford a better view into the house, Leona waved at Milo still seated on the couch. "I wouldn't interrupt if it weren't really important."

"Come in, come in." Tori stepped back, letting Leona pass. "Is something wrong?"

Waving her hand in the air, the woman kept walking, her signature a-man-is-in-the-room posturing in full force. "I just need your help."

Pushing the door shut, Tori trailed her friend into the living room. "With . . ."

"My project." Stopping beside the plaid armchair that was her favorite, Leona perched on the edge, an off-white clutch purse in her hand.

"Project?" Tori echoed as she raised a confused eyebrow in Milo's direction.

Waving Tori off, Leona addressed Milo, her false eyelashes fluttering rapidly. "I'm making a wedding present for Ella May Vetter. I simply have one little detail left before I can bring it by her home tomorrow morning."

Tori's mouth gaped open. "Bring it by . . . tomorrow morning? Why?"

As if she hadn't spoken a word, Leona continued, her obvious flirtation with Milo bringing a grin of amusement to the man's face. "I seem to have stumbled across something that belongs to Ella May and I figured it would be best to bring the gift at the same time I bring back . . . well, I bring back the item she's misplaced."

Tori snorted. "You're going to bring back the"—she moved her fingers up and down to simulate quotes—"item she misplaced?"

Leona glared at her. "I was threatened within an inch of my life if I didn't return it by tomorrow."

Rolling her eyes upward, Tori sat down beside Milo once again. "Milo, I'm terribly sorry. I need to help her with this project."

He planted a kiss on the top of her head in understanding.

"Can we continue this again soon?" she asked.

Again he nodded, his smile chasing away any worry Leona's unexpected visit had stirred inside her heart. "I look forward to it." Rising to his feet, he reached a hand in her direction and tugged her off the sofa. "But walk me out, okay?"

"Absolutely." She trailed him toward the door, her thoughts vacillating between tossing Leona out on her ear and asking Milo to hang around until they finished. But in the end, she opted to call it a night. Besides, Leona had a lecture coming.

They stepped onto the porch, the decreasing sun casting their bodies in shadows. "I had a wonderful time with you tonight, Tori."

She looked up at him. "I did, too. Very much. I'm just sorry Leona chose tonight to develop a sudden urge to sew."

"It's okay. We have tomorrow. And every day after that for as long as you want me around."

Aware of the sudden moisture in her eyes, Tori simply nodded, her voice too constricted to speak.

"Good night, Tori. I'll call you in the morning."

"You might want to make it after ten. I suspect I'll be accompanying Leona on her all-important mission."

"Have fun with that." He reached for her hand and gave it a gentle squeeze, his lips finding hers in the looming darkness.

"Fun?" she asked as he pulled back, the touch of his lips leaving her dazed. "You haven't spent much time with Leona Elkin, have you?"

Chapter 22

"Tell me again why I'm here?" Tori eyed the woman in her passenger seat. "Why I'm an accomplice in a crime I didn't commit?"

Leona pouted her perfectly plump lips as she peered inside the straw bag on her lap. "Because you're the one making me bring him back."

"Uh, Leona? He doesn't belong to you . . . that's why I'm making you bring him back." She looked up into her rearview mirror, her guilty conscience making her wary of anyone who could be watching.

"Why? So he can be one of hundreds instead of his own special little bunny?" Leona's cheeks rose as she made a playful face at the bunny peeking out through the tiny opening she'd made with her fingers. "Isn't that right, my sweet little Paris?"

Good grief.

"Okay, what gives? What's with the name?"

Leona gazed down at the rabbit. "He just reminds me of someone."

"Don't you mean somewhere?"

"No. Someone."

"Who?"

Leona puckered her plump lips and made kissing noises at the bunny. "A man I met the last time I was in Paris."

Tori cast a sidelong glance at her friend. "A bunny reminds you of a man you met?"

"Yes. My little Paris here has the same warm chocolate eyes . . . whiskers that tickle my skin . . ."

She bit back the urge to laugh as she swung her focus back to the road. "So then why didn't you just call him the same name as this man?"

Leona waved her hand in the air. "Good heavens, dear . . . I don't remember his name."

"Just his eyes and his whiskers?"

"Exactly." The woman looked from Tori to the bunny and back again. "Why can't I just keep him? Ella May will never notice."

"He's not yours, Leona. That's why." She pulled into an abandoned turnoff less than a quarter of a mile from Ella May Vetter's home and cut the engine. "Couldn't I just drop you off? Let you walk back to town when you're done?"

Leona raised her free hand to the base of her neck and feigned surprise. "You'd ask me to walk back to town while my heart is breaking?"

She rolled her eyes. "Oh, c'mon, Leona. Giving this bunny back is not affecting you that much."

The woman huffed. "Shows how much you know, dear." She pulled her hand from her neck and wiggled her manicured fingers at the soulful brown eyes peering out from the bag. "Besides, don't you want to see how my first sewing effort is received?"

Damn.

"Okay. Okay. I'll do it. But how are you going to explain the bunny?" Tori leaned across her friend for a better look at the seemingly willing prisoner.

"If we're not able to make it to the porch without being seen, I'll gently drop the bag, make it appear as if Paris just hopped in." Leona leaned against the seatback, a self-satisfied look on her flawlessly made-up face. "It's really quite genius."

"Don't forget to pat yourself on the back," Tori mumbled as she turned the key in the ignition and pulled back onto the road, Ella May's Victorian springing into view behind a large grove of trees.

"Must you be so snippy this morning, dear?" Leona chided. "Paris likes positive, happy people."

"Then what's he doing with you?"

Leona slowly shook her head. "And here I thought I'd made some progress in teaching you how to conduct yourself as a proper southern belle."

"Do southern belles make a habit of helping one another steal things? Do they stalk around people's homes trying to get a glimpse into a personal life that is none of their business?" The questions sprang from Tori's mouth as she slowed the car once again before turning into Ella May Vetter's driveway.

"Leave it to a northerner to disguise their accusations in sarcasm." Leona pulled the straw bag closer to her body as the car bumped its way down the gravel driveway.

"Ahhh yes, because out-and-out accusing people of crimes they didn't commit simply because they don't look and act like everyone around them isn't wrong?" She knew her teasing had crossed into bitterness but she didn't care. Some things just needed to be said. "Wait. Don't answer that. I forgot we're living in a place where decent men are murdered for telling the truth."

Leona waved her free hand in the air. "I still intend to work on Harrison."

Tori shifted in her seat. "When?"

"After my date with William."

"After?" She bit back the urge to scream, her irritation at her friend's constant man-chasing nearing its limit. "I thought you said you learned a lesson last time . . . that friends come first."

"Did I say that?" Leona asked with surprise.

"Yes. You did. And spending time with Harrison could give us some much needed insight into what happened to Colby."

"I did try. When you first brought it up. But . . ." The woman's voice trailed off for a moment only to return as a near whisper, "he didn't seem interested."

Tori gasped. "A man didn't jump when you asked?"

"Stop it, dear. Perhaps he's involved with a new woman and he's trying to resist temptation."

She couldn't help but laugh at the way Leona shifted uncomfortably in her seat, the notion a man might not be interested just about more than the woman could take. "Do you know who?"

"He acted very secretive."

She straightened behind the wheel, her radar pinging loudly. "Secretive?"

"Not in the I'm-hiding-a-dead-body kind of way, dear. Rather in an I'm-dating-someone-but-don't-want-anyone-to-know kind of way. But it won't last. When he realizes the opportunity he was given, he'll come around. They always do, dear." Leona jutted her chin upward as she wrapped her fingers around the door handle and pulled, the door swinging open simultaneously. "Enough of that for now. Let's get snooping . . . I mean going."

"No, you meant snooping." Tori followed suit, stepping onto the gravel driveway in her new woven wedge heels as she moved her hand upward to shield her eyes from the midmorning sun. "I think you might be in luck. Though I suppose that's contingent on what you consider luck . . .

Ella May being home so you can spy, or Ella May not being home so you can return the bunny without fear of getting caught?"

Leona walked around the front of the car to join Tori, her hand shaking ever so slightly as she held the bag outward one more time. "I'm going to miss him."

"We can get you your own, you know." Tori slid a sympathetic look in Leona's direction as the woman peered forlornly down at the bunny. "We could call a few pet stores in the county, see if they have one."

"He wouldn't be my Paris."

"Your Paris?" Tori echoed in surprise.

"I got attached."

"I'll say." Realizing her friend wasn't acting, Tori slipped a reassuring hand around the woman's shoulders. "Think of all the friends he has here. And the flowers he can trample through and the organic carrots he'll eat."

Leona nodded sadly.

"He really is better off here." Tori rested her head briefly on her friend's shoulder before letting her hand drop to her side.

"How should I do this?" Leona asked, her voice barely audible over the chirping of the birds and the whir of Ella May's air conditioner clicking to life.

"Just set the bag down. Let him hop out just the way he hopped in." Tori gently wrestled the bag from Leona's clutches and set it on the ground.

Moments passed. The bunny remained in the bag.

"See?" Leona asked, her mouth widening in a smile. "See. He loves me."

Seconds later a second bunny appeared, hopping its way past the bag and toward the house. Paris emerged and followed suit, stopping every once in a while to munch on something green and leafy.

Tori laughed. "He really is your bunny, isn't he?"

"Why is that, dear?"

"He's interested in that one"—she pointed at the rabbit who'd lured Paris from the bag—"yet playing coy at the same time."

Leona's hands found her hips. "I don't play coy, dear."

"Oh, yes, my mistake." Tori turned on her heels and walked toward the car, looking back over her shoulder as she did. "Leona? Aren't you coming?"

"No."

She stopped, her shoulders slouching. "Why not?"

"Because I have a gift to deliver, dear. Remember?"

"How could I forget," she mumbled under her breath as she retraced her steps. "Couldn't you just wait until there's an actual date for the wedding? Give it to her then?"

"And miss all the fun?" Leona shook her head. "Not on your life, dear."

Ahhh, yes, the many polite overtures of a proper southern belle . . .

Tori trailed her friend as the woman made her way toward the wide front porch that spanned the front side of Ella May's Victorian, her thoughts skipping ahead to the work that awaited her at the library that morning—cataloguing, ordering, reading to a summer school group, and making her first delivery out to the nursing home.

Yet as they mounted the stairs, she couldn't help soaking up every detail of the woman's home—a woman who was both sweet and a tad bit odd all at the same time. When they reached the top step, she looked around, noted the two rocking chairs that stood side by side, positioned to watch the sun as it set over Sweet Briar. A window overlooking the porch stood open a few inches, the glimpse of the country kitchen it afforded lit only by natural light.

"I don't think anyone's home, Leona."

Leona knocked, first quietly and then more insistent, the sound bringing curious bunnies from around every corner.

"I don't think anyone's home, Leona," Tori repeated,

looking over her shoulder at the driveway that was empty save for her own car. "There's not another car anywhere."

"Ella May doesn't own a car, dear." Leona rolled her eyes while simultaneously shaking her head as if Tori's lack of knowledge in that area was due to pure stupidity.

"Still, I don't think she's home. There aren't any lights on."

"It's daytime, dear. And Ella May believes in natural everything." Leona placed her hand on the door and turned the knob to the right.

"What are you doing?" Tori hissed through clenched teeth. "You can't just walk inside."

"Didn't you see, dear? The door was partially open . . . I'm just being a good neighbor and calling it to Ella May's attention." Leona stepped inside, gestured for Tori to follow.

"It was not! You just turned it. I saw you!"

"I most certainly did not. It was open." Wrapping her hands around Tori's forearm, she pulled her inside the large country kitchen decorated with a blue and white border of bunnies. "Hmmm, isn't this quaint? Ella May is quite the interior decorator." Leona pointed at a picture in the middle of the table. "And, as it seems, an artist."

Tori leaned forward and studied the beautifully illustrated picture of a family of bunnies frolicking in a knoll. Despite the use of crayons, the attention to detail was impossible to ignore. "Wow, she's good. Really, really good."

"It's okay, I sup—"

A fast rhythmic thumping from upstairs cut Leona off midsentence.

Thump-thump-thump-thump . . .

"What was that?" Tori whispered.

Thump-thump-thump-thump . . .

The mirrored surprise on Leona's face morphed into a knowing smile as she shooed Tori back outside, the rhythmic sound increasing not only in speed but volume as well.

Thumpthumpthumpthump.

Feeling Leona's hand beneath her arm, Tori looked a question at her friend.

"Don't they know about the birds and the bees in Chicago, dear? Or must I teach you that as well?"

"The birds and the bees?" Tori asked as she felt Leona's pace quicken, urging her forward as well. "Of course they . . ." She slapped a hand over her mouth as she peeked back over her shoulder. "Wait. You think . . . you think that was them?"

"Yes I do. And a good southern belle respects the privacy of her fellow belles." Leona reclaimed the passenger seat as Tori slid behind the wheel.

"Since when are you a proponent of privacy, Leona?"

The woman reached across the center console and gave Tori's leg a mothering pat. "There's a time and place for everything, dear."

"A time and place for everything," she repeated as she backed her car slowly from the driveway.

"You'd know that, dear, if you'd stop being so rigid around Milo."

She hit the brakes. "Rigid? Did you just say I'm *rigid*?"

"Yes, dear. Rigid."

"One minute you tell me I'm too rigid, the next you tell me I wear things that show too much bosom," she said as she bopped her head against the seatback in frustration.

"There's a time and place for bosom, dear."

"And when, Leona, is that?" She lifted her head, looked both ways over her shoulder, and then backed onto the main road, her mind whirling from the outlandish conversation taking place inside her car.

"Why don't you ask Ella May? She seems to be well versed in the subject."

Chapter 23

She probably should have felt guilty for leaving Leona standing in the library parking lot without a way to get back home, but she didn't. She'd spent far too much of her morning traipsing all over God's creation when she had a mountain of work to do.

Rounding the corner of the information desk, Tori flung her backpack purse onto the lowest shelf. "I'm sorry I'm a little late, Nina. I got . . . sidetracked." *Bamboozled* was a better word but it would have resulted in questions. Questions she had neither time nor desire to answer.

"Not a problem. We've only been open ten minutes, Miss Sinclair." The woman she'd come to count on as far more than a part-time assistant moved effortlessly between piles of books. "It was just enough time for one visitor to return some books and another to ask a question." Nina pointed toward a forty-something woman with dark brown hair and a high schooler in tow.

"I'm glad." Tori looked from pile to pile, noting the

slip of paper Nina had placed on each one. "Are the orders all ready?"

"Yes, Miss Sinclair. And only one of the requested books was already checked out. So I made a substitution with a similar book and tucked a note inside saying we'd send the requested book when it comes back." Nina leaned against the counter long enough to eye Tori closely. "Are you okay, Miss Sinclair? You look a little . . . tired."

"Long morning." She squatted down in front of a large binlike drawer and slid it open, a stack of homemade bags springing into view. "I guess we better get these orders bagged up and ready to go. I'll take them over to the nursing home on my lunch break."

Nina took some bags from Tori's hand, examining them carefully. "These are wonderful, Miss Sinclair."

She couldn't help but smile. For as crazy as the past week had been, some good had come of it, too. "They are, aren't they?"

The door opened, followed by the sounds of young children who didn't have a firm enough grasp on the concept of quiet voices. Looking quickly at the clock on the counter, Tori's eyes widened as they met Nina's.

"The summer school group."

She nodded along with Nina's words, her own voice dipping to a near whisper. "They're early, aren't they?"

"By almost thirty minutes," Nina whispered back. Pushing off the counter, Nina rubbed a hand on Tori's shoulder. "I can read with them if you'd like . . . give you time to take care of the bags."

She hoped her sigh wasn't too obvious, especially to the approaching ears of the overanxious summer school teacher who'd run out of things to keep her charges busy. "That would be great. My mind isn't really in the right place to make exciting voices and sound effects."

"I'll take care of it." Nina left the desk area, her shy smile greeting the students on the other side. "Hello, boys and girls. Let's head on into the back for some fun with books, okay?"

A chorus of agreement rang out as the children followed Nina down the hallway toward the children's room Tori had created in an old storage area. The hard work that had gone into transforming the room had paid off as the addition was one celebrated throughout Sweet Briar.

Forcing her attention onto the stacks of books in front of her, Tori began the slow process of matching a bag to each order form—the nursing home director's description of each resident making the process somewhat easier. There was the bag with the fishing motif for Mr. Donaldson, the floral pattern bag for Ms. Thomas, a pastel colored bag for Mrs. Richmond, and the cartoon characters for Mr. Zane. Eunice Weatherby, an avid painter, would adore the bag boasting an artist's palate and a rainbow of paint colors.

She opened Ms. Weatherby's bag and placed the first two books inside, her throat constricting as she stared at the third—*In a Split Second* by Colby William Calhoun. Setting the bag down on the counter, Tori reached for the book, turning it over in her hands to look at the publisher's name that had captivated her two days earlier.

If only she'd been right. Then maybe Debbie wouldn't have to hurt any longer . . .

"But you weren't right," Tori whispered to herself as she shoved the book into the bag and set it aside in the plastic bin she'd purchased specifically for the purpose of transporting the bags to the nursing home.

One by one, she went through each pile, placing the correct order form and books into the bag she'd selected for that particular resident. When she'd finally placed the last bag in the container, she scanned the counter for anything she may have forgotten, her gaze coming to rest on a stack of books with oddly familiar titles to the right of the computer.

Scooting the stack to the side, Tori searched for its order form and accompanying resident description but to no avail.

"Things are going well, Miss Sinclair. The kids are delving into the dress-up trunk to act out the story I just read to them." Nina peeked over the counter. "Could you hand me my purse. One little girl wants to clip her hair up to look like a princess."

"Yeah, sure." Tori pulled her attention from the unmarked pile long enough to grab Nina's purse and hand it over to the woman. "I'm almost done up here. Except I can't find the order form to go with this pile," she said, pointing at the stack of books containing everything from a Stephen King horror title to a Beatrix Potter storybook. "Do you have any idea where it might be?"

"Oh, that's not one of the nursing home piles." Nina scanned the empty countertop to the left of the computer. "Looks like you got all of those."

"Then what are these?" she asked.

"Those are the books Ella May Vetter dropped off just before you got here."

"Oh, okay." She pushed them off to the side and returned to the bin of book bags on the floor beside her feet. "I'll shelve those later."

"I set those aside so you could take a look at the top one. It has a slight rip in the cover."

Tori looked back at the stack of books, *Misery* looking no worse for the wear. "I don't see a tear."

Nina shrugged. "I told Miss Vetter the same thing. But she insisted on jotting you a note of apology anyway."

She studied the tiny tear more closely. "What happened?"

"It got caught on those gloves she wears. Anyway, here's the note."

"What's with the crayon?"

Nina shrugged. "It's what she grabbed when I handed her the pencil holder and that piece of paper."

"Oh."

"She said something about starting your day with a splash of color."

A splash of color . . .

Nina tapped her hand on the counter before turning back toward the hallway. "I better get back. I've got a show to watch."

To start her day . . .

"To start my day?" Tori whispered, as she glanced up at the clock, her eyes confirming what she knew to be true. "Nina . . . Wait!"

Her assistant stopped, turned around. "Yes, Miss Sinclair?"

"You said Ella May dropped these off this morning?"

The woman nodded. "Not more than five minutes before you walked in." And with that, Nina turned on her heels and disappeared down the hallway.

"How could she have gotten here before I did?" The words poured from her mouth in a near whisper, the answer hitting before the question was fully worded.

She couldn't have.

Which meant one thing. The thumping she and Leona had heard must have been the mysterious Billy . . .

Billy who wasn't one and the same with William Clayton Wilder.

He was simply Billy.

William . . . Willy . . . Billy . . .

Tori grabbed hold of the counter as a terrifying picture began to form in her head. A picture that was at once ludicrous, yet . . .

Entirely possible?

Dropping to the ground, Tori dug through the gift bags, lifting Eunice Weatherby's from the bin and pulling its contents out and onto the floor. *A Cry in the Night* by Mary Higgins Clark, *To Kill a Mockingbird* by Harper Lee, *In a Split Second* by Colby William Calhoun.

"*In a Split Second* by Colby William Calhoun," she read aloud as she stared at the name in the middle.

William.

Colby William Calhoun.

As the room began to spin around her, bits and pieces of conversation filtered through her thoughts, a bizarre reality taking root.

"For goin' on ten years now we've all heard about this amazin' man she's been datin'. He's smart. Good-looking. Funny. Charmin'. Well traveled. Even famous. He is—to hear her talk—the epitome of every woman's dream."

Rose's description of Ella May's Mystery Man had elicited laughter, yet now, in hindsight, those same words could surely describe Colby Calhoun . . .

He was drop-dead gorgeous.

He was funny.

He oozed charm.

He was well traveled.

And he was, in fact, famous. Especially around Sweet Briar.

"Billy can be used for Willy."

But why now? After living in the same place for—

"Ten years," she whispered. The same time Colby moved to Sweet Briar to marry Debbie . . .

But still. Why now?

Because an opportunity presented itself . . . Because Colby had finally earned enemies who'd actually threatened him . . .

She bit back the urge to scream as each subsequent thread came together. . . .

Enemies deflected suspicion . . . enemies she and Milo had discussed in front of Ella May at the festival.

Feeling the room begin to spin faster, Tori leaned her head against the wooden drawers and shelves of the information desk. But how could she get Colby out of his house by herself?

"People in la-la land can be coaxed without really having a clue . . ."

She sucked in her breath. Someone like Ella May—a person who seemed so harmless—could probably be very coaxing. Especially with just the right ploy.

But the knife and the threat . . . And the lack of fingerprints . . .

"Oh, and we can't forget the frilly gloves."

The gloves.

The gloves Ella May wore to keep the oils from her hands from harming the bunnies . . . Gloves like she wore when she ripped the book . . .

Pushing off the ground, Tori steadied herself against the counter, her gaze falling on Ella May's note. Her *crayon-written* note.

It couldn't be. It just couldn't be. . . .

She looked at the ripped book on the counter beside the note, the title hitting her with a one-two punch.

Misery.

"Nooo." The word passed through her lips as her stomach twisted and flopped. "The thumping . . . was that—"

She stopped, refusing to allow herself to put too much hope into something that might be nothing more than a series of strange coincidences. But if it wasn't . . . if she was right . . .

Grabbing the phone from its holder, Tori dialed the Sweet Briar Police Department, each ring in her ear bringing the frightening puzzle she'd assembled in her mind into undeniable focus.

A puzzle that was still missing one monumental piece . . .

A piece that was tinged bright red with the blood of Colby Calhoun.

Chapter 24

It was hard not to feel a sense of excitement and pride as she passed beneath the large paper banner hung between two moss trees on the edge of the town square. Unlike its predecessors though, this sign didn't welcome people to a festival started so long ago no one could remember its actual origin. Instead, it beckoned to residents with its spontaneity and its newness.

For more years than anyone could recall, Sweet Briar had celebrated traditions that were handed to them by people long gone—people who had rebuilt the town with their own blood, sweat, and tears after a devastating loss that would have sunk those with less character. Their achievements were worth celebrating, worth remembering.

But they were by no means the only ones with any merit. Every accomplishment—big or small—was worth noting whether it happened a hundred years ago or the day before yesterday. If the town's rebirth was meant to teach future generations a lesson, it was in the power of working together. For a common goal.

"Victoria! Over here."

Tori looked to her left, felt a surge of joy at the sight of Debbie and Colby Calhoun waving to her from a picnic table amid a sea of familiar faces. With several quick strides, she joined her friends, who looked as if the weight of the world had been lifted from their shoulders.

"I don't know how I can ever thank you enough," Debbie whispered in her ear as the woman wrapped her arms around Tori. "Getting that call from Chief Dallas . . . hearing that Colby was alive and okay . . . I can't even explain how that felt."

"You don't have to. Your smile says it all." Tori took a step back only to be enveloped by another set of arms—tanned, muscular arms that felt as good as they looked.

"Victoria, thank you. For being on the ball. For noticing details. For following your hunch." Colby hugged her close, his breath warm against her hair. "I can't tell you how grateful I am."

She fought the stinging in her eyes as she stepped back again, her gaze lingering on Colby's handsome face. "I'm only sorry we didn't respond to your thumping. I just didn't know . . ."

Colby's wide mouth stretched into a smile, dimples forming in his cheeks. "Leona told us what you thought my thumping was. It gave Chief Dallas and me a good laugh when it was all over."

"What *I* thought it was?" she asked as she tried desperately to keep her teeth from clenching.

He nodded, the slight curl to the ends of his hair brushing the collar of his soft blue button-down shirt. "It's okay. You figured it out eventually, that's all that matters."

She scanned the crowd, searched each and every familiar face for the cosmetically enhanced liar she called friend, but Leona was nowhere to be seen. Shaking her head free of various strangulation methods, Tori focused on Colby once again. "So why did she do it?"

"Who? Ella May?" His smile disappeared as his shoulders rose and fell. "She had a crush that developed into an obsession somewhere along the road. She'd been content to speak of her relationship in cryptic fashion for much of that time . . . but when she saw people's anger toward me and heard their criticism, she decided she could kill two birds with one stone."

"Two birds?"

"Being with me and keeping me safe." Colby's smile returned as Debbie came up beside him, the red swollen eyes of four days earlier replaced with the infectious sparkle that was synonymous with her bubbly personality. Tori watched as he slid his arm around his wife's shoulders and pulled her tight to his side. "We were just talking about Ella May."

The sparkle faltered for a split second before Debbie waved it away. "What she did was wrong, but I do believe she was trying to help in a twisted kind of way."

Tori slowly shook her head, her friend's willingness to try and understand the unthinkable an overture she hadn't expected. Even from someone as sweet and caring as Debbie Calhoun.

"You're not angry?"

Debbie was silent for a moment as she seemed to consider Tori's question. Finally she shook her head. "Hurt? Yes. Upset for my children's unnecessary heartache? Of course. But angry, no. She didn't hurt him. And I"—she pressed her cheek against her husband's broad chest—"got him back. Safe and sound."

"But there was blood on the kitchen floor," Tori reminded, her thoughts traveling back to the night they'd found the note and the knife.

Colby pointed at his nose. "I had a nosebleed."

"Are you serious?" She looked from Colby to Debbie and back again, all final traces of stress dissipating from her body. "She didn't hurt you?"

"Nah. Ella May wouldn't hurt a fly." Colby brushed the top of his wife's head with his lips.

"She's gonna be charged with kidnapping though . . . right?"

"I guess. But we're not going to make things any rougher for her . . . it's up to the chief what to charge her with. I'm home now. That's all that truly matters." Colby squeezed Debbie once again, his free hand gesturing toward the long linen-draped table near the town's signature gazebo. "Can you believe all this hoopla over Margaret Louise's recipe?"

Tori nodded, a smile stretching her face wide. "Yeah, I can. It's tremendous."

"But a town festival so everyone can try it? Bill has never given me that kind of treatment."

"Bill's his publisher—you know, William Clayton Wilder." Debbie wiggled out from beneath Colby's arm as their son Jackson skipped over with a group of boys at his heels. "Hi sweetie, are you having fun?"

Jackson nodded, his mouth opening to reveal two missing teeth. "Nobody's mad at me and Suzanna anymore, Mama."

"I'm glad to hear that, sweetie." Debbie tapped her son on the nose. "Now go play. We'll call you when it's time to eat."

Tori watched the little boy run off, his sneakers flashing little red lights every time his feet smacked the ground. As he disappeared in the crowd, she looked back at her friends. "So no more real fallout from the article?"

"Nah, not really," Colby said with a shrug. "I still feel some tension from some people but that's to be expected. I shook their truth."

"But it wasn't the truth."

"It was their truth, Victoria."

Colby was right. Historical truth or not, the story surrounding Sweet Briar's incineration during the war was a legend, passed down through the generations as fact. And for those who'd only heard the story, it was the truth as they'd been told it. They were no more responsible for the lie than Colby was for the truth.

"Can I catch up with you later? I'd like to track down Margaret Louise and ask her how the photo shoot went earlier today."

"Have fun." Debbie and then Colby each leaned forward and hugged her one more time, their heartfelt appreciation misting her eyes.

Picking her way through the crowd, Tori stopped every few feet to greet a familiar face from the library, people who stopped their own conversations to seek her out and say hello. Six months ago, she'd never believed the people of Sweet Briar could ever truly embrace her as one of their own. But she'd been wrong.

She may not have been born and raised in this town, but she cared about it nonetheless—the people, the enviable pride, the community spirit. And whether she was a resident or not, Sweet Briar was very much her home.

As she neared the open-air tent imprinted with the Lions Publishing logo, Tori couldn't help but feel a sense of pride for the heavyset woman standing inside. Margaret Louise Davis was the kind of person everyone wanted to be—energetic, creative, positive, loving, loyal, and true.

"Tori, you made it." Margaret Louise's voice bellowed across the lawn as she did a little stationary jog. "I was hopin' you'd come."

"I've tried these potatoes, remember? I wouldn't miss another helping for anything." She leaned over as she reached the woman, brushed a kiss on her cheek. "So this whole thing is really so the town can try your sweet potatoes?"

"Well, kinda . . ."

Tori tilted her head to the left, studied the way the woman's eyes cast downward.

"Margaret Louise, what aren't you telling me?"

"You'll find out soon enough."

"Can you give me a hint?" She knew she was prying but she couldn't help it. Margaret Louise was up to something. Something big.

"I can tell you that you were right about Hank Jameson, I mean Harrison James."

She narrowed her eyes. "No I wasn't. It was Ella May."

"No. I mean right in the fact he's furious at Colby."

"Still?" She searched the crowd for the man but didn't see him anywhere.

"He's representin' Ella May."

Tori shrugged. "That's okay, I guess. If it helps him blow off steam then it's worth it. And besides, maybe he'll learn something from Colby's willingness to go easy on Ella May." She pointed at the tent and the crowd assembled around the town square. "So all of this is about your sweet potatoes?"

"Sweet Briar has good taste," Margaret Louise gushed before shaking her head in regret. "Why would you listen to me crowin' about myself? If I don't watch it, people might mistake me for—"

"Leona?"

The woman's hearty laugh shook her body from head to toe. "Can you imagine"—she trailed her hands down her round body—"people mistakin' chubby ol' me for Leona?"

"If Leona could only be so lucky," Tori said as she reached out and patted her friend's hand. "Speaking of Leona, where is she? I've got a bone to pick with her."

"She's over there"—Margaret Louise pointed toward a suit-clad man near the back of the tent—"with William Clayton Wilder."

His back to a tent pole, the strikingly tall man was staring down into Leona's large doe eyes with obvious fascination.

"She doesn't waste any time, does she?" Tori asked, her head shaking as she spoke.

"She'll be bored with him by Sunday." Margaret Louise turned back to Tori, her eyes wide with excitement. "She showed me the handkerchief she made for Ella May."

Tori looked past the woman to her reluctant sewing pupil. "And?"

"Well, it was a little cockeyed, and she used glue on the patch . . . but—"

"She told me she was going to use an iron," Tori protested.

Margaret Louise raised an eyebrow.

"She has used an iron before, right?"

The woman's eyebrow rose even more.

She looked back at Leona for a moment as reality dawned. "She doesn't even own an iron, does she?"

"She dated Winston Hohlbrook for a few weeks after movin' here. She now gets free dry cleanin'."

She felt her mouth gape open. "Are southern men just that clueless?"

"Hey! Who are you calling clueless?" Milo grabbed her around the waist and poked his head over her shoulder to greet Margaret Louise. "Should my ears have been ringing just now?"

Tori spun around and kissed Milo's chin. "No. But Leona's should be."

Margaret Louise glanced down at her watch and made a high sign in the air at Leona's latest conquest. To Tori and Milo she said, "I think it's time."

"You mean I'm finally going to get to taste these sweet potatoes Tori told me about?"

The woman grinned. "Soon."

Tori gestured toward her friend. "Margaret Louise is up to something. What, I have no idea. But she's up to—wait! Does this have something to do with turning someone else's rags into riches?"

A knowing smile crept across the woman's face.

"It does, doesn't it?" she prodded.

"You caught me." Margaret Louise pulled a folded sheet of paper from her pocket and waved at William Clayton Wilder as he approached. "I gotta go."

"Go, go where? And I still don't know what that rags and riches thing means . . ." Tori's voice trailed off as Margaret Louise's back disappeared into the crowd beside Colby's publisher. "Why must I always have to figure everything out for myself?"

Milo grinned. "Because you're so good at it." He turned a hairbreadth as Leona approached, the woman's near-flawless face sporting a flirtatious glow. "Were your ears burning, Leona?"

"My ears? Good heavens, no. Though"—she cocked her head to the right and batted her eyelashes—"William's breath was quite lovely against my skin when we spoke."

Tori rolled her eyes at Milo. "Hey, I have a bone to pick with you, Leona."

Leona's shoulders drooped as she met Milo's gaze. "Can you please translate, darling? I don't know anything about picking bones."

"I have an issue to take up with you, Leona. Do you find that easier to understand?"

The woman released a sigh. "What have I done now, dear?"

"The thumping . . ."

Leona's eyebrows furrowed.

"At Ella May's the other morning . . ."

The woman's eyebrows relaxed as the color deepened across her cheeks.

"You told Colby and Police Chief Dallas that I was the one who thought it was coming from Ella May and her Mystery Man?"

The woman shifted from foot to foot then settled her hand at the base of her neck. "Did I? I don't recall."

"Wait." Milo pointed at Tori, his lips turning upward. "You thought they were—"

"I didn't think anything," Tori corrected. "Leona is the one with the gutter mind."

Milo laughed.

"She's also ignorant to common basic household appliances."

Leona stared at Tori. "Excuse me, dear?"

Tori reached out, grabbed hold of Leona's clutch, and snapped it open, her hand reaching inside and extracting the misshapen blue handkerchief. "Would you mind telling me how you applied the bunny patch?"

The woman mumbled something inaudible beneath her breath.

"I'm sorry, did you hear that Milo?" Tori asked as she kept her gaze locked on Leona's.

Milo shook his head in amusement.

Leona's mouth opened only to close once again.

"You glued it, didn't you?"

The woman swiped the handkerchief from Tori's hands, stared lovingly down at the patch, then stuffed it back in her purse. "So what if I did?"

"You're a piece of work, Leona."

"A piece of art, dear," the woman corrected. "And there's a very big—"

"Hey, I hate to interrupt but it looks as if that Wilder guy is about to say something." Milo pointed toward a podium set up inside the gazebo.

"We'll talk later," Tori hissed at Leona as they trained their focus on the publisher.

"Good evening, Sweet Briar. For those of you who don't know who I am, my name is William Clayton Wilder. I am the CEO of Lions Publishing—the company that publishes your own Colby Calhoun and magazines like *Taste of the South*, which will soon feature the woman right beside me . . . Margaret Louise Davis."

The applause that had started at the mention of Colby's name took off as the people of Sweet Briar shed the trauma of the past two weeks in favor of something positive, something different.

"I stopped by your town to see Colby a few weeks ago and ended up staying for the festival that honors your town's historic rebirth."

The applause stopped. Bodies shifted uncomfortably as more than a few sets of eyes searched the crowd for a visual of Colby Calhoun.

"I've come to learn that the story of that rebirth may be different than once thought. Or, rather, I should say the story of the incident that caused the rebirth may be different than once thought."

A few throats around them cleared uncomfortably as the man continued from his spot behind the podium.

"As a man who's built an empire on stories, I know what matters and what doesn't. And while the incineration of your town is the kind of ambulance-chasing story that gets people's hearts pumping, it's also the one that eventually fades into bits and pieces of a vague memory."

Tori scanned the crowd, her gaze coming to rest on Dirk Rogers. If the publisher's words were striking the right note with the garage owner, it was hard to tell. But the angry sneer she'd seen on his face at the garage had definitely softened.

"But the story that lives on . . . the story that inspires and motivates . . . the story that equips you with a can-do spirit long after the words are told is the part about the actual rebirth. The part about the town's forefathers—your kinfolk—coming together to start over. That's the story."

"Rags to riches," Tori whispered.

"What was that?" Milo asked as he leaned close.

"Just something Margaret Louise said that's finally starting to make some sense."

"So Colby Calhoun didn't take your history from you . . . he put it in focus." William Clayton Wilder nodded his head at the local author before turning to the woman beside him. "And Margaret Louise Davis here . . . well, she took the leftover bad taste and sprinkled a little magic on it."

"What's he talking about?" Milo whispered from behind his hand.

"I'm not sure."

"Next month, Margaret Louise and her recipe for Sweet Briar Sweet Potato Pie will get the feature spot in *Taste of the South* magazine. And trust me, all of you will soon taste for yourselves why she's earned that spot."

Tori glanced at the woman to the side of the podium, felt the pride well up inside her heart for her friend's accomplishment.

"But what's taken this recipe to a whole new level is the story behind it. A story not unlike your town's history." The man shifted the note cards in front of him before looking back out at the crowd. "While I truly believe it's of little importance whether this town was burnt to the ground by Yankee soldiers or a mishap with some moonshine . . . the truth is, it was the moonshine. Truth is truth."

A series of coughs sprang up among the crowd as the man continued on. "But just as your forefathers focused on creating a silver lining from that mishap, so, too, has Margaret Louise Davis." William Clayton Wilder pulled an envelope from behind the podium and held it out to Margaret Louise. "I asked her to take what was a spectacular recipe to start with and give it a uniquely southern twist. And she did . . . however, she took it one step forward and gave it a uniquely *Sweet Briar* twist."

The crowd's focus shifted from the publishing giant to Margaret Louise as, once again, the man continued. "And just as your forefathers regrouped from tragedy, so, too, did she. You see, the very thing that burned this town to the ground is the very same thing that this town will be celebrated for in *Taste of the South*'s next issue."

"Huh?" Milo asked, his confusion and sentiment echoed by those around them.

"That's right, Sweet Briar, there's moonshine in my Sweet Potato Pie!" Margaret Louise's voice bellowed out from the podium as she gestured toward the head table now covered with casserole dish after casserole dish of her soon-to-be famous recipe.

Pockets of laughter were drowned out by the sound of wild applause as the crowd cheered and made its way over to the table.

"One man's rags are another man's riches."

"What was that?" Milo asked as he looked down at her.

"One man's rags are another man's riches . . . it's something Margaret Louise first said to me a few days ago."

"Well, she certainly hit that home today, didn't she?"

"She sure did." Tori rose up on tiptoe so he could hear over the increased noise level around them. "I'll meet up with you over by the picnic tables in a little bit. I want to congratulate Margaret Louise."

He raked a hand through his hair and smiled. "I'll save you a spot. But give her a kiss for me, too. Okay?"

"Absolutely."

Step by step Tori made her way through the passing crowd. When she finally reached the gazebo she stopped, Leona having beaten her to the punch.

"We're both so very proud of you," Leona said as she released her sister from an embrace.

"Both?" Tori asked as she offered her own hug to Margaret Louise.

Leona looked down, her cheeks suddenly crimson.

"Leona?" She shifted her gaze to Margaret Louise's equally guilty face. "Margaret Louise?"

"It was the right thing to do considering the circumstances."

She narrowed her eyes on Margaret Louise. "What was?"

"We couldn't leave him out there to fend for himself."

"Him?" She shifted her focus to Leona once again.

"Without his mama to look out for him, he was bound to end up a target for Carter Johnson."

She held up her hands, palms outward. "Wait. You're not talking about—"

"Paris. He needed me." Leona clasped her hands in front of her body and smiled up at Tori angelically. "I mean, with Ella May facing possible confinement in a loony bin, what else was I to do?"

"You went back out there and snatched him?"

Leona's eyes rolled upward. "No, I didn't snatch him. I don't need to snatch men, dear."

"She really doesn't. They just flock to her," Margaret Louise insisted on behalf of her twin.

"So you're saying—"

"I'm saying that I set my bag—"

"Actually, it was my bag, Twin."

Ignoring her sister, Leona continued on. "I set it down and he"—she rose up on the balls of her feet and did a slight bounce—"hopped right in."

"Just like that, huh?" Tori asked.

"Yes, just like that." The woman turned toward her sister, her hand gesturing in the direction of the various tables playing host to Margaret Louise's prized Sweet Potato Pie. "While I certainly look forward to that being included in some of my suppers, I definitely must insist on a side dish of organic carrots each and every night."

"Organic carrots?" Margaret Louise clamped her mouth shut and shook her head. "Oh no, you didn't win the bet."

Without so much as a single word, Leona opened her clutch, pulled out the pale blue handkerchief, and waved it in front of her sibling's face.

"You didn't . . . That's not . . ."

Tori shrugged. "She may have glued on the patch, but she did sew on the edging."

Mumbling something about the need for a quick swig

of her special ingredient, Margaret Louise stalked off in the direction of the tables, her loveably plump frame disappearing among the crowd of adoring fans.

As they watched her go, Tori shook her head, a smile tugging at her mouth despite her attempt at disdain. "You really are a piece of work, you know that, Leona?"

"Art, dear. Art."

Sewing Tips

- Avoid the temptation to moisten the end of your thread before threading a needle. This can cause it to swell up and make it more difficult to fit through the needle's eye. Instead, trim the end of the thread at an angle before trying to put it through the needle. Working in front of a white background can also be helpful.
- Before sewing around tight curves, change the setting on your machine to use a shorter stitch so that it will be easier to sew a smooth seam.
- If it is difficult to tell the right side of your fabric from the wrong side, apply a small piece of blue painter's tape or use a safety pin to attach a brightly colored fabric scrap to the wrong side to help you quickly distinguish the difference.
- You can reduce or prevent fraying when you preshrink your fabrics if you use pinking shears, a zigzag stitch, or serge along the raw edges before washing.

- If your sewing project involves different types of materials, make sure all of the fabrics can be washed in the same way. Avoid mixing machine washable and dry clean only fabrics in the same garment. Be sure to prewash your fabrics.

- If you are having difficulty ironing out a stubborn crease in a fabric, try spraying the area with a mixture of equal parts water and white vinegar before pressing the crease with a pressing cloth. Straight vinegar can be used on especially tough creases. (Test a discreet area of your fabric before spraying a large area.)

- Many carpenters use the phrase, "Measure twice, and cut once." The same is true for sewing.

- Cover your sewing machine when you are not using it since dust and lint—in and on—your machine, are a big cause of machine breakdowns.

- To achieve cleaner cut lines on fabric, don't let the scissor tips shut completely before reopening them to continue cutting.

- You don't need to purchase a fancy plastic gadget to keep your bobbin and thread spool together for convenience in storage. Take a rubber band and loop it through the bobbin and around the spool enough times to secure it.

Have a sewing tip you'd like to share with readers? Stop by my website at www.elizabethlynncasey.com and let me know.

Sewing Pattern

Tori's Gift Bag Pattern

Experience:

Some sewing experience needed

Materials:

½ yard of 54" wide fabric can make 3 gift bags of this size
Sharp scissors
Pinking shears
Straight pins
Thread
Sewing machine
Chalk
Ribbon, twine, or raffia

Cut two 8 ¾" x 17" pieces of fabric. Using pinking shears will help keep seams from unraveling, but regular scissors can also be used.

Pin front to back with right sides together. Sew a ½" seam around the sides and bottom of bag. Clip corners. Press seams.

With bag still inside out, fold side seam back onto the bottom seam, keeping seams matched. Pin in place. Measure one inch from the tip of the corner along the seam toward the center of the bag. Use chalk to mark a line at that one inch point that is perpendicular to the seam and goes from one edge to the other edge. Sew from edge to edge along the chalk line. This will create a triangular-shaped flap and will give your bag some depth. (Measuring and sewing across the seam closer to the center will create a deeper bag. Likewise, sewing across the seam farther from the center will create a shallower bag.) Repeat on the other side.

Turn bag right side out.

Get creative when finishing your gift bag.

If you used pinking shears when cutting out your fabric, you can leave the pinked edges along the top for a casual look that won't unravel.

For a more finished look, hem the top edge.

You can tie ribbon, twine, or raffia around the top of your bag for a closure.

You could also use ribbon to create handles.

This pattern can be used to make gift bags in any size you want. Just change the dimensions keeping in mind seam allowances, the depth you need for your bag, and how much extra fabric you will need above your gift.

WELL-CRAFTED MYSTERIES FROM BERKLEY PRIME CRIME

- **Earlene Fowler** Don't miss this Agatha Award–winning quilting series featuring Benni Harper.

- **Monica Ferris** This *USA Today* bestselling Needlecraft Mystery series includes free knitting patterns.

- **Laura Childs** Her Scrapbooking Mystery series offers tips to satisfy the most die-hard crafters.

- **Maggie Sefton** This popular Knitting Mystery series comes with knitting patterns and recipes.

penguin.com

M5G0508

Cozy up with Berkley Prime Crime

SUSAN WITTIG ALBERT

Don't miss the national bestselling series featuring herbalist China Bayles.

LAURA CHILDS

The Tea Shop Mysteries are the toast of Charleston, South Carolina.

KATE KINGSBURY

The Pennyfoot Hotel Mystery series is a teatime delight.

For the armchair detective in you.

penguin.com

M6G0708